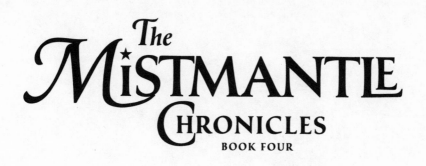

The Mistmantle Chronicles
BOOK FOUR

Urchin and the Raven War

by

M. I. McAllister

Illustrated by

Omar Rayyan

HYPERION BOOKS FOR CHILDREN
New York
AN IMPRINT OF DISNEY BOOK GROUP

For the Northumbrian saints, past, present, and to come

PROLOGUE

CORR WAS TIRED OF WAITING. He needed to do something new.

Corr was one of a large clan of otters living beyond the Rough Rocks on a far tip of Mistmantle. He had so many brothers, sisters, cousins, half cousins, and sort-of cousins that the adults were always counting them in case any of them got lost and nobody noticed. They taught each other to swim, fish, row, and sail, make boats and nets and repair them, and all the other skills an otter needed to get along "well enough." That was what everyone said, time and again. "We get along well enough."

Corr was young, and didn't want to get on well enough. His head and heart were full of dreams, stories, and questions, and he wanted excitement. What he yearned for was to see the world, but that was no good, living on Mistmantle. Enchanted mists circled the island, making it impossible for anyone who truly belonged there to leave by water and return by water, so unless he learned to fly—unlikely for an otter—he could never leave. But if he couldn't explore the world, couldn't he at least explore the island?

On long summer evenings he would sit with his great-aunt Kerrera outside the smokehouse, and she would tell him of the terrible times of Lord Husk, when weak and disabled babies had been put to death, and little Prince Tumble had been murdered. On winter nights when even the starlight was bitter with cold, they would settle by the fire and, in a haze of fishy-smelling smoke, she would tell him of the wonderful Spring Festival when King Crispin (but he had been Captain Crispin in those days) had flown home to Mistmantle on a swan and saved all the island. When snow fell, she would tell him of the night when Urchin of the Riding Stars, Juniper the priest, and Captain Lugg the mole had sailed home through snow and riding stars, and the mists had let them through, bringing Cedar of Whitewings, who had married King Crispin. He loved that story, partly because it had a night of riding stars in it, when the stars flew from their orbits and swooped about the island. Nights like that always signaled a great event, for good or for harm. But he liked it, too, because it was about sailing through the mists, and the thought of that thrilled and frightened him.

In all these stories Brother Fir had been there with his wise, kind eyes, his limp, his way of saying "Hm!" and his friendliness to all animals, from the king and queen to every young hedgehog, otter, mole, and squirrel. Corr had seen him from a distance and knew the priest had been at his naming ceremony, but he couldn't remember it. With all his heart he wanted that kind, wise smile turned to him.

I want him to know about me, he thought. Even if there isn't much to know.

He had heard breathtaking tales of King Crispin and Queen Cedar at Mistmantle Tower, and of their captains and the Circle, the animals closest to the king who helped and advised him. Corr wanted to meet Captain Padra and his brother, Fingal of the Floods. They were otters, like himself. He dreamed of meeting his hero, Urchin of the Riding Stars, the pale squirrel who had crossed the sea and returned again.

There were stories, too, of the distant past, and Voyagers. There had been very few Voyagers in the history of the island. A Voyager—usually an otter—could travel freely through the mists and back, and visit islands beyond the sea.

He'd never meet a real Voyager. But he might meet Brother Fir. One day, he would go to the tower and meet them all. One day, he would have the adventures he could only imagine as he carried baskets of herring up the hill to the smokehouse and mended nets. But each day was filled with fishing, repairing, and tramping up and down the hill to the smokehouse.

The warm, dark smokehouse, where Great-aunt Kerrera cooked fish over woodsmoke to preserve it, was on a hill with the fumes of oak, peat, and fish hanging around it. Great-aunt Kerrera was always good for a cordial, a biscuit, and a story of old times, and occasionally, Filbert would be there, too.

Filbert was a stout and solid squirrel who seemed old to Corr but probably wasn't really. He was too shy to mix with the otters on the shore, but he liked to help Great-aunt Kerrera in the smokehouse, where he, too, was rewarded with a drink and a biscuit. When he could be persuaded to talk at all, he sometimes talked of Mistmantle Tower.

On this particular spring day, when Corr had carried so many baskets of fish to and from the smokehouse that he smelled of singed oak and never wanted to look at a kipper again in his life, Filbert was there. They sat outside in the sunshine, drinking cordials that tasted smoky.

"Can you tell me anything else about the tower, Filbert?" asked Corr.

Filbert was silent for a while, looking into the cordial. He always did that.

"I was there when we all had to give our clawmarks and Crispin was sent away," he said at last, shaking his head at the cup. "Bad, that. Bad. Bad days. I remember old King Brushen crouched over on his throne."

Corr had heard that story before, and wanted something new. "Did you ever do anything really exciting?" he asked.

"Me?" Filbert made a little grunt that was probably meant to be a laugh and continued talking into his cordial. "Would have liked to. No time for adventures, though. When I was young, I was like you, fetching and carrying. Might have liked an adventure. Never got around to it, really." There was a long silence and Corr thought he had finished, when Filbert added, "I hear Brother Fir hasn't got long. Must be very old. Getting frail."

"Corr!" shouted Great-aunt Kerrera. "I've got some nice big fish bones and oil here. Take them to your ma; they'll come in handy for mending."

That evening Corr trudged downhill with his paws full of fish, fish bones, and oil for waterproofing, and his head full of Brother Fir, who was old and dying. How many other animals would grow old and die before he had the chance to meet them?

One day, he thought, I could be like Filbert. I could grow old and look back wishing I'd done more with my life. It's no good waiting for a chance to get away. I have to make my own chance, and do it now.

At home, he found a boat so old and shabby that nobody else wanted it. He patched it up with sap and seasoned bark and put in fresh water, food, and a cloak. Then he found his parents, who were struggling to put his brothers, sister, and a few cousins to bed. When he told them he was going to the tower to see Brother Fir before he died, his mother said that Brother Fir was a lovely old soul, bless him, give him our love, take a warm cloak, take care, and don't be too long. After he had gone, she winked knowingly at his father and said that Corr would be back when he was hungry.

At sunrise, Corr the otter took to the water. What he hadn't told anyone was that he wasn't going *straight* to the tower. There was exploring to do first, and adventures to be found. He couldn't go to the tower without any stories to tell.

CHAPTER ONE

IN MISTMANTLE TOWER all went on steadily and peacefully, but with a little sadness. Brother Fir might live as long as the winter, but he would never leave the tower again. One side of his body was numb and paralyzed, and his heart and limbs had weakened, but his sight, his hearing, and his mind were as sharp as sword points. He lay on his small white bed in the highest turret of Mistmantle Tower while animals took turns to keep him company. They had moved his bed to give him a good view of the shore. Two young squirrels, Juniper (the younger priest) and Whittle (the apprentice historian and lawyer) opened windows so he could feel the sea breeze, and the scent of flowers in the window boxes would drift in for him. On cool evenings they lit the apple-log fire in the grate, mixed cordials the way he liked them, and told him the news of the island.

Urchin of the Riding Stars would tumble through the window to visit between having advanced fencing lessons himself, teaching the new pages, and keeping an eye on the young animals in Anemone Wood. Crackle, the squirrel pastry cook, sweetened rice puddings with red berry jam the way Fir liked them, and learned to cook seaweed because apparently he liked that, too. (Seaweed was becoming very popular.) Sepia of the Songs called between looking after the king and queen's children and teaching and practicing her music. In the workrooms where the Threadings were made—the woven, stitched, and painted pictures showing the story of the island—Thripple and Needle and the small hedgehogs said little as they worked. Hope, the shortsighted hedgehog, seemed to have given himself the job of fetching and carrying, fire lighting, and washing up for the priests. On a spring morning he stirred the bilberry cordial and put it into Brother Juniper's paws.

"It's just the way Brother Fir likes it," whispered Hope with a glance at the bed.

Brother Fir gave a weak, lopsided smile without opening his eyes. "Don't look so worried," he wheezed. "I'm not dead yet." He took the cup in his good paw when Juniper had helped him to sit up.

"That's a very good cordial," Brother Fir remarked. "He will come, you know."

"I know he will, Brother Fir," said Juniper, who had no idea what Fir was talking about. Brother Fir had been murmuring on for days about somebody who would come, and Juniper had given up asking who he meant. He never got an answer.

"It's a beautiful day," remarked Fir, looking down at the shore. "Are they having a race down there?" He chuckled, then leaned forward with great interest. "Juniper! Look up! What do you suppose *those* are?"

There were always animals on the shore beside the long wooden jetty, especially young animals. On this particular morning, when the turning tide carried drifting seaweed to the sands, Fingal was swimming in and out of the wharves on one side of the jetty with Padra's son, Tide, racing him on the other. Swishing her tail in the water, Tide's sister, Swanfeather, opened her mouth to shout for Tide, then thought she might support her uncle Fingal instead, then couldn't decide and shouted herself hoarse for both of them. Princess Catkin and her brother, Prince Oakleaf, leaned from either side of the jetty to watch, and the race looked so close that all the otters in the water had stopped fishing and swimming to see who won. Catkin, her tail curled high over her back, sprang up as Tide won by a nose and a whisker. (Swanfeather thought Fingal had lost on purpose.)

"I declare Tide the winner!" cried Catkin.

Glossily wet, dripping, and laughing, Fingal bobbed up. "Oh, are you declaring again?" he said. "You do a lot of declaring, Catkin." He winked at Prince Oakleaf, then disappeared underwater again and presently emerged on the dry sand, where he rolled and shook himself dry. Princess Catkin was telling Swanfeather something very important, and hadn't noticed what he was doing.

"Fingal, now I'm soaked!" she cried.

"It must be raining!" said Fingal. He looked innocently up at the sky and suddenly stopped being flippant. "Swans!" he said. "Four—five of them!"

Five swans drifted down from the sky and skimmed onto the sea so smoothly that a graceful track flared through the water behind each one. But they looked weary and ragged. Swans usually held their necks tall and their heads high, but these drooped over the waves. Their badly ruffled feathers were smudged with mud, blood, and weed. Their eyes were hollow with strain and tiredness. Their leader—bigger than the rest and still struggling to hold his head and wings high—swam to the shallows and stepped on great webbed feet to the shore. Fingal, as a member of the Circle, went to greet him. The swan lowered his beak just a little.

"I am Lord Arcneck of Swan Isle," he announced, and there was pride in the tired voice. He glanced at the gleam of silver from the bracelet on Fingal's wrist. "My greetings to King Crispin of Mistmantle. You wear silver. Are you a lordling of this island?"

"Not exactly," said Fingal. "But can I help you? You look as if you've had a rough journey." He glanced over his shoulder. "Tide, will you find . . ."

"Thank you, Fingal," said Catkin's clear, commanding voice behind him. "I'll do this."

Fingal wanted very much to say, "Certainly, Your Princess-ship," but he bit his tongue, fought against a smile, and moved aside for

10

her. Young Princess Catkin had flame-red fur like her mother's, a heart-shaped face, long ear tufts, and immense determination. The swan lord stretched out his neck and lowered his hard, bright beak as he looked down at her.

"What is this?" he croaked. "A youngling?"

"I am Princess Catkin," she said before Fingal could introduce her. "The firstborn child of King Crispin and Queen Cedar, and the Heir of Mistmantle. Anything you have to say, my lord, you may say to me."

Fingal winced silently. Lord Arcneck regarded Catkin with cold, sharp eyes, as if wondering whether she were worth speaking to.

"Then kindly take me to your father," he said. "King Crispin and I have been allies from long ago."

"Oh, of course!" said Catkin. "You're from *that* island. You'd better come with me."

"Er . . . Catkin" —began Prince Oakleaf— "do you think . . ." but Catkin was already marching to the tower with a weary procession of swans waddling behind her. Looking over her shoulder, she realized she was leaving them behind, and had to wait.

"Don't worry, Oakleaf," said Fingal quietly. "I'll go with them. You and Swanfeather nip into the kitchens. Find out what swans like and whether we've got any. Good lad."

It could have been worse, he thought as he loped up the sand. *That* island. At least she hadn't said, "Oh, you're *that* swan."

"Excuse me, my lord," he said as he reached Lord Arcneck's side,

11

"the tower steps may be awkward for swans to climb, but you're welcome to fly up if you have room to spread your wings. I'll send someone to get you some springwater; it's very good." He waved at a young squirrel page near a window. "The king needs to know that there are visitors from Swan Isle on the way. We'll need springwater brought to the Gathering Chamber."

"The Throne Room," called Catkin over her shoulder.

"Are you sure that's the best place, Catkin?" he asked. The Throne Room might be the likeliest place to find the king at that time in the morning, but it would be a tight squeeze for five swans.

"Of course it's the best place," said Catkin, and Fingal didn't argue. It would be unkind to show her up in front of visitors, and anyway, she wouldn't listen.

"Springwater to the Throne Room, please," he said. "Lots of it."

The Throne Room windows looked down on trees just beginning to show shy green buds, and conifers frilled at the tips with new growth. The fire had been newly lit, and small flames flickered around the logs. Opposite the throne hung a Threading of the famous Captain Lugg the mole wearing his captain's gold circlet and a blue cloak, with a spray of oak leaves at the neck. Woven into the background were a clump of borage flowers and meadowsweet, a golden yellow lapwing, and a spray of black broom, and one paw was edged in gold.

Nobody was seated on the tall, carved thrones. Queen Cedar knelt on the floor as Princess Almondflower took wobbly steps toward her, fell over, and giggled. King Crispin and his oldest friend, Captain Padra, sat in the window seat, cups of wine in their paws, looking down on the island. There were three captains just now—Padra; his wife, Arran; and Docken the hedgehog.

"Docken's a good captain," Crispin was saying, "but try telling him that."

"He's been a captain for a long time now," said Padra, "but he still seems to think it's just a temporary arrangement. He doesn't believe that he's suitable. Fair enough, he doesn't have the dash and sparkle that animals like in a captain, but he doesn't need it. The ordinary animals find him easy to approach."

"Dash and sparkle?" The queen laughed.

"Mine's worn off," said Padra.

"Not a bit of it," said the queen, rolling a ball to Almondflower. "Doesn't Docken want to be a captain anymore?"

"The way Docken sees it, he doesn't mind being a captain until we have someone better," said Crispin. "But I don't want him to resign. We could have a fourth captain, but the best of the moles won't do it because they still don't feel they could follow Lugg. There's the squirrel brothers, Russet and Heath, but they've said that neither of them would accept it because of the other. And the rest are too young, except possibly Fingal."

"Let him have fun for a bit longer," said Padra. "And the same goes for Urchin. It's really Urchin we're talking about, isn't it? We both want him to be a captain one day, but it isn't his time yet, and I don't want—"

A knock at the door interrupted him. When Crispin called, "Enter," a guard mole marched in.

"A message from Fingal to tell you Princess Catkin's on her way, Your Majesty," he said, "with a party of swans seeking an audience."

"Swans!" said the queen, and picked up Almondflower as if afraid they would eat her. "In here?"

Padra and Crispin looked at each other, then around the Throne Room for any furniture that could be moved. They jumped up, pushed a table against the wall, and slid a few toys under Cedar's throne.

"How many swans is a party?" called Padra.

"And why in here?" wondered Crispin. "Quill, take the extra chairs outside, we won't need those—that's better—Lord Arcneck! Welcome!"

The swans were undignified on land. Lord Arcneck managed better than most, but he had to press his wings tightly against his back as he padded on large webbed feet into the Throne Room. Pressing himself into a corner to make more room, Padra saw the cold displeasure in the swan lord's eyes.

"Lord Arcneck," said Crispin, "you and your companions are most welcome to Mistmantle. I fear this chamber is not a suitable place to receive you all." He couldn't see very well past Lord Arcneck, but more swans were squeezing into the chamber. It would have been unsuitable for a king to stand up on his clawtips or hop on to the throne to see over their heads, but he could just see Catkin following like a small swan herder.

"Catkin!" he called. "I think the Gathering Chamber would be better. Will you take our visitors there, please, and have all the windows opened? Swans are creatures of air and water. Quill, send for Urchin to come to the Gathering Chamber."

Lord Arcneck inclined his head. The other swans shuffled back into the corridor to let him pass.

"Creatures of air and water, and proud as moles on mountains," whispered Crispin when they had gone. "They've just had their dignity ruffled. Not a good start."

"Shouldn't we have met them on the beach?" said Padra. "Much more their sort of place, and it would have saved them tramping up here."

"Yes, we should," said Crispin. "But now they're indoors, the Gathering Chamber is the next best thing. I don't know why Catkin dragged them up here." He adjusted his crown and followed them, redirecting the hedgehogs who were struggling along the corridors with slopping bowls of springwater.

The Gathering Chamber was high, wide, and airy. Light poured in through the long windows, which tower attendants were opening. Threadings and candleholders were mounted on the walls, but the furniture had been cleared away, and only the thrones on the dais remained. In this room, there was room for the swans to lift their wings, stretch, and drink, long and thirstily, from the bowls set before them. With two wing beats Lord Arcneck had alighted on the windowsill and turned to face the dais, but even there he seemed to dominate the chamber, and the squirrels and moles in attendance shrank back from the power of those wings. At a nod from Crispin, the thrones were turned about so that he and Cedar could take their places facing their visitors.

"Lord Arcneck," said Crispin, "and all of you, you are welcome to Mistmantle. Will you tell me your cause?"

Lord Arcneck began a speech about how great a king Crispin was, and how much they had done to help each other in the past—it would clearly take him a long time to get to the point. As he was speaking, a young squirrel slipped into the chamber. His fur was unusually pale except at his ears and tail tip, he carried a sword at his hip, and on his left wrist was an old squirrel hair bracelet. For less than a second, King Crispin glanced into the mirror. He saw the young squirrel, caught his eye, and smiled.

Good. Urchin's here. And Lord Arcneck's finally coming to the point.

CHAPTER TWO

O ur island," said Lord Arcneck, "has been peacefully governed by swans for years before years before years, since the trees were small and before the"—he hesitated— "the squirrels came." (Urchin knew they were called "tree-rats" on Swan Isle.) "But long, long ago, the swans had to fight for the island against the tyrants who kept all creatures in slavery. These tyrants were ravens. My great ancestor Strikewing fought for many years in a war against them. They were unlike all other creatures—cruel, treacherous, and greedy. Destruction and devouring was all they understood

"When, at last, the ravens knew they had no hope of victory, they begged for merciful terms of surrender. They made a solemn and binding promise that they would forsake all claim to the island for themselves and their descendants forever, unless they had a Silver Prince to lead them. This was, of course, impossible. There

17

were stories of silver-gray ravens in the past, but they were always female, and so rare nobody had ever seen one. Lord Strikewing agreed to this clause.

"Now ravens have returned. They claim that a Silver Prince was born to them, the son of their king the Archraven, and he has been raised to lead them."

Lord Arcneck raised his head with a little shake. "They call him the Silver Prince," he said. "He is gray, Your Majesty, simply that. A gray bird. What does a flash of sunlight on a wing matter? But they take him for their Silver Prince. He is only an excuse for the Archraven to attack our island, and there has never been such a bird as their Archraven, so proud, so strong, so terrible in battle! His sister, the Taloness, is always at his right claw. The Silver Prince is nothing, but he has the power of their protection. They came"— he raised his voice— "they came with their wings grazing the face of the sun and darkening the sky like thunder! The trees bend under their weight! They will destroy every living creature on the island, and seek more islands to devour! They feast on our squirrels and our cygnets, King Crispin! With every death and every tree destroyed, our island is dying!"

His cry rang in the air, followed by silence. Crispin let the stillness hang in the air.

Urchin understood. Long ago, the swans had carried Crispin and himself home to Mistmantle to fight against the tyrant Lord Husk. Now Lord Arcneck wanted Crispin to come to the help of his island, but he was too proud and honorable to ask for the return of a favor.

Crispin turned to the mole standing to the side of the throne. "Fetch me Mistress Tay and Master Whittle, please, Burr," he said. Presently, two animals stood before him—Tay, a dark-whiskered female otter turning gray at the muzzle, and Whittle, who had a look of intense attention.

"Lord Arcneck," said Crispin, "here are Mistress Tay, our senior lawyer and historian, and Master Whittle, her junior. We must hear their opinion."

Crispin outlined Lord Arcneck's story very briefly, and there was a quiet conference between Whittle and Tay, after which Whittle scurried forward to the swans, put some questions to Lord Arcneck, and hurried back to stretch up and whisper the answers to Mistress Tay. Finally Tay drew herself up.

"The ravens may have an ancient claim to the island," she said. "That point is uncertain. There may also be some doubts as to whether the Silver Prince is, indeed, a Silver Prince at all. But . . ." She paused for effect, bestowed a solemn glare on Crispin, and glowered at Lord Arcneck. Then she spoke very slowly and precisely, as if they were not at all bright and needed to have things explained very simply.

"The ravens have no authority over the creatures who live there," she said. "There is a faint possibility that they may have rights over the *island*, but not over the islanders. No right to rule over them, and certainly no right to harm them."

Slowly and gracefully, Lord Arcneck inclined his head. He seemed most impressed with Mistress Tay.

"Thank you, Tay," said Crispin. "Lord Arcneck, I had thought that ravens ate only food that is already dead—carrion eaters."

Lord Arcneck inclined his head. "That is their custom," he said, "but they are great in numbers and in size, and no amount of carrion will satisfy them. 'Kill and devour' is their call."

"I see," said Crispin gravely. "We will talk further of this. Now, Lord Arcneck, refreshments will be prepared for all of you, and you are welcome to fly over the island and choose where you wish to rest tonight. I shall be with you soon. Padra, Arran, Tay, Whittle, Urchin, please stay. Burr, have all the available Circle animals assembled here." Before the swans could make a clumsy exit across the Gathering Chamber he added, "Perhaps you'd prefer to fly down to the shore. Fingal, Heath, will you attend our guests?"

Fingal and a tall, rather handsome squirrel stepped forward and bowed. Lord Arcneck inclined his head graciously, then stretched out to look over the heads of the crowd.

When Urchin realized that those cold, hard eyes were looking for him, he felt smaller than Princess Almondflower and less important than an earwig, just as he had when he had first met the swan lord. But many summers and winters had passed since then. Urchin was now as tall as Crispin, and his pale fur was brushed and gleaming. The red fur on his ears and tail tip had darkened as he grew, and were now deep auburn.

"I have met this squirrel before," remarked Lord Arcneck. "The strange-colored servant who came to your aid? He was smaller then."

"Yes, Lord Arcneck," said Crispin. "He is now a trusted adviser and helper to me. Urchin of the Riding Stars."

Lord Arcneck never looked surprised, but his eyes did seem to widen a little.

"I have heard that name before," he remarked. "The same pale squirrel who set free the swans on Whitewings?"

"Yes, Lord Arcneck," said Urchin. Slowly, elegantly, Lord Arcneck bowed to him.

"Then you are a friend to all swans," he said solemnly, and his long neck stretched as he raised his wings. "Swans! To the shore!"

Wings beat with a wild swish that sent a draft through the chamber as the swans soared from the windows. Heath and Fingal hurried down the stairs to meet them. Crispin and Cedar left their thrones and sat down on the edge of the dais as the other animals gathered around them, and steadily, with hurrying paws, more Circle animals arrived to have the situation explained to them.

"If everything is as Lord Arcneck says," began Crispin presently, "we must help him. It's only a question of how to go about it."

"That's the thing, Your Majesties," said Docken. Under a captain's circlet, his prickles looked untidier than ever. "Last time another island asked for our help, we ended up with Urchin and Juniper carried off and a mole invasion."

"And a queen," said Crispin.

"And freedom for my home island," added Cedar.

"Aye, well, I'm not saying we shouldn't help," said Docken. "I'm just saying we have to be wary, that's all."

"We have to know they're telling the truth, Your Majesties," said Mother Huggen the hedgehog, folding her paws neatly. "The last lot didn't, begging your pardon, Queen Cedar."

"That's quite all right, Huggen," said the queen.

"But, Your Majesties, these are swans," Urchin pointed out. "They're proud and bossy, but they believe in honor and they respect you, sir. I'm sure they're telling the truth."

"The truth as they see it," said Docken. "If it's just a skirmish between ravens and swans, they should be left to sort it out themselves."

"I can't see Lord Arcneck coming all this way for our help because of a bit of a skirmish," said Crispin. "He's too proud."

"And they look terrible, sir," said Urchin. "Worn out and in a mess. And thin."

"Yes, that's what I thought," said Crispin. "They wouldn't let us see them in that state if they weren't desperate for help. He wouldn't ask if he didn't have to. Tay, you're sure his cause is fair?"

Tay frowned so that her whiskers stood out in a thin, dark line. "As far as I can judge, yes," she said. "A thorough examination of history as revealed in the most ancient of the Threadings would clarify the situation."

Urchin caught the queen's eye, smiled, and looked away quickly. Tay couldn't just say, "I'll see what the Threadings say," could she?

"Then, assuming that a good look at the Threadings proves us right," said Crispin, "we have to help Lord Arcneck, and not only for his sake. If the ravens are as bad as he says, they won't be content with one island. When they've finished killing and feasting there, they'll start on the next, and the next. Sooner or later it would be Whitewings, Mistmantle, and every other island in the sea. Battle plans, then. There are only two ways to travel—underground, or flying on swans. Swans such as Lord and Lady Arcneck don't normally allow themselves to be ridden on, but they have been known to cooperate"—he smiled at Urchin— "and they certainly will, to save their own island. Are there any tunnels—Moth, do you know?"

Moth the mole was the daughter of Captain Lugg, who had taught his family a great deal about tunnels under the sea. She had spent much of her life looking after other animals' babies before marrying Twigg the carpenter and having two little daughters of her own.

"We can't get to Swan Isle that way, Your Majesty, at least not quickly," she said. "Father said all the tunnels going that way were ancient, and a long time ago the swans stopped anyone using them, so they've collapsed. They'd need digging out again and putting new roof supports and everything in."

"So we fly on swans!" said Crispin, and smiled brightly up at the Circle animals. Some gasped with excitement, while others looked worried or, like Tay, appalled. "But we can't send much of a fighting force with only five swans, even if one can carry two of us. Tactics, anyone? Very *good* tactics?"

"They'll have to be brilliant tactics," said Captain Arran, Padra's wife. Her gold circlet was half hidden by the rough, tufty fur around the top of her head. "A lot of vicious creatures who can fly against a handful who can't."

Silence followed as Urchin tried hard to think of an idea, and couldn't. He could see that everyone else felt the same.

"No ideas?" said Crispin. "Then we all have something to exercise our brains with." He stood up, and so did everyone else. "Tay, Whittle, kindly go now to check the Threadings. The rest of you, *think*. We need to move quickly, if anyone on Swan Isle is to be left alive. You may go, all of you, and Heart keep you."

Urchin waited until the others had gone.

"Your Majesty," he said, "however we get there, we should attack by night. Not many birds are at their best at night."

"Well thought of," said the king. "I'll bear that in mind. And I need Catkin kept out of Lord Arcneck's way before she force-marches him across the island."

"She needs to be kept busy," said Cedar. "If we don't watch her, she'll jump on his back and try to fly off to Swan Isle on her own. Urchin, could you give her a little fencing lesson or something?"

Urchin wanted to ask if that was a good idea, but didn't feel he should question the queen where the princess was concerned. Crispin seemed to read his thoughts.

"She does have to learn to use a sword, Urchin, if only in

self-defense," he said. "So she needs to know how to use it correctly. And with my orders that she's not to try it out on anyone."

"Yes, Your Majesty," said Urchin. In the past he'd faced a mad king and an evil sorcerer, and nearly died in a landslide. Now he had to teach Princess Catkin to use a sword. He had taught sword skills and tower duties to the deft and the clumsy, the bright and the dim, but he wasn't sure if he could teach Catkin anything.

CHAPTER THREE

T WILIGHT SETTLED. Instead of the usual dinner at the tower, a banquet had been spread on the rocks, as the swans were much more at ease outside the tower than in it. Otters had been sent to fetch pondweeds, which the swans had nibbled delicately, and Fingal had managed—by a huge effort—to listen without yawning to Lord Arcneck's stories of his mighty ancestors. Now the swans had flown to a pond to rest, the dishes had been cleared, and small Mistmantle animals were listening to stories and snuggling into their nests.

In the highest turret of the tower was a faint light. Brother Fir was sleeping, watched over by Mother Huggen and Hope the hedgehog. In the royal chambers, candles and lamps glowed. Juniper and Urchin, who had snatched a few minutes at the end of the day to walk down to the shore and skim stones, glanced up at those lighted windows and wondered what was happening behind them, but they could see only two silhouetted figures with their backs to their window.

Crispin and Cedar were in the window seat. Facing them, Princess Catkin sat on the floor with her elbows on her knees and her little pointed chin in her paws. The only other person in the room was Sepia of the Songs, a friend of Urchin and Juniper and a Companion to the Queen. She had been like a young aunt to Catkin.

"We're not angry with you, Catkin," the queen was saying, "but this is important. You've been behaving in a way that simply won't do. You can see that, can't you?"

Catkin wrinkled her nose and said nothing.

"You do like to take over, don't you, Catkin?" said Crispin gently.

Catkin said nothing.

"Sometimes," said Cedar, "you don't let anyone else get a word in."

Catkin looked up at last, her eyes wide and her lips parted in astonishment.

"Yes, I know you're being as quiet as a feather now," said Cedar, "but that's because you're sulking. Yes you are, dear. You like to organize, don't you?"

"What's wrong with that?" demanded Catkin.

"Nothing, when things need to be organized," said Crispin. "But most animals like to sort out their own lives, and they usually do it pretty well. But the *swans*! They're visitors! Sweetheart, you rounded them up and marched them into the tower!"

27

"Well, I didn't know they were *that* special!" cried Catkin.

Crispin managed not to sigh. He wasn't sure if any of this made sense to Catkin.

"All guests are honored guests," he said. "Just as all animals are your equals. How would you feel if you arrived in a strange place, tired and distressed, and they started bossing you about? Think, sweetheart, think of how other creatures feel. This island is a good place to live because we all care for each other."

Large tears formed in Catkin's eyes. "But that's all I try to do!" she protested. "I only try to help! I'm not bossy!" She looked at Crispin and Cedar in turn, hoping that they would say, "Of course you're not!" but they didn't, so she looked at Sepia, who took her paw.

"You never mean any harm," said Sepia gently. "We know you only want to look after other animals, we just want you to know the best way to go about it. And sometimes, Princess, it's best to leave them alone."

A fat tear rolled down Catkin's cheek.

"I try to do everything right," she said, and sniffed. Sepia took a pawful of petals from a dish and offered them to her. Catkin dried her eyes and looked up at her parents with reproach in her pink-rimmed eyes, pouting dramatically. "It's not easy being a princess."

Cedar looked down at her paws to hide a smile. Crispin knelt on the floor beside Catkin and hugged her.

"I wouldn't know," he said. "I've never been a princess. But I think you're a very nice one."

Catkin wriggled free. "You're laughing at me!" she said. "Nobody on this island has ever been a princess, so nobody can tell me what it's supposed to be like!"

Crispin realized that she was right about this. "She has a point there," he admitted.

"Just be yourself, Catkin," said Cedar.

"But I don't know what that is," said Catkin, in a much smaller voice than usual. "I want to be a really good princess—I mean, I want to be a very good whatever I am, but I never get the chance. I want to do—you mustn't laugh—something really brave, and special, and noble, and *exciting*!" She looked her father in the eyes. "Everyone's always talking about the things you did, riding a swan and fighting Lord Husk, and all that stuff with Whitewings, and then the floods—and you, Mum, you did all those really dangerous, exciting things when you lived on Whitewings. And you saved animals when there was fouldrought. And Urchin and Needle, and you, Sepia! You rescued me when I was a baby! Wasn't that exciting?"

"I don't remember being excited," said Sepia. "Just very frightened."

"All the same," said Catkin, "you've all done wonderful, scary, dangerous things, and I don't get the chance, because you've done the exciting things already!"

"Your parents have made this island a safe place to live," said Sepia. "I don't think you'd like it if it were different."

"Yes, but it's so safe I never get to do anything really special!" wailed Catkin.

"Of course you do!" said Cedar.

"I mean, *really* special! Hero sort of special! Daddy, you're laughing at me!"

Crispin bit hard on the inside of his lip before answering. "No, darling, I'm not."

Catkin looked at him suspiciously, but went on. "The only adventure I ever had was being stolen when I was a baby, and I was too little to do anything about it. I can never go anywhere on my own for long. I want to do things *for* myself, *by* myself. Big, brave things."

"Most of life is doing little things," said Cedar gently, "and doing them really well."

"They might be little *brave* things," said Crispin.

"I'm sick of little things," snapped Catkin. "I wish I were a Voyager; then I could go anywhere. A Voyager can go away through the mists and come back again as much as they like."

She didn't know why she'd said that. There had only been three Voyagers in the entire history of the island, and none of them had been squirrels. It wasn't fair. She wrinkled her nose again and scowled. Crispin looked at her, and went on looking at her. She tried to keep the scowl on her face, but couldn't—a smile was growing inside her, and she couldn't hold it back, so she covered her face with her paws and found that the smile was too big for her, and she was laughing. She tolerated a hug.

"We'll have to think hard about this, Catkin, and talk," said Crispin. "Off you go, now. And send for Urchin."

"Shall I go and look after the swans?" she offered helpfully.

"No!" said Crispin. "Go and find your brother, and see what he'd like to do. *Ask* him, don't tell him. Let him make decisions."

"But he never does!" argued Catkin.

"He will," said Cedar. "He will if he gets the chance to learn. Away you go."

Catkin dried her eyes again, blew her nose, smoothed her ear tufts, and left the chamber. Sepia, at a nod from the queen, curtsied and went with her.

"Is she right?" she asked. "Do we watch her too carefully? After she was missing when she was a baby I couldn't bear to let her out of my sight. Now she wants to take risks, and I want to keep her safe."

"It's good that she wants to take responsibility," said Crispin. "She just has an unfortunate way of going about it."

Padra arrived at the royal chambers at the same time as Urchin. Burr brought cups of wine on a carved wooden tray, drew up chairs for Urchin and Padra and, as the evening was getting cooler, took a flint from a basket and lit the fire.

"Thank you, Burr," said Crispin. "You may go now. Good night! Move in closer to the fire, everyone, and tell me how our guests are doing."

"Lord and Lady Arcneck are keeping to themselves," said Padra. "Their son's completely different. He's pleasant and friendly, and said you rescued him from a water snake when he was little. He's called Crown."

31

"Crown!" repeated Cedar.

"His feathers sort of stick out around the top of his head," explained Urchin. "They regard that as a sign of his noble breeding, so they call him Crown."

"Arran's fur sticks out, but she calls it a nuisance," said Padra. "But Crown is a very likeable swan. His parents do rather look down their beaks at everyone, but he's not like that at all. He fits in well with the animals here. And he's very keen to be useful, especially to you, Crispin. He's been telling the whole island how you saved his life, and his mother's. If you've sent for us to suggest a brilliant strategy for fighting ravens, sorry, I haven't got one. And Urchin doesn't look inspired, either."

"Just now we're thinking about Catkin," said Crispin. "It seems that she's only bossy because she wants to prove herself, to meet challenges, and she wants the freedom to do it. That's what she *wants*. What I think she *needs* is to learn to live on the same terms as any other animal."

"Couldn't she do both?" suggested Padra. "If she had the freedom to explore, to make her own mistakes—ordinary, everyday mistakes, like everybody else's—she'd fall into a few challenging situations. She'd fall into lots of things."

"My father was a tower squirrel, but I wasn't a prince," said Crispin. "I don't know what it's like, growing up as royalty. We've tried to treat her perfectly normally, but it isn't normal, not really."

"She's never had the chance to run about in Anemone Wood and choose her own tree to climb," said Urchin. "The sort of thing other squirrels do. Needle and I built our own Mistmantle Tower in a tree."

"What happened to it?" asked Padra.

"It fell out of the tree and Needle landed on it," he said. "And I landed on Needle."

"Ouch," said Padra.

"Yes, she's the sharpest hedgehog on the island," said Urchin, still feeling that he should be calling Padra "sir," even though he was a member of the Circle and it was a long time since he'd been Padra's page. "Could Catkin go somewhere where she wouldn't be recognized? Nobody would treat her differently. She'd be the same as everybody else, like an ordinary squirrel."

"And fall on ordinary hedgehogs," said Padra. "That sounds good to me."

"She doesn't want 'ordinary,'" said Crispin. "She wants 'exciting.'"

"Oh, she'll find that as she goes along," said Padra.

"And ordinary won't be ordinary for her, Your Majesty," said Urchin. "It'll be an adventure."

"I think Urchin's idea is excellent," said Padra. "Let her go to some remote corner of the island where she won't be recognized, take a different name, and say . . . oh, I don't know . . ."

"Say her parents work at the tower?" suggested Urchin.

"Brilliant!" said Crispin. "She'll have to promise to cooperate, to keep her identity secret, and be willing to learn from the other animals. And she's not to go looking for heroic things to do. As Padra suggests, trouble will find her in its own time."

"That's what worries me," said the queen. "You're all in a great hurry to let her lose herself in a strange place and fall out of trees."

"We'll give her a bodyguard," said Crispin. "But nobody will know he's a bodyguard. An animal who'll keep her identity secret, keep his distance, and help her only if necessary. Brindle of the Circle, the hedgehog, would be good. He's young and new to the Circle, he gets on with people easily, and he's ready to take responsibility. And perhaps we'll have a quick, reliable mole to watch secretly and report back to us now and again."

"That would give me some peace of mind," said Cedar. "There's a bright young mole maid called Swish who could watch her discreetly. And how long should this go on?"

"Oh, until we think she's had long enough," said Crispin. "We can pack her off as soon as she likes."

"Should we wait until the swan war is over?" asked Urchin.

At once, he wished he hadn't asked. It had made the atmosphere change, as if the sun had clouded over—or, he thought, as if Crispin had clouded over.

"No," said Crispin. "She should go now."

Urchin was aware of the look that passed between the king and the captain. It was as if they were holding a solemn conversation he could not hear.

"Yes, I see," said Padra, although Crispin had not spoken. "If you've finished with us, Urchin and I will go and work out a plan that will not only defeat the ravens, it'll fling every last one of them into the sea.

34

Unless, Your Majesty"—he bowed to Cedar—"you would like one kept as a souvenir."

"What would I want a dead bird for?" said the queen. "But, Urchin," she went on, "you do understand, don't you—about Swan Isle? About leaving Mistmantle?"

Once again Urchin felt as if the sun had passed into shadow. "Yes, Queen Cedar," he said. "I'd thought of that."

"To work, then, Urchin," said Padra. "Shall we go back to my chambers?"

"What was that about?" asked Urchin as they walked along the corridor. "When Crispin said Catkin should go away before the swan war, and then neither of you said anything."

"Think, Urchin," said Padra, striding briskly past the rows of Threadings. "It's a war, it's an army. Who's going to lead it?"

"Oh," said Urchin. Of course Crispin wouldn't stay in Mistmantle and send other animals to fight this war. He would lead the Mistmantle armies, taking the greatest risks himself. If—and it hardly bore thinking about—Crispin was killed in this war, Catkin would be queen.

"So she needs to have her freedom while she can," he said.

"And she needs to grow up quickly," said Padra. "Your turn. What was it that the queen wanted you to understand?"

Urchin scowled. "That I can't go," he said, and kicked open the next door.

"Of course you can't!" said Padra. "You've already been beyond

35

the mists twice and returned, and nobody has ever done it a third time."

"I know the king's going into danger, but I envy him riding a swan again," Urchin admitted. "It won't be easy watching them all go and having to stay behind." He glanced toward a window and, seeing a swan sweep past, stopped. "Just look at that! Can you imagine riding a swan? It's as near as you could be to flying! The air rushes through your fur, and even when it's terrifying, it's . . ."

"Urchin!" said Padra. "That's not one of the swans who came before. It's another one. And . . . and look, Urchin!" His eyes brightened. "Let's tell the king!"

CHAPTER FOUR

NEEDLE, THE PRICKLIEST hedgehog in Mistmantle and Urchin's oldest friend, was one of the best needle-hedgehogs on all the island. At her first coming to the tower she had been taught by Mistress Thripple, the wife of Docken the hedgehog and mother of Hope and Mopple. (Now that Docken was a captain she was Lady Thripple, but she didn't expect anyone to call her that.) Thripple had a hunched and twisted look about her, but the longer Needle had known her, the less she noticed what she looked like. They had become great friends. If anything in the workrooms troubled Needle, she would ask motherly, sensible Thripple about it. So now she sat on a workroom bench when everyone else had left, surrounded by uncompleted tapestries, skeins of wool and silk, cord and ribbon, pale blue, deep blue, midnight blue, pale pink to deep pink, and every shade of green. Before her was a half-finished Threading of the tower, stitched on canvas.

"You wanted to see me?" said Thripple.

"Oh, yes, please!" said Needle, and shuffled along the workbench to make room. "Will you look at this, please?"

Thripple turned the Threading toward the light.

"It's by one of the new apprentices, isn't it?" she said.

"Yes, just a little bit of background," said Needle. "I gave it to that shy little hedgehog Myrtle."

"Oh, I know," said Thripple. "She hardly ever says a word. I thought at first she was too young to work here, but she was longing to start, and she loves it. And she's so talented. And such big eyes, more like squirrel eyes than a hedgehog's."

"And not—er—well, I don't think she's very bright," said Needle.

"But a sweet nature," said Thripple, examining the Threading. "This is very neat and even." She ran her paw along the back. "And nicely finished. What am I supposed to be looking at? Oh!" She bent to look more closely. "Has she added something, here, in the window? Is it a sword?"

"Yes," said Needle. With a claw she outlined the tiny shape worked into the stitches of the tower window. "At first I thought it was just a bit of highlighting, but it isn't; it's a sword. And nobody told her to put that in."

"She isn't the sort to think of it on her own," remarked Thripple.

"No," said Needle. "And when I asked her why she'd done it she went all scared and worried—I thought she was going to cry! She said she didn't mean it, and she didn't know she *had* done it.

38

She turned those big frightened eyes on me and asked if she should take it out, but I told her to leave it. I said I wanted you to see it. I calmed her down, too, and told her she hadn't done anything wrong."

Thripple frowned a little in thought. "Does Myrtle know any of the symbols in the Threadings Code?" she asked. "It doesn't seem likely."

"That's the other strange thing," said Needle. "We haven't got past the first lesson, and that's hard work where Myrtle's concerned. She just about remembers which color stands for which animal, and she knows that anything to do with the Heart is outlined in gold, but that's it. She certainly doesn't know what a sword means. It really is as if she didn't know what she was doing."

"Sword for battle," said Thripple thoughtfully. "And it seems that there really is going to be a battle, from what I hear about these swans. And she's shown the sword pointing upward, which means victory. Could she have known there would be a battle?"

"She did it first thing this morning," said Needle. "The swans hadn't even arrived."

"This is all very strange," said Thripple. "And rather unsettling. If she does anything like it again, we should tell Brother Fir . . . I mean, Brother Juniper."

Something passing across the window shadowed the tapestry. Thripple and Needle looked up and gasped. Swan after swan after swan, flocks and hosts of swans, flew past the tower.

Padra and Urchin hammered at the door of the royal chambers and, as soon as Crispin called, ran in.

"Pardon us, Your Majesties," said Padra, "but come to the shore!"

Already the sands were white and gray with swans. The sky was filled with them. Cygnets carried on their mother's and father's backs whimpered with weariness. Under Arran and Docken's orders, animals ran to bring food and water to the birds.

"They're worn out," said Padra. "They'll take some time to recover their full strength, but we needn't worry about how to get an army to Swan Isle. You'll get your battle, Crispin."

More swans arrived the next day, and the next, with outstretched necks and white wings beating slowly, slowly, until they sank to the sea with tired eyes and bedraggled wings. Mistmantle animals fetched clean water and pondweed, and helped them to find the fresh water they needed. Tipp and Todd, Captain Lugg's grandsons, led pond patrols to find the most suitable habitats on the island. Padra and Arran's bright-eyed daughter, Swanfeather, having been named after swans, wanted desperately to help, and staggered up the shore with slopping buckets of water. She yearned to pick up the cygnets and cuddle them, but Arran urged her not to.

"The parents are fiercely protective of them," she warned.

"You'll get a badly bitten paw if you try to touch their young."

Swanfeather looked as if she'd very much like to try it, all the same, but it wasn't worth the risk.

"When the adult birds have rested and recovered," said Arran, "they can fly back to Swan Isle carrying Mistmantle warriors."

"Is Daddy going?" asked Swanfeather.

Arran laughed. "Not otters," she said. "We're too big."

"Not even small otters?" suggested Swanfeather.

"Not even *one* small otter," said Arran firmly. "Sword-skilled animals and archers. Animals who have excellent balance, and can keep their heads in a crisis."

"Are Catkin and Oakleaf going?"

"Certainly not!" said Arran. "They're much too young!"

"Well, where *is* Catkin, then?" asked Swanfeather, picking up an empty bucket. "I never see her now. Where's she gone?"

"I have absolutely no idea," lied Arran.

Animals from all over Mistmantle gathered at the tower to join the war band, to say farewell to their warrior friends and relations, or simply to admire the swans. As their health and strength returned, the swans' wings grew strong and smooth, their feathers gleamed white, and their eyes were bright as they prepared for battle. Even from the small, curved little bays on the northwest of the island, where animals lived contentedly and minded their own business, they hurried off to the tower to see the magnificent visitors and their own king and captains, who, they said, were worth more than a dozen swans.

In Curlingshell Bay, there was so much talk of the swans that they barely noticed the new hedgehog who had moved in. —*Nice fellow, though. Brindle, pleasant young chap, easy to get on with, always ready with a helping paw.* He was something to do with the tower, but had moved to the bay for some peace and quiet. Quite right too, they said. There was a young squirrel lass with him, whose parents worked at the tower. Apparently her mother made salves for the healers, and her father—what did her father do?—oh, he was a guard or something of that sort. Her name was Lapwing. She'd soon settle in, they said. There were plenty of youngsters about for her to make friends with.

Having said that, Lapwing hadn't made a good start. The other young ones said she was bossy. They didn't like a newcomer who behaved as if she ran the whole island, let alone Curlingshell Bay; but in time, and after a few tears, Lapwing seemed to understand this and settle down. They weren't taking much notice of her anyway. They were much more interested in the great happenings at the tower than in one young squirrel.

Pennants flew from the tower, swords flashed, cloaks swished. The fighting force was to be made up of squirrels and moles, so it was squirrel and mole families who hugged each other long and tightly. Mothers told their sons and daughters to take care, the sons and daughters laughed, hugged them, and looked forward to the adventure, or pretended to. Animals gathered around Juniper for prayer and blessing. Near the jetty, King Crispin and others of the vanguard—including the mole brothers Tipp and Todd, and Russet of the Circle—sat in gently bobbing boats, speaking with the swans who drifted around them. On the jetty, gazing with yearning at the high white wings of the swans, stood Urchin and Sepia, trying to answer Prince Oakleaf's questions. Prince Oakleaf was very much like a younger version of Crispin, and full of questions such as "How does that work?" and "How do they know?" Questions Urchin hadn't thought about and struggled to answer. He couldn't easily answer "What's it like to ride a swan?" How could he describe flying?

"Perhaps one day you'll do it yourself, Oakleaf," he said.

"Father says swans don't like being ridden; only if there's a real need," said Oakleaf. "Urchin, isn't that your mum . . . I mean, your foster-mo . . . Sorry, I didn't mean . . ."

Urchin's foster mother, Apple, sticking out her elbows, pushed her way through the crowd and waddled along the jetty. It creaked and wobbled a little.

"Never seen—" she began, then stopped to get her breath back. "Afternoon, Prince Oakleaf, ooh, you get more like your father every day, never seen so many swans—hello, Sepia! There's going to be feathers everywhere when this lot flies off, island's full of feathers, beautiful feathers, I've got some for me hat, don't get too close to

43

them swans, Prince Oakleaf, just as well they're going, don't know how we'd go on feeding them all. I'm right glad you're not going, Urchin, aren't you, Sepia?"

Sepia nodded, knowing that there was no point in saying anything, as Apple would go on talking. She was glad, very glad, that Urchin couldn't go. But Crispin was going, and she felt desperately sorry for Prince Oakleaf. Apple clasped the prince's paw in both of hers and leaned to look earnestly into his eyes. "Don't you worry, son, your father'll soon get the better of them ravens, nasty old birds, they're only—"

A clang of metal made her, and everyone, jump. The jetty shook. Arran and Fingal had clashed their swords together to call for quiet. Crispin leaped from the boat to the jetty (Apple ducked), and ran to the nearest high rock, where all the animals could see him.

"We leave now," cried Crispin, "to aid the swans who have been our friends in time of need, and deliver them from the cruelty and injustice that claims their island and attacks their families. Cedar the Queen will be regent while I am away. The captains will advise and assist her and continue their duties as present. Should I not return to you—"

"Oh, it won't come to that!" whispered Apple.

"—I declare my daughter, Catkin, as the true Heir of Mistmantle, who will rule after me. The queen, with the help of the captains, will be her regent until she is old enough to rule alone, and I ask your support and your prayers for them all. Heart keep you!"

44

Through the lift and fall of swan wings, Urchin could hardly see Juniper as he limped through the crowd toward Crispin. But he saw the king kneel, and presently Juniper was standing on the rock with his paw raised.

"Heart keep you, swans, creatures of Mistmantle, King Crispin. May the swans of Swan Isle be free and at peace. May all be restored to their own. May this army return safely! Lord Arcneck, King Crispin, we pray for your victory and a joyous homecoming!"

At first Urchin could only see a confused flapping of wings, but the noise of it grew like a calling of drums, and a draft rose that left Apple holding on to her hat with both paws as she gazed open-mouthed. But the swans only flew as far as the shallows, where they settled on the pure blue-green waters, drifting and gliding until they had formed rank upon rank of swans, all with their wings curved high over their backs, their necks arching, and their bright beaks high. From boats and rafts, the Mistmantle warriors mounted.

The watching animals stretched up on clawtips, peering around each other. —*Look, there's our Chaffie. Look, there's Mallow, can you see?* —*Oh, look at Trey, he looks so different with his sword . . . doesn't he look grown-up? —Don't they look splendid?* There was waving, and dabbing of eyes, and calls carried across the bay. —*Take care, Heart bless you. —Come home safely. —Don't worry about me, Mum . . .* Then the first flight of swans stretched out their necks, skimmed across the water, and, to the gasps and cries of the Mistmantle animals, rose higher and farther, farther and higher, until they were only specks rising above the mists. There were a few sniffs and sighs, and some very young animals saying they were bored and could they go home now? Sepia rubbed her eyes with her paw. Apple sat down heavily.

"Heart bless the king, but it don't seem right." She sniffed. "I remember half them guards and archers and that when they were little, it don't seem right at all, they just want to go on living their own quiet lives and they have to go out and fight them ravens, it's a terrible thing. And there's the little ones with their brothers and sisters and uncles and aunties going off with them swans."

"But not parents, Mistress Apple," Prince Oakleaf pointed out. "My father said no parents of very little ones were to go—apart from himself, and that's different, and besides it's only Almondflower who's still little. He really does have to go."

"Heart love him, course he does!" exclaimed Apple. "Never said he didn't. All the fault of them ravens for starting it. Let me tell you, Your Highness, if I could ride a swan I'd sort them out myself, but I don't reckon there's a swan in all the islands could carry me and I wouldn't want to sink one, would I? Mind you," she added, "I reckon they'll have to fly through the night, and won't they bump into each other?"

"I don't think they ever do," said Sepia.

"They're too clever," Urchin reassured her. "And the king will attack at dawn."

It grew late, but nobody in the tower felt like going to bed. They wouldn't sleep. In the royal chambers, Prince Oakleaf stayed up late, arranging wooden figures of squirrels and moles as Urchin explained the battle strategy to him. Oakleaf had asked where Catkin was, and Urchin had lowered his voice and said, "Secret princess training. So secret that I do't know where she is. And I mean *secret*. Understood?"

There was a knock at the door so soft that Urchin wasn't sure he'd heard it, but when the queen called, "Come in," a very small female mole slipped into the chamber as smoothly as if she were on wheels. She was dark gray rather than black, with bright, happy eyes as she bowed to the queen.

"Oakleaf," ordered the queen, "go to the turret, please, and see how Brother Fir is. Then you can go to bed."

"He'll be asleep," said Prince Oakleaf.

"Just do it, please," replied the queen. Prince Oakleaf looked ready to go on arguing, but thought better of it and left the room. The queen and Urchin huddled near to the mole.

"Welcome, Swish!" whispered the queen. "How's Catkin?"

"She's all right now, Your Majesty," said Swish the mole. She had a quick, breathless way of speaking and a ready smile. "Learning to keep her mouth shut, Majesty. Nearly gave herself away once or twice. Stopped herself in time. When the king flew away, she stopped and looked up to watch, same as all the others, but she never said a word."

"Well done, Swish," said the queen, and offered her a cordial and biscuits from a tray on the table. "Keep up the good work."

CHAPTER FIVE

FEAR HUNG IN THE SLOW GRAY dawn over Swan Isle. Deep in reeds and in hidden nests, swans hid their young and watched, their eyes fierce and weary, for the harsh beat of blue-black wings. They sheltered their young from the cruel raven beaks and from the sight of slaughtered swans and shattered eggshells. The island smelled of blood. When mother swans wept for their young, they cried quietly. The squirrels had hidden deep in the trees, rationing out the stores of food, seeking water only from underground or collecting it from the leaves at night. Nothing must attract the attention of the ravens.

When an animal or swan was caught by the ravens, there were two possible endings. The first was to be killed and eaten at once. The second was to be forced to work—*Bring water, more water. Bring meat, more meat, faster. Bury the bones*—until they staggered with exhaustion and were killed, and more animals would be dragged miserably to slavery. Nights were long and days were worse.

Caw! Caw! The ravens called to each other as they completed each night patrol of the island. Swans and squirrels, just starting to fall asleep, jerked awake. To Pitter, a young squirrel hiding in a tree with her uncle, aunt, and cousins, it seemed that they did it on purpose so that nobody would sleep properly.

Pitter had never known her father. Now she no longer had a mother. So what if her mother had been so careless and lazy that she had never cleaned the nest or prepared food, and Pitter had to do it? So what if she had spent more time with her friends than with Pitter, and never seemed to care where Pitter was? She was my mother, thought Pitter. The only one I could ever have. They had no right to kill her. She imagined herself standing up to the ravens and terrifying them, even fighting the Archraven himself. But, of course, she couldn't. She hid and cowered with everyone else, and despised herself for it. She lived now with an uncle, aunt, and cousins, who plainly resented her.

Knowing that she wouldn't go back to sleep, she put both paws to a hole in a tree and peered out, leaning to one side, then to the other. If she pressed far enough to the left, she could just see a corner of the princess's grave.

Since the ravens had come, hope had drained from the island. Every new day brought wretchedness, and every new day was too long. Like all the squirrels, Pitter looked for little things to bring brightness—a few flowers opening before the ravens could rip them up and use them for nesting; a little sunlight through the leaves before raven wings blocked it out; a mouthful of hazelnuts—and, for Pitter, there was the princess's grave.

The Swan Isle squirrels were a forgetful bunch, and nobody seemed to know who the princess had been. They just shrugged and said that the neat mound of stones in the clearing near the sea was "the princess's grave," but nobody could remember her name. —*It was, you know, her.* —*I think I sort of know who she was.* —*Oh, yes, whats-her-whiskers.* —*If you ask me, she threw herself at that stranger as soon as he got here.* —*Didn't she wear that gold thing on her head?* There was a story that a squirrel had once come to the island, and he was a prince or a lord or something, and he married a squirrel here, but she died, and nobody could remember what had happened to him. —*Suppose he just went away.* —*Don't know.* —*Wonder what happened to that gold thing.* —*That was pretty.*

Pitter thought there must be a wonderful story in all this. She wished she knew more of the story of the poor young squirrel and how she had died, and what happened to the prince. She imagined how good it would have been if the princess had been her sister, or even better, her mother. One of the things that held her up, in these miserable times, was to see the princess's grave, and know that the young princess slept there quietly, where the ravens couldn't get her. In her head, she made up stories about the princess. She imagined the squirrel princess leading them into battle against the ravens, a sword in her hand and a crown on her head, and herself fighting at the princess's side.

Caw! Caw! That was the sentries again. They always cried out twice. A third call meant that they were alarmed about something and were calling for help and reinforcements, but there was nothing here to trouble them for long. The swans had fought against the ravens at first, but those who survived had flown away. Lord and Lady Arcneck had abandoned them. It was all right for swans, who could fly. One band of brave squirrels had built a boat and tried to escape, but the ravens saw them and tore them to pieces. The thought of the ravens feasting on the bodies made Pitter's stomach lurch. She pressed further against the tree, craning her neck to see the pile of stones, wishing that the princess could help.

High above in the gray dawn, Crispin of Mistmantle rode with Russet of the Circle on his right and Tipp the mole on his left. Three by three, swans and their riders circled the skies.

A little closer. Closer. Crispin crouched lower over the swan lord's neck and strained his eyes through the grayness to see the swans take their places above the island.

"Now," he whispered.

Caw! Caw! Before the sentries could utter a third cry, the swans had gripped them by the throat. Crispin's sword ran through one, Russet's through the other. As the bodies tumbled to earth, a few raven wings ruffled, but none of them fully woke.

"The ravens are very big, Your Majesty," whispered Tipp.

"They're only birds," Crispin whispered back. "But you're right not to underestimate them." He wouldn't tell Tipp that he, too, was astonished by the size of the ravens. Those huge sharp beaks were terrible weapons.

He would not kill a sleeping enemy, but they would wake in his time, not their own. With the island ringed by archers on swans, this was his time. Wherever a sentry strutted, a swan threw it from its perch. Squirrels scrambled down trees, and a rush of swan wings made the ravens wake, yawn, and look about them, raising their wings to attack, tipping back their heads to rasp out war cries, and opening their beaks to the deadly rain of arrows. Crispin and Lord Arcneck swerved away from the raised wings, then soared and swooped. Lord Arcneck bit into the neck of the raven flying down on Tipp.

"Fire!" yelled Crispin, as the three swans soared above the Mistmantle archers. The next wave of arrows sang from the sky. Black shapes, losing the rhythm of flight, tumbled raggedly to the ground. From every part of the sky came the enraged screeches of the ravens. Those who fell were finished off by the squirrels and moles on the ground—those who tried to fly above the archers were met by swans and warriors.

Crispin, Russet, and Tipp wheeled higher and looked down over the swans' necks. Below them, the ground grew black with feathers.

"They'll soon have the sense to stop flying into our arrows," yelled Crispin. "We won't give them time to choose the ground. Just give the moles a bit longer."

He leaned sideways to have a better look. Mistmantle squirrels and moles were running into cover in the undergrowth, ready to spring out with sharp swords. He could feel the eyes of Tipp fixed on him, ready for a signal. *Not yet. Not yet . . .* From the corner of his eye he saw a dark shape to the right, and heard the swish of Russet's sword as a raven fell to the ground.

Now! At the raising of Crispin's sword for the attack, the swans dived toward the earth, a flurry of black wings following them. Squirrels and moles leaped and rolled to the ground. As the swans rose to battle in the air again, the Mistmantle animals fought with swords, teeth, claws, and all their strength and determination. Tipp slashed wildly about, fell, scrambled to his paws, then remembered all he had been taught—*Go for the belly or the throat, whichever is nearest as it lands. If the bird tries to peck you, slice off its head as it darts forward. Strike quick and clean. Stand together, watch each other's back.* A bird's head, with cruel black eyes and a savage beak, leaned toward him, and he lashed out with a blow that only overbalanced it, but the next killed it instantly. He staggered back, tripping over the outstretched claw of a dead raven, and plunged his sword two-handed into the neck of the bird that squawked over him. Then another mole was dragging him to the cover of the heather.

"Well done, son," whispered the mole. "Now we lie low and get our breath back, and do it the easy way." He pushed Tipp deep into the heather. "Get down."

The ravens were searching for them. One harsh black beak tore at the heather and stabbed hard into the earth.

"It's looking for us!" whispered Tipp. The other mole rolled onto his back and stabbed upward.

"Found us, then, didn't it?" said the mole. "Keep moving about, now. Don't give 'em a chance."

From a straggling nest high in a birch tree, the Archraven watched, flexing his talons. He had sharpened them for such a battle as this, and their edges were jagged. They could rip an enemy open. On one side of him was his son, the Silver Prince and, on the other, his sister, the Taloness.

"Kill and devour!" cried the Silver Prince. "Kill and devour!" It was the call that served the ravens for everything. It was their anthem, their battle cry, their solemn vow, their cradle song and their death lament, their celebration and their reason to live.

"Kill and devour!" rasped the prince. His father looked down through heavy, hooded eyes. This was his son, his only son. He had killed his wife, the prince's mother. She had not been careful enough of the prince, not respectful enough. She had not understood how honored she was to be the mother of the Silver Prince, so he had killed her. The Silver Prince did not need a mother. He was a true raven, proud, vain, greedy, bullying, and noisy. He was the Silver Prince.

The Archraven and the Taloness jerked their heads left, right, forward, and back, watching the scene. The flash of weapons was beautiful. Such shining, such silver, such glitter and slash! It set the battle hatred in a hard, fast pulse through their veins. Stretching out his wings, the Archraven wheeled over the island. Near the shore, the fighting was fierce. The clang of swords was a challenge that rang and stung like sword points. Those flashing swords, and the warriors wielding them—he would have them all. He flew back to the Taloness and the Silver Prince. The Prince had much to learn.

"Watch me, Silver Prince!" he croaked, and held a wing over the prince as they flew. "Come! Learn!"

"Pitter!" squealed her uncle. "Get away from there!" When he tried to drag her from the hole in the tree trunk, she shook him off, and with a mutter of "Get yourself killed, then!" he retreated farther into the tree with her aunt and cousins. Pitter's claws curled, and she bit her lip. Moles darted up from the ground with their bright swords, squirrels leaped from branches to slash and stab, and swans seized ravens by the neck to finish them with a bite and a shake. Around the princess's grave, the fighting was furious. When a raven landed on it, Pitter growled, but a squirrel jumping from a tree landed on the raven's back and speared it before springing to the ground. Another raven flew down, and again a mole jumped up to strike.

The raven turned its head, and Pitter saw, too closely, the power of the curved beak. With a stroke of that beak, the raven flung the sword from the mole's paw. As the disarmed mole struggled to rise, the raven raised its talons, stretched and sharpened to kill.

Pitter ran from her hiding place, sprang across the open ground, and grabbed the raven's claw with both paws. As the raven lowered its beak to strike at her, she swung clear but clung on, biting and tugging. It gave Tipp the mole the moment that he needed to find his sword again. As she ducked and swerved, there was a terrible sound like tearing and a rasp from the raven's throat, and the bird lay dead, its wings still spread.

Pitter looked up. The young mole had picked himself up from the ground again, when with a cry of "No!" Pitter pushed him over, rolling with him across the outstretched black wing of the dead raven. A stone thudded down on the place where they had stood.

"The princess's grave!" screamed Pitter in fury. "They're on the princess's grave!" She had looked up just in time to save him, and had seen the ravens scratching and pulling at the stones on the princess's grave, rolling them to fall on the enemy.

"Get your head down!" shouted the mole, and pushed her under cover of the heather. "And humble thanks for saving my life; consider me in your debt. Tipp of Mistmantle at your servant, Mistress . . . ?"

"Pitter," she gasped. "Never mind that; they're destroying the princess's grave!"

Tipp raised his head a little to squint through the heather. "The swans have seen them," he said.

Swans swooped down to grab at the ravens as they tore up the stones. In a blur of red, a squirrel leaped from the back of a swan, twirling his tail for balance as he landed on the cairn. With two swishes of his sword, two ravens toppled to the ground.

"The king!" gasped Tipp, scrambling to his paws to fight beside him. "I have to defend him!"

A hoarse shriek, as if the clouds were being ripped apart, made every animals and every bird stop fighting and look up. There were fewer ravens now. The swans and Mistmantle were winning, and dead ravens were heaped on the open ground. The Archraven, circling the island, had seen who led the squirrels, his attention caught by the flash of gold from his head. If he killed and devoured their leader, they would lose heart, but he must do it unaided. The glory of this kill must be his alone.

Crispin, sword in hand as he stood on the cairn, kicked away a raven's body to make room for Lord Arcneck. Above them wheeled the Archraven.

"Kill and devour!" he cried. "We will kill and devour you, tree-rat! Who dares come against us?"

"Lord Arcneck of Swan Isle and Crispin of Mistmantle," cried Crispin. "We come for the creatures of this island, for their freedom and their right to live in peace."

A terrible sound broke the air all around them—crackling and cackling like swords sharpened on stone, strident and harsh. Crispin couldn't tell what it was—a war cry? Behind him, Lord Arcneck hissed as he lifted his wings.

"They are laughing! The ravens laugh at us!"

He rose into the air, but as he did so, six ravens fell on him, seizing him by the beak, the wings, the feet, and grappling him to the ground. Swans and squirrels rushed to help Lord Arcneck, but this was what the Archraven had hoped for. For a few seconds, the squirrel leader on the cairn stood alone. The Archraven flexed his talons, lowered his beak, and swooped.

"Your Majesty!" cried Tipp, lurching through heather toward him. Until the last split second, Crispin stood still. Then with a twist and a spring he was high in the air, flinging himself onto the Archraven's back and raising the sword in both paws. He stabbed down with a sword thrust that ran through the raven's body.

"*Treachery!*" screeched a voice above them. "*Treachery, treachery!*"

There were more ravens above them, swooping down to strike as Crispin heaved the sword from the dying Archraven, but Russet and Tipp were scrambling up the cairn to the king's side. Pitter stumbled after them. In one horrible moment that made her cold to the bones, she saw what would happen next and cried out, but it was too late. As Crispin turned, raising his sword again, the dying Archraven raised a claw and ripped into Crispin's shoulder.

"He is dead!" cried Crispin. "Your leader is dead, and his troops lie dead around him!"

His voice seemed to come from far away, and he felt he was swaying. With his sword he pushed the Archraven's body to the ground, noticing blood on his claw and wondering why he suddenly felt weaker.

58

But the ravens knew they were defeated. Already they were gathering above the trees, crying and wheeling, until they were only specks of pepper in the sky and, at last, were gone.

The Mistmantle animals hardly saw the ravens go. They were scrambling onto the cairn where Crispin lay, his eyes closed, blood seeping into the stones.

"Move him carefully," ordered Russet. "Lord Arcneck, please help me get him to the ground. Find something to stop the bleeding."

Pitter was pulling moss from the stones. She was astonished at herself, damaging the princess's grave when she had just defended it, but this was important.

"Please, sir, listen, sir," she gabbled to Russet. "This moss is good for stopping bleeding. There's more of it on the ground, please, sir, it's what we use all the time."

Russet turned over the wounded king, and Pitter pressed her paw to her mouth. She could see no white fur at all. There was only dark blood and a deep ragged tear running from shoulder to hip. With both paws she pressed the moss hard against the wound.

"This is moss from the princess's grave," she said, though she didn't know if he could hear her. "Our princess will watch over you."

The squirrel king did not move.

CHAPTER SIX

FREEDOM! CORR WAS LOVING freedom, the taste of it in the air, the feel of it in the sand under his paws, the touch and smell of it every morning as he woke. No nets to mend, no fetching and carrying, and, most of all, nobody telling him what to do, how to do it, and where and when to do it, then nagging him for not doing it well enough. He could choose where to row his boat and where to land. He caught his own fish, and lit fires to cook it on if he felt like cooking it at all. He found that there were at least a dozen different kinds of seaweed—pink, purple, black, and every shade of green—that he'd never seen before. The Island of Mistmantle, with its bays and rock pools, was more varied and beautiful than he had ever imagined.

At first he chatted mostly to other shore animals. As he became bolder, he made his way farther inland to explore woods and hills. He saw the way the light changed on trees and water, and how skies were different every morning and every night. When his boat became battered, he patched it up again.

He was enjoying it all hugely, but there wasn't much in the way of adventure—not unless you counted getting lost a few times and having to find his way back to his boat and campfire. And he killed a water snake, but he'd done that before; rescued a rather frightened little mole that had lost its home tunnel; and helped a family of hedgehogs move into a tree root. It was fun, but it wasn't enough. He needed more than that to tell them about when he turned up at the tower. And he would like to take a present, a really special present, for old Brother Fir. The trouble was, he didn't know what was special. The bushes inland were bright with flowers he'd never seen before, but they might be commonplace at the tower.

On a night of cloud and mist, when Corr slept curled against the shelter of his boat, Urchin of the Riding Stars lay in his chamber at the Spring Gate and decided that if he couldn't get to sleep, he may as well stop trying. Before dawn he got up and wandered down to the shore.

Were those swans in the sky? Between cloud and darkness, it was hard to tell. He strained to look into the grayness, then took a run at the tower, ran halfway up the wall, stopped, looked, and ran higher. And higher. And higher. At the window of the priest's turret he climbed in, nudged Juniper awake, and said, "They're coming home!" Then he ran onto the battlements.

The sun had been fully up for hours, and animals were gathered on the rocks by the time the swans landed. Boats were ready to ferry the warriors from swan to shore. In the kitchens, animals worked furiously to prepare food the returning heroes would like.

The healers were ready, too. Under the queen's instructions, rooms had been prepared for the wounded. Clean white beds, bandages, water, salves, and medicines were neatly arranged in rows.

Urchin stood beside Prince Oakleaf, a little behind Juniper and the queen. The breeze that chased the mists away flapped at his deep red cloak and ruffled his ears. Animals whispered to each other, shading their eyes as they peered into the sky. As the swans drew nearer, the chatter stopped. Animals held tightly to each other's paws. Needle, with her brother, Scufflen, beside her, remembered the Threading with the picture of a sword pointing upward and hoped it told the truth. At a tower window, Sepia cradled Princess Almondflower, singing softly as she watched.

The swans flew smoothly and steadily, close together. No riders waved from their backs. Standing on clawtip, craning his neck, Urchin saw at last the figure of Russet of the Circle leaning to the right of his swan, and a small squirrel he didn't recognize doing the same opposite him. Then he realized that they were both watching, very carefully, the back of the swan between them, where no rider could be seen.

The swans were close now, almost at the tower. Something lay on Lord Arcneck's back—something white, and heaped up. Padra called an order to the stretcher bearers as Lord Arcneck landed at the queen's paws and Prince Oakleaf ran forward. From the white heaped-up blanket, a little of Crispin's face showed.

Juniper and the queen knelt, their faces taut with fear. Each put a paw to Crispin's neck, feeling for a pulse. A girl squirrel Urchin had never seen before stood beside them, her paws full of moss.

"Heart hold you, Crispin," said Padra, bending over him.

Crispin's eyes opened. He almost smiled.

"We won," he whispered. "Padra, help me sit up. They need to see I'm still alive."

"You mustn't move!" said Russet, and bowed to the queen. "He's badly wounded, madam."

"Obey orders, Padra," muttered Crispin with a faint smile, but he gritted his teeth and winced as Padra raised him. He lifted a paw to greet the animals, but the movement made him sway. If Padra had not been holding him, he would have fallen. In the tower, Sepia turned Princess Almondflower away from the window.

"Take him to our chambers," ordered the queen, and raised her voice. "Animals of Mistmantle, the king needs your prayers!" The other animals ran to greet their friends and families, but they did so in subdued quiet.

Urchin dared not think how close Crispin might be to the line between life and death. The thought of Mistmantle without him was unbearable. In the royal chamber, he watched as the queen gently unwrapped the blanket, and gasped. Dried blood caked the king's chest. Half covered by moss, a deep and jagged gash seared him from shoulder to hip.

"What's all this moss?" demanded the queen.

The small squirrel scurried forward, her voice trembling with shyness. Her paws shook as she held out the moss.

"Please, Your Majesty," she whispered, "it's called mendingmoss. It stops the bleeding. You'll need more, please, Your Majesty; you have to keep taking it off and changing it so I brought some fresh, Your Majesty."

For a moment, the queen only looked at her as if she were speaking a foreign language. Then she wrung out a cloth in a bowl of water and began to gently wash away the moss and blood from the king's deep wound.

"Your Majesty," whispered Urchin, "shall I fetch Catkin?"

"No," said the queen, then thought again. "Yes. She'd better be here. Squirrel, tell me about this moss."

Urchin bowed and slipped to the door. He'd fetch Catkin himself, praying that she would not be queen by morning. Juniper was just coming in with a small oval box in his hand. It was made of pale pink stone, with flecks of gold and silver.

"The Heartstone?" whispered Urchin.

"He needs it," Juniper whispered back. "It has properties that none of us understand."

Around Crispin stood Russet, Padra, the queen, and the little stranger squirrel with her moss. Nobody cried, nobody fussed.

64

Quietly, steadily, with watchful eyes and skilled paws, they attended the king. Juniper, joining them, took the Heartstone of Mistmantle from its box and folded Crispin's claws over it.

"Hold the Heartstone, Your Majesty," he said. "Hold the Heartstone, and live." But he had to hold Crispin's paw closed. There was no strength in it.

Animals gathered around the tower. From Fir's turret to the Chamber of Candles, from Mistmantle Tower to the North Shore and the Rough Rocks in Anemone Wood. In the Tangletwigs, on hilltops and on sands, at the rivers and the waterfalls, candles were lit and prayers were said. Urchin brought Catkin to the royal chambers. Prince Oakleaf refused to leave his father's side. Juniper, Padra, and Urchin took turns staying by the king as Cedar changed dressings, cleaned the wound, and raised the king's head to give him sips of medicines and water from the Spring Gate. Animals left flowers, berries, and bottles of their best cordials at the tower for him. Every morning, Pitter looked out of her window and pinched herself to see if she had woken up.

She was in awe of the queen, who seemed so efficient and so clever that Pitter adored and feared her at the same time. On that first day she had stammered out to the queen everything she knew about mendingmoss, please, Your Majesty, and how she had come to Mistmantle with the other animals because, please, Your Majesty, they didn't know about it and she did. Then she had been taken to

65

another room where somebody had brought her food and a drink, which was very nice—but she didn't know what it was and what she would do next. Then a kind-faced squirrel had come in and said, "You're Pitter, aren't you? I'm Sepia. We've made up a bed for you in my room for tonight. I hope you don't mind sharing, but it means you won't be lonely."

A day passed, and the king fought to stay alive. Nobody saw the queen. She stayed beside Crispin, changing the moss, talking to him, urging him to live, praying, not telling anyone that she had never known anyone to survive a wound as terrible as this. Other Mistmantle animals had been wounded, and the healers worked steadily. Lord Arcneck and the swans were preparing to leave. Realizing how interested the queen was in mendingmoss, Prince Crown, who desperately wanted to help Mistmantle, promised to send bundles of it to Mistmantle as soon as he could find where it grew; but the swans knew little about it. It was, they said, a squirrel thing.

Mistmantle animals knew that life must go on and it was best to keep busy, so they went back to their gathering, building, and fishing, and burrows, nests, and gardens. Needle and the other workroom animals sketched designs for new Threadings. Mistress Tay, visiting the workrooms to inspect the new designs, snapped at little Myrtle and demanded to know what on the island she thought she was up to, sewing a flower in the sea? Myrtle, who hadn't realized what she was doing, shrank down, stammered out earnest apologies, and unpicked it.

The Taloness settled on the high bare branch of a stricken tree and surveyed the ground beneath her. She had gathered together the remains of the raven army and settled for a brief rest on the first island they came to, though it was almost barren. Hardly anything lived here but snakes—writhing, treacherous things, and hardly worth eating; but the snakes themselves must be feeding on something. Sharp eyes detected small, scurrying animals, and sharper beaks finished them off. The Silver Prince strutted among the others, pushing them aside, giving orders—*Bring me that one. Kill that for me.*

This would only be a rest. The Taloness jerked her head from one side to the other as she scanned the horizon. There were other islands far from here, where colonies of ravens thrived. They would gather strength, for ravens of all islands would gather to support the Silver Prince, keen to show themselves his friends. They would be willing to die for him, and some of them would have to before revenge was complete. The Archraven had thought himself the greatest leader they had ever known, but under the Taloness, the ravens would have a power her brother had never dreamed of. The Silver Prince was still too young and inexperienced to make his own decisions. She would guide and instruct him.

When they had fed and slept, she led them on to the next island where ravens lived. She made sure that the prince always flew with the sun on his wings so that he would appear silver, not gray. Everywhere they went, their followers increased.

If Crispin of Mistmantle had lived, he would regret it. She would make him wish he had died on the cairn at Swan Isle.

Pitter was determined to make the most of every day on Mistmantle. Every time a swan prepared to fly back to Swan Isle she hid, in case anyone remembered that she was still there and tried to send her home. She had made friends with a squirrel called Scatter—a great friend of the otters—who came from Whitewings, the same island that the queen came from. Scatter knew what it was like to be new to Mistmantle, and was just introducing her to some very friendly otters, when a messenger came to say that the queen wished to see Miss Pitter "at once."

Pitter swallowed hard, and her legs felt wobbly. *The king's dead, the queen thinks the moss killed him, she blames me, it will be all my fault, I did something wrong, they'll put me in a dungeon. . . .* But the messenger was smiling.

She stood outside the Throne Room door, her paw in her mouth. There hadn't been time to brush her ears or smooth her fur. When the page opened the door, Pitter whipped her paw out of her mouth, pattered in, and saw the queen rush toward her. She managed a shaky curtsy and was saved from falling as the queen took her paws.

"Pitter!" she cried. "Come and meet King Crispin!"

The Throne Room, with its two carved wooden thrones, small tables, and open windows, was simple and beautiful. She gasped. King Crispin was there! He was seated on the throne, his face thinner than she remembered it, and the dark red seam still running from shoulder to hip. Pitter couldn't resist a glance up at the top of his head, and was a little disappointed that he wasn't wearing a crown. When he spoke to her, it wasn't the ringing call of the warrior who had challenged Lord Arcneck, but there was authority and kindness in his voice, even though it was weak. His eyes seemed deep with suffering.

"Dear Pitter," he said, "for saving my life when I was careless enough to nearly be killed, more thanks than I can express! All the island loves you."

Pitter wondered what she ought to say. "Ooh!" really wouldn't be suitable.

"Are they looking after you well?" asked the king. "Are you happy on Mismantle?"

"Yes, Your Majesty," said Pitter, almost too shy to speak.

"I believe Sepia, the Queen's Companion, is looking after you?"

"Yes, Your Majesty. She's very kind."

"And she's shown you the tower?"

"Yes, Your Majesty," she said. "It's very . . . um . . . nice."

The king smiled warmly, and there was laughter in his eyes. "And the shore, have you been down to the shore?"

"Yes, Your Majesty."

69

Aware of him glancing over her head at the queen, she looked at the floor, bit her lip, and curled her claws with embarrassment. But the queen brought a chair and cushion, and she suddenly found herself sitting in a comfortable seat with the queen beside her.

"Dearest Pitter!" said the king. "I can tell you've lived on Lord Arcneck's island! We do things differently here. Cedar and I are both squirrels, like you, and neither of us was born to be royal. You can talk freely with us."

"Tell us about your home, Pitter," said the queen. "And your family. And that moss!"

Pitter found she could speak quite freely about her life on Swan Isle. It wasn't a very interesting subject, though, and she was glad when the queen changed it.

"Pitter," said the queen, "King Crispin can't remember anything much after he challenged the raven. Can you remember?"

"Oh, yes!" said Pitter. She had relived that day over and over. With shining eyes and growing confidence, she told them about the battle, and the young mole, Tipp, who had leaped from the heather with his sword in his paw.

"Then they started throwing stones at us!" she said. "And that was what made me so angry, because it was the princess's grave!"

"The princess's grave?" asked Crispin.

"Yes, Your Majesty!" said Pitter. "I'm afraid I don't know anything about the princess, because nobody can tell me. I only know that it's her grave."

Crispin looked past her as if he were concentrating on something far away.

"Near the shore?" he said.

"Yes, Your Majesty, in the clearing."

"And I think it's built out of stones from the shore—from that little sheltered bay that nobody goes to. . . ."

"Yes, Your Majesty. Please, Your Majesty, they say that the princess was lovely, and she married a prince from another island, and then she died."

Crispin became so quiet that she was afraid she'd annoyed him. Then he smiled, but the smile seemed to make the pain show even more in his eyes.

"I remember now," he said. "I saw the ravens on the cairn—what you call the princess's grave—and it made me angry, too. You're quite right, Pitter. It's a sacred place, and no evil thing should touch it. So, did I kill the Archraven on . . . on the princess's grave?"

"Yes, Your Majesty!" she said, and added, not sure whether she should say this, "And that's where the mendingmoss came from."

The king leaned forward, sharp-eyed, though the movement made him catch his breath. "Really?" he said.

"Yes, Your Majesty. It grows very well there."

The king smiled quietly down at her. "She wasn't exactly a princess," he said. "But I'm pleased they call her one. She saved me before, and it's as if she's done it again now. It wasn't so very long ago. I'm surprised that they've forgotten so quickly, but that's the way they are."

71

He tried to stand, but there was pain on his face, and the queen stopped him. "The door," he said. "Pitter, look at the Threading on the door."

She turned to see the Threading hanging there. It showed a pretty young squirrel with flowers all around her, rowans, and a circle of gold on her head.

"Is that . . . ?" she whispered in awe.

"She's your princess," he said. "Her name was Whisper. She was married to a captain of Mistmantle, not a prince, and she wore his circlet as a sign of their marriage. Would you like to know what the flowers mean?"

"Yes, please!" gasped Pitter.

"The rowans are a sign of love," he said. "And there are marigolds for joy and feverfew for healing, because she brought both, lily-of-the-valley for gentleness, pink-edged daisies for laughter, and lavender for marriage."

"There's a butterfly by her head," she whispered.

"For beauty," said King Crispin. "And a hellebore behind her paw. The hellebore means danger, and the very tiny nightshade behind her right paw is treachery, because treachery killed her." He looked at the Threading for a long time, in a quietness she knew she must not interrupt. Finally he said, "She was my first wife. The last thing I did on Swan Isle was to build that cairn over her grave."

Pitter gasped. She looked up at him and thought there was something different about his eyes.

72

"Thank you for defending Whisper's grave," he said. Then he pressed her paw and said very quickly, "Off you go, now, Pitter. Heart keep you."

Kindly but quickly, the queen ushered her from the chamber.

"And Pitter," said the queen, "the swans are leaving us. We need to get you home."

"There's no hurry, Your Majesty," said Pitter. "I mean, I don't want to bother the swans—I mean . . . and Mistmantle . . ." She wasn't sure how to say this, but gabbled out, "Please, Your Majesty, I promise I won't be any trouble!"

Needle and Thripple found Myrtle crying quietly in a corner. When she had told them why, Needle's spines bristled.

"I will speak to Mistress Tay," said Thripple gently. "In future, if you seem to be sewing something different, something you haven't been told to do, you're not to unpick it. You're to leave it just as it is, and they must send for me or Needle to come and have a look at what you've sewn. Can you remember what flower you were sewing in the sea?"

Myrtle screwed up her face in such concentration that Needle worried.

"No," she said. "I didn't even know what it was when I was sewing it. Sorry."

"Never mind, dear," said Thripple. "You've done a lovely piece of work. That's a beautiful sea."

Needle examined the Threading, but Myrtle had unpicked her own work so neatly that it was impossible to see what flower she had stitched in the sea. And why in the sea? It troubled Needle. She slept badly that night.

The news spread across the island that the king was recovering. It reached the ears of a gray, hoarse-voiced mole whose name was Grith. Grith growled softly in his throat when he heard of it. He had reasons to wish Crispin had died from the wound that tore through him on Swan Isle.

Grith was a good spy. He had learned the skill from his brother, long ago.

CHAPTER SEVEN

THE MORE CORR EXPLORED, the more he was astonished. He found narrow inlets, where sandbanks reared up and willows dangled their fingers in the water. There were wide, shallow bays rippled with the tide and scattered with tiny shells. The next day he found dark rearing rock faces clothed with green weeds. The next, there were pale cliffs with waterfalls. Getting to Mistmantle Tower was taking him far longer than he had expected, but it was fun. Lonely, though. He often met other animals, who told him about the war and the return of the army, but a friend to share the journey with would be good. Another day was drawing late, and he had found a sandy bay surrounded by cliffs, with a sloping path. There would be time to explore that path before dark. He was climbing up past rough bushes when a cry startled and stopped him.

"Let go, raven!" cried a young female squirrel. "Evil death wing, I will fight you to the last drop of my blood!"

Raven! Ravens had nearly killed the king! Corr ran, pushing through brambles that scratched and tore at him, realizing as he did that he had nothing to fight with. Picking up a stick, he lurched on until he saw the squirrel perched on the branch of a tree, pelting down beechnuts as she cried out her challenges. She darted back, flattened herself against the tree trunk, then began her attack again.

She must have scared off the enemy, thought Corr, who couldn't see a single raven in sight. But there might be more of them hanging around, waiting to attack—in the treetops, probably. The squirrel now skimmed down the tree, snatched up a fallen branch, and brandished it like a sword.

"As long as I breathe," she cried, "I will defend this island!"

"And so will I!" called Corr as he ran to her side.

The squirrel shrieked, dropped the branch, and picked it up again. It was bigger than she was.

"Who on all the island are you?" she demanded, raising the branch.

Corr looked from one side to the other, and finally up at the sky.

"I thought you were fighting ravens," he said. "I can't see anyone."

The squirrel glared at him. "I was practicing," she snapped.

"Practicing?" repeated Corr.

She gave a little twist to her face and wriggled her shoulders.

"It's very important to practice," she said crossly. "You have to be able to react if you're attacked."

Her self-importance made him want to laugh. "Do you attack each other much here?" he asked.

"I'm talking about enemies," she said, sounding very superior. "Real enemies. It's no good waiting for them to turn up and then realizing you don't know what to do."

Corr glanced around in case any other animals were nearby. If this squirrel belonged to a family as big as his own, there could be any number of them like this—but he saw only a male hedgehog, who smiled brightly, waved a paw, and appeared to ignore them.

"Are all the squirrels around here like you?" he asked.

She put her head on one side. "Not exactly," she said. "It depends on what you mean."

"I mean, bossy," said Corr.

The squirrel's ears twitched. Her eyes flashed.

"Bossy!" she repeated.

"Well, you—"

"Just go away, can't you!" She threw away the branch and turned her back on him to kick the tree.

Corr shrugged. If she felt like that, he may as well go and explore a bit farther, and maybe have a chat with that hedgehog who'd just given him a friendly wave. He'd leave the squirrel to throw a tantrum at her imaginary ravens. A few hedgehogs and squirrels came past, picking berries, playing games, and carrying birch-bark boats, and he was soon chatting with them. They told him that this was Curlingshell Bay, and the hedgehog he'd seen was called Brindle, and invited him to go with them to sail their boats in rock pools. (He didn't tell them that he'd just had an argument with that squirrel, in case she was a friend of theirs.) But as the boats floated along, it didn't look as if anything exciting would happen. Nobody fell into the pond, so there was no chance of a brave rescue. The biggest adventure he'd had today was a row with that bossy little squirrel. Now he came to think of it, that had been fun.

It was getting late, so he'd stay the night here. He'd catch some fish, and look about for strong reeds and sticky sap for patching up the boat. He was on his way back to the shore when he heard a sort of squeaking from behind a gorse bush. It might be none of his business, but he couldn't help taking a look.

It was that squirrel again! But she wasn't angry now. This time she was curled up, holding her tail in both paws and crying quietly. Corr knelt down beside her. She dried her eyes on her tail.

"I'm sorry," he said. "I didn't mean to upset you."

"Go away," she said, but he didn't because she might not mean it.

"You said I was bossy," she said with a sniff.

"Sorry," he said again.

She finished drying her eyes. "I don't mean to be bossy," she said.

"Of course you don't," said Corr. She was probably born that way and couldn't help it, and he shouldn't have teased her. "It was really good, the way you ran down that tree."

She shrugged modestly.

"You don't live here, do you?" she said.

He told her about his journey, and his aim to go to the tower at last. He left out the bit about wanting adventures, in case she laughed at him.

"What's your name?" she asked.

"Corr," he said.

"I'm Lapwing," said the squirrel. "Are you staying here long?"

"I want to go on in the morning," he said, "but my boat needs patching up first."

"Can I help?" she said eagerly. "Can I see your boat?"

She didn't seem to have a clue about how to mend a boat with rushes and sap, but she was willing to learn, pulling up reeds and warming sap over the fire as Corr told her how to do it. She brought enormous bunches of reeds, half of which were too soft or too hard, and he had to rescue the sap before she could overheat it and set it as hard as rock; but she was trying her best to help. Spreading the sap over the reeds on the upturned boat was something she found unpleasantly messy, so she held the reeds in place while Corr did it.

"They do this differently at the shore near the tower," she said, leaning away from the sticky mixture as she watched. "They use bark and things."

Corr looked up suddenly, getting sap on his paw.

"The tower?" he said. "You've seen them mending boats at the tower?"

Lapwing looked most uneasy. It was as if she hadn't meant to say that.

"Not the tower, exactly," she said. "The shore near the tower, the jetty and all that."

"That's close enough!" said Corr. He smoothed the last of the rushes into place, washed his paws in the sea, and sat down beside her at the side of the boat most sheltered from the wind. "You've been to the *tower*! Have you ever seen King Crispin?"

Lapwing laughed. "Yes, I've seen him," she said, then suddenly stopped laughing and changed the subject. "I used to live near there, but, anyway, what I was going to tell you was, there's a really good boatbuilder there. Twigg the mole. If you can get there, he'll sort out your boat."

Corr sat up straight and turned to face her. "Do you really *know* these animals?"

She shrugged and wriggled a bit. She'd come a bit too close to giving herself away.

"I told you," she said, "I used to live around there."

Corr took a deep breath. Suddenly, he had a new friend who had set eyes on King Crispin, Captain Padra, and Fingal of the Floods. And . . . ?

"Ever seen Urchin of the Riding Stars?" he asked breathlessly.

"Oh, him!" she said, and laughed again. "He's really nice. You'd like him."

"What's so funny?" asked Corr.

"Nothing," she said.

It was all too much, really. Lapwing had brought him within reach of his dreams. He felt he was pushing his luck, but she didn't seem to mind him asking about tower animals.

"Brother Fir?" he asked.

"What about him?"

"Well . . . is he all right?"

"Last I knew, he was getting very weak," she said. "He never leaves his turret now." She saw the disappointment on his face, and added, "But if you want to see him they might let you go up there to visit, if he's not too bad, and if you don't stay long. Is the boat dry yet?"

It wasn't, and they were hungry. Lapwing gathered berries and nuts while Corr fished. Brindle joined them and brought bread, and together they cooked supper over the fire. As darkness fell, they sucked stickiness from their paws. Brindle went to settle down to sleep in a shallow burrow, and Corr and Lapwing curled up against the boat.

"If you do want to see Fir," said Lapwing, "don't wait. I don't know how long he's got."

Corr lay gazing at the sky, considering this. He remembered Filbert talking about all the things he'd never got around to. *Don't wait*, Lapwing had said. He wanted desperately to visit Brother Fir, but not to arrive at the tower with nothing to tell, no adventures, and empty paws.

"I should take him a present," he said. "Do you know what he'd like?"

81

Lapwing rolled over in her cloak. "I'll think about it," she muttered, and appeared to fall asleep.

She wasn't asleep. She just didn't want to go on talking about the tower.

When Catkin first came to the bay and took on her new identity as Lapwing, she'd been just a little homesick. Then she had made friends, become accustomed to the place, and settled in, and been quite happy until that terrible day when they had all stood craning their necks and watching the swans return. She had known something was wrong as soon as Urchin had arrived to take her home.

Urchin had stayed calm and focused, but he had not pretended that everything was all right when it wasn't. As he hurried her home to the tower, he had told her how ill her father was, how serious things were, and why she must go home so urgently. Since then, her father had recovered and she had been sent back to continue living as a normal animal. But this time, leaving had been hard. More than the first time, she missed her parents, her tower friends, her chamber, the aromas of cooking from the kitchens, the familiar Threadings, and the floating calls of music when Sepia and her friends rehearsed. She longed for her own bed and the people who loved her most. A tear squeezed its way through her closed eyelids. She must not think of that first sight of her father, King Crispin of Mistmantle, Crispin the Seafarer, the Swanrider, lying wounded and as helpless as a child. Instead she tried to think of what present Corr could take to Brother Fir. She fell asleep thinking about it, and woke in the morning knowing the answer.

"*Seaweed!*" said Corr.

"I didn't just say 'seaweed,'" said Catkin coldly. "Weren't you listening? I said, '*a particular kind of seaweed.*'"

Corr looked at her and tried to judge whether to believe her. She might be teasing him. On a cool, damp, and misty morning, in a boring little bay with his boat all ready to go, he didn't have time for any silly joke Lapwing might be playing.

"What would he want seaweed for?" he asked.

She regarded him with a cool stare before going on. "I was about to say that seaweeds are very popular at the tower just now. Fingal started it. He was going on about some particular seaweed cake that his granny used to make, and then all the otters started remembering the different seaweeds that their families used to gather, and how they cooked them. Not just otters, either. All the animals used to eat seaweeds. And Brother Fir remembered a kind of seaweed cake that he liked when he was young, but you need a very special seaweed to make it, and it's hard to find. Fir's mother called it kingsmantle."

"Kingsmantle?" said Corr, trying to remember if he'd ever heard of it.

"It's called kingsmantle because it's very deep purple with a crinkly gold edge, like a royal robe," she said. "You can use it fresh or you can dry it out and put it in cakes and things."

"Deep purple with a crinkly edge?" replied Corr. He had heard of something like that but never seen it. "I think it's what they call Queen Bramble's Robe where I live. My auntie told me about it, and I asked her why I could never find any, and why it was never washed up on the shore. She said it grows a long way out to sea."

"Must be the same thing," she said. "Anyway, if you can find any of that, he'd love it. I don't know where you find it, but it doesn't grow anywhere in the seas near the tower." She frowned. "If it grows that far out, it may be a waste of time to try."

Corr decided that she wasn't teasing. It would be worth a morning's search to make Brother Fir happy, especially if nobody else could find kingsmantle for him. It would also be a good reason for arriving at the tower.

"I'll wait for you," said Catkin.

Corr looked around at the misty sky, glanced at the shoreline, and sniffed the wind. When he had worked out all he needed to know about the weather, the time of day, and most important, the tide, he slipped into the water.

Oh, how long since he'd had a really good swim? For pure pleasure he twisted under the waves, enjoying the long thorough soaking of it, surfacing now and again to fill his lungs before swimming on. With a deep breath he plunged down toward the seabed so he could swish far along it, sleek and fast, before he needed to come up again. Fishes shoaled past him, weaving and flicking as they changed direction. Weeds floated, green and deep-plum, but nothing that looked remotely gold and purple.

He should go back to where Lapwing was waiting. He bobbed up to see where he was—farther out than he had realized, and coming near to the mists! But he could still get a little farther. Beyond the green fronds and the silent fishes, something gleamed gold.

There was a tightness in his chest, and he kicked hard to the surface to gasp at the cool, damp air, wishing the day could be fresher. On a morning like this it was hard to tell the fog from the mists. Shaking water from his whiskers, he glanced about and sniffed.

Safe enough. He filled his lungs, somersaulted, and plunged down, down, bubbles streaming from his nostrils, fishes flicking away from him, until he saw the deep purple-and-gold weeds drifting gently with the pull of the tide. Seizing all he could carry in paws and teeth, he swam for the surface and, when everything above him darkened, twisted onto his back to look up. If the sky was suddenly dark, he needed to know about it. There could be thunderclouds gathering.

No, not thunderclouds. The darkness was not in the sky. It was nearer, and solid. It looked . . .

Can't be, thought Corr. But it looks just like the hull of a boat.

He swam closer. He'd been right about that! The curves of a strong, black-painted hull sat above him in the water, and from it came noises he struggled to recognize. There was rustling and rasping—then a harsh grating of voices that sent him kicking furiously to the surface.

Lapwing sat on a rock, kicking her paws restlessly. She had inspected the repairs to the boat, put in some bread, kale, and very sandy cake that Corr might enjoy on his journey, then wrapped herself in her cloak and settled herself down to wait for him.

Brindle the hedgehog was nearby, chatting to a stout squirrel who had turned up, apparently lost. The squirrel was saying that he'd never got around to anything much. *"No time—but there's a young otter I know who's just gone off in search of adventure, and I thought if that young chap can do it, so can I. . . ."*

Bored, Catkin wandered down to the shore to practice sword drill with a stick and watch through the fog for Corr.

He'd been a long time. The tide was coming in, which would carry Corr quickly to land, but perhaps she should pull the boat farther up the shore in case it was a very, *very* high tide. The fog was lifting, and, standing with her clawtips in the water, she saw the bobbing of a smooth, dark head.

"Corr!" she cried, and began wading out to meet him. But why was he swimming so fast, with that urgent light in his eyes? Why was he scrambling furiously up the shore, heaving for breath?

Flopping onto the wet sand, his breathing raw and hoarse, he gasped, "Ravens!"

CHAPTER EIGHT

W HY DID ANIMALS in the tower go about that morning with their ears and whiskers twitching? King Crispin woke with a sharp pain in his chest, though the wound had healed. Princess Almondflower was fretful, and nobody could settle her. Perhaps it was because the last of the Swan Isle swans, Prince Crown, would need to leave them soon—but why should that make them uneasy?

Prince Crown was reluctant to leave. He wanted to talk to Juniper about the role of a priest on Mistmantle, and to almost everyone about how the island was governed. The tower's youngest choir was restless, quarrelsome, and ready to burst into tears. Even Sepia's patience with them was wearing so thin that she decided to stop trying and let them all go home early. Brother Fir had spent a restless night, waking often and muttering to himself. As the fog cleared, Juniper leaned from the window to look down at the shore. He felt ill.

In the workrooms, wool and threads snagged, frayed, and tangled; paint was either too thick or too thin. The light was poor and kept changing. Needle, who had unpicked the same picture twice, gave up and went to see how the apprentices were managing. She sat down, folded her paws in her lap, and watched Myrtle very, very carefully, not wanting to startle her as she stitched steadily and rhythmically at a flower.

The flower began to take shape. Needle's paws tightened in her lap.

It mustn't be.

She leaned forward, watching intently.

Don't draw that.

Pointlessly, she knew, she was willing Myrtle to stop. Steadily, stitch by stitch, the flower took shape.

White, green. Please, thought Needle, not pink. Without taking her eyes from the fabric, Myrtle reached for the pink thread.

Needle slipped away. She found Thripple repairing an old Threading, crouched at the frame with a frown of a headache across her face. Needle hated herself, having to bring her such alarming news, but Thripple just stood, stretched her stiff limbs, and went with her to Myrtle's bench.

"Don't be afraid," said Thripple gently. "We've just come to see how you're doing." She leaned forward to inspect the picture. "It's very neat, Myrtle. And you've put in a little flower."

Myrtle seemed to shrink. She began to stammer an apology.

"No, Myrtle, it's all right," said Thripple. "I just wondered why you put it there. Do you know what that flower is?"

"No, Mistress Thripple," whispered Myrtle.

"It's a hellebore," she said. "A very pretty plant, but highly poisonous."

A cold shiver ran down Needle's spine as she ran to tell the king and Juniper. Myrtle didn't know the Threadings Code, but *she* did.

Hellebore for danger.

Corr had never swum so fast in his life, fighting the turning tide and the burning in his limbs, his tail, and his lungs. He pushed his way around the coast, took the shortcut through a river that Lapwing had told him of, slipped back into the sea, and finally, with all his limbs burning, faced the last stretch of seawater to the tower.

Lapwing had said it wasn't far. Not far! Raising his head from the water, Corr saw the fluttering pennants on the tower, but such a long way away that his heart and limbs felt too heavy to go on. He filled his lungs, flicked his tail, and fought on with all his strength.

The tower seemed no nearer, but that wasn't the hardest thing. Coming from this direction took him to the side of the tower rising from high rocks, with no door and few windows. There were four guards, but it would be no good hailing them. They'd only think he was waving, and they wouldn't hear him if he tried to shout from the water.

He dared not glance up. A great black-winged bird might be flying above him. He had once in his life seen a crow, and it had terrified him. Ravens, he had heard, were bigger and worse.

There were two choices now, and Corr wasn't used to having choices. He had always been told what to do. He could swim out of the water, climb up onto the shore and find someone, or he could go on swimming until he rounded the bay and other animals were in sight. Knowing he was faster in water, he pressed on. Lapwing had told him exactly what the shore and the jetty were like.

But she was young, and a squirrel, not a sea animal. She could not have known how powerfully the current churned at the shoulder of the island at Whirl Point, at the turning of the tide. For an hour before and after low tide, sea animals left it alone.

In the turret, Juniper was leaning heavily on the sill with both paws. Hope, who had come in with clean sheets and towels, slipped to his side.

"Are you all right, Brother Juniper?" he asked.

"Yes, Hope," said Juniper, but he was taking deep breaths and struggling to keep a clear head. A sense of menace was about, making him nauseated. But Hope was being very helpful, looking after Fir and keeping him company, and Juniper didn't want to alarm him. He shouldn't be looking down, which would only make it worse—but there was a young otter bobbing about in the water, alone. He'd watch to see if the otter needed help—but a cry from Brother Fir made him dash to the bed, where the old priest sat upright, staring in front of him.

"They will call him!" Fir cried out.

Juniper seized his paws and stared into Brother Fir's eyes.

"The enemy will come upon us!" called Fir, and though he had grown thin and weak, his voice rang with authority. "The enemy will call for the Voyager, and the Voyager will come! He will bear the clothes of a king!"

The fur on the back of Juniper's neck prickled. He waved a paw in front of Fir's eyes, but the old priest did not blink.

"Brother Fir?" he said urgently. "Can you see me? Do you know what you said?"

Brother Fir remained sitting up. He said nothing more. Carefully, because it was most important to remember this word for word, Juniper repeated the prophecy.

"The enemy will come upon us.
The enemy will call for the Voyager,
And the Voyager will come!
He will bear the clothes of a king."

He said it once more, looking anxiously into Brother Fir's face, holding his paws. Fir did not move.

"Hope," said Juniper urgently, "repeat those words exactly as I said them. It's most important that whoever was in this room remembers precisely what was said."

Hope repeated it faultlessly, but before Juniper could say "well done," Fir had slumped on to the pillows. Juniper felt his wrist as Hope padded around to put a paw close to Fir's chest.

"His heart's beating, Brother Juniper," he said. "And he's breathing. He's all right, Brother Juniper."

"I need to tell the king about this," said Juniper. "Hope, stay and look after him, please. If there are any problems, shout for a page to fetch me."

As he limped down the stairs to the Throne Room, he heard a step far below on the stairs. He had already worked out that it was a hedgehog, when Needle shuffled into sight.

"You need to see this!" she gasped.

Myrtle sat nervously, her paws on the workbench, her hind paws not touching the floor. She wasn't sure what she'd done, but the king had called her a good girl as he looked at her work. Captain Padra was there too, and they were very interested in a detail on a window of the half-finished tower.

"That's a sword," said the king.

"Yes, Your Majesty," whispered Myrtle. "I think it sewed itself. It isn't new, Your Majesty. I put it in before you went to the war."

"It's pointing upward," said Crispin. "Do you know what that means?"

"I do now, Your Majesty. Lady Thripple told me. It means Mistmantle won."

"And when . . ." began Crispin, but stopped as Juniper ran in, followed by Needle.

"Your Majesty!" said Juniper. "Fir has just received a prophecy!"

"And so has Myrtle," said Crispin quietly. "Danger, and from the sea. Throne Room, everyone."

"The sea!" said Juniper, remembering. "I just saw a young otter swimming around the northwest corner of the island! He looked tired. I was watching in case he needed help; then Fir sat up and gave the prophecy."

"Heading this way?" asked Padra.

"For Westree Bay, I think," said Juniper. "Hard to tell; he was quite a way off."

"Tide's on the turn," said Padra briskly. "Excuse me, Crispin!" As the other animals hurried down to the Throne Room, Padra dashed to a window, leaned out to bark orders, then rushed to the shore.

Though the current was dragging Corr from the island, he struggled against it with fury and desperation. He was losing the battle. The heartless power of the whirlpool dragged him under the water, held him down and spat him out, each time farther from the shore. From deep inside he screamed to the Heart to help him. Every heartbeat and every breath were needed—not to reach the shore, not any longer—just to stay alive. Each relentless pull lasted longer. Corr was good at swimming underwater and staying there, but this was too hard, too cruel, too much. His lungs ached, and all the thrashing of his paws and tail were useless against the bullying tyrants of current, tide, and whirlpool. With every drag and hurl he found something, some strength, some anger, to fight back—but his strength was failing, and the tide was not. He had to fight even to keep his eyes open. If he closed them, they would never open again.

Somebody was shouting, but they couldn't be shouting to him because nobody here knew him, nobody knew anything about him. All his friends and family were far away, and with wretched longing he remembered his mother and father, his brothers, Great-aunt Kerrera. . . .

Something splashed across the water beside him.

It was a rope. But it was too late now. He no longer had the strength to catch a rope. He was too cold, too weak, too battered, and too broken.

"Grab the rope!" It was a male otter's voice, used to giving orders. "Can you hear me? Grab the rope!"

Hardly caring, Corr turned his head. Before the water dragged him down again, he saw a boat holding off a little way from the whirlpool, carrying two otters who still shouted to him to grab the rope. As the water swamped him again, he saw the gleam of a gold circlet.

A captain. An otter captain—Captain Padra! Corr found new strength. The captain had given him an order—*Grab the rope!*—and he had to obey it. When he rose to the surface again and the rope slapped onto the water beside him, he reached out to it with numb and feeble paws and, because he wasn't sure he'd be able to hold it, rolled over to wind it around himself. Before the whirlpool could swallow him again, the rope heaved him to the solid wooden safety of the boat—there were leaves painted around it—and strong paws were reaching out for him, pulling him into the boat, where he gasped and spluttered.

"All right now," said a voice.

Corr raised his head. Captain Padra was wrapping a cloak around him and rubbing warmth into his chilled shoulders. He tried to thank the otters and apologize for being a nuisance, but his teeth were chattering.

"No problem, you're welcome," said the other otter airily. "Let's get you home."

Corr took a deep breath that left him wracked with coughing. Finally, struggling and gasping, he managed to say something about ravens in ships, but wasn't sure if he was making any sense.

"I have to get back to the tower," Captain Padra was saying. "Fingal, look after him."

"Please," gasped Corr hoarsely, "tell the king . . . they're here!" A beating of wings above him made him twist to look up.

"It's all right, young otter," said Captain Padra. "That's only a swan."

CHAPTER NINE

GUARDS AND PAGES STOOD OUTSIDE the Throne Room door. King Crispin, Queen Cedar, Captain Arran, Urchin, and Juniper were there. Captain Docken had been sent for, and a squirrel messenger who arrived at the Throne Room door at the same moment as Crispin whispered something urgently to him before dashing away.

"An enemy, and danger from the sea," said Crispin briskly as he sat down. "And Brindle has just sent a message about a ship full of ravens! Apparently a young otter swam underwater and saw the hull, but nobody on land has seen it."

There was a knock at the door, and Burr the mole called, "Captain Padra!" But Padra was already through the door, breathless and with damp fur.

"Fingal's on the shore with a half-drowned otter," he said. "He's nearly killed himself trying to warn us about a ship full of ravens."

Something flew across the window, casting a shadow. Every animal took a step back with paw to sword.

"It's all right, it's Prince Crown," said Crispin. "Open the window for him."

"Your Majesty!" cried Crown as he settled on the sill. "The mists are surrounded! There are boats everywhere, thronged with ravens!"

The island prepared for attack. Weapons were sharpened, bowstrings were fitted. At night, the youngest animals of Mistmantle slept in the arms of their older brothers and sisters as they were carried through secret ways to the old Mole Palace, or to hidden burrows and tunnels. The strongest moles dug deep in the damp-smelling earth, shoring up new tunnels and hanging lamps along them. Twigg the Master Carpenter mole sent apprentices running to the tower with wood for boarding up the windows, leaving just enough space for arrows. Animals crammed the stair to the armory as they lined up to collect their weapons.

Every animal who could fight was sent to defend the tower, the coasts, and the animals' homes. Orders were sent out around the island —*Take food, water, blankets, and candles.* —*Get underground, or deep into hollow trees.* —*Block the entrances to make them too narrow for ravens.* —*Take particular care of the very young, the very old, and the frail.*

Timidly, Pitter asked for an audience with the queen. Scatter went with her because she was nervous to approach the queen at such a busy time.

"Please, Your Majesty," she said, "do you still have any mendingmoss?"

"Probably not enough," said the queen. "I've cultivated it and it's starting to grow, but if the ravens attack, we'll soon run out of it."

"The thing is, madam," said Pitter shyly, "if you soak it and keep the water till the next day, it gets a hot, sour taste, and the ravens don't like it. On Swan Isle, if you did that, they didn't want to eat you."

The queen seized a leaf from a basket beside her and tore her clawmark into it.

"Take that as my token," she said. "Get the messengers to tell all animals to put something on their fur—the children's first—to taste nasty. We can't get enough mendingmoss distillation, but we can use whatever we've got. It's what I used to do with Urchin on Whitewings. King Silverbirch was afraid of catching lice, so we pretended Urchin was crawling with them and had to be treated all the time. Well done, both of you."

"Thank you," they said in unison. They bobbed curtsies and ran away to give their message, while the queen lifted Princess Almondflower from her cot, wrapped her in a blanket, and kissed her before passing her to Mother Huggen to be taken into hiding.

Crispin sent another order through the island. *Don't wear jewelry. The ravens are attracted to anything that shines and sparkles. Hide anything that would draw them to you.*

Fingal took off the silver bracelet the king had given him as a reward, and hid it under his bed. The captains took off their circlets.

Hope the hedgehog trotted steadily up and down the tower stairs between Fir's turret and the underground Chamber of Candles carrying blankets, pillows, and mattresses. When he had prepared everything he could think of to make Fir comfortable and happy, including flowers in a vase and bottles of cordial, he told Juniper, and together they carried Brother Fir from his turret down to the Chamber of Candles. The turret could be too easy a target for hard raven beaks, and if worse came to worst and he had to be carried from the tower, it would be easier to do it from the Chamber of Candles.

Sepia watched as Mother Huggen carried little Almondflower away. *She'll be safe. I needn't worry about her.* Sepia would stay in the tower, whatever happened. She knew she could be helpful to Juniper, and Juniper had so much responsibility to carry. She would take her place in the Chamber of Candles, where she could help to care for Fir, keep Hope and Juniper company, and pray. She could do that anywhere, but she found she could concentrate better in the Chamber.

She couldn't bear to think of what might happen to her friends in the fight against the ravens. Quietly, she prayed for Urchin.

Swish, the quick and bright-eyed mole who had been sent to watch Catkin, arrived at the tower. She was taken to the Throne Room, where the king was giving instructions to Padra, Urchin, and Juniper.

"The princess is well, and she has a cave to hide in, Your Majesty," said Swish, her voice soft and breathy. "And there are burrows and tunnels, so she can get straight underground. She's as safe as she can be."

"She could do with being farther inland," said Crispin, "but the tunnels are full of animals being taken to safety just now. We don't want any unnecessary movement cramming them. When everyone else has settled down, Swish, get her moved inland. Urchin, Juniper, I need you to witness that if the tower and everyone in it is lost, Catkin becomes queen. Cedar, Padra, and Arran should be regents for her, but if there are no captains left, it'll have to be you."

"But . . ." began Urchin.

"No time to discuss it," said Crispin. "Obey orders."

"Yes, Your Majesty," said Urchin.

"Juniper," said Crispin, "we need prayer in ever part of the tower and around it. No enemy is ever stronger than the Heart. And animals will want to come to you for a blessing."

"Yes, Your Majesty," said Juniper. "I'll go to the turret. It'll be safe for the next few hours, then I'll go to Fir. Heart keep Your Majesty." He gave Urchin a quick pat on the shoulder as he left the Throne Room.

"Swish, you may go as soon as you've had some refreshment," said Crispin. He took a leaf and scored his clawmark through it. "Take that to Brindle, tell him all I've told you, use that token if you need to prove the orders are from me. Heart keep you."

"Yes, Your Majesty," said Swish. "Heart keep you, too."

She ran away, swift and sure, through the tunnels. Was there a vibration somewhere near? But the earth to her left smelled freshly dug. New tunnels were being built all over Mistmantle, and old ones filled in so that the ground would not weaken. There was nothing alarming about somebody digging one more. She ran on, clutching her token.

Crispin, Cedar, Padra, and Urchin remained in the Throne Room. Still awaiting orders, Urchin could feel the readiness in the air.

"Urchin," said the king, "go straight to Curlingshell Bay. I'm sending Heath, too. I need a couple of good animals to lead the defense of the bay, if the ravens attack it."

Urchin's heart slumped. He wasn't sure if Crispin really wanted him to serve as a warrior at Curlingshell Bay. Maybe he was just being sent to a place of safety, like the youngsters. With an effort, he looked Crispin in the eyes.

"Do I have a choice, Your Majesty?"

Crispin placed both his paws on Urchin's shoulders.

"I'll insist if I have to, Urchin," he said. "I'd rather not have to. Cedar and I will feel a lot better about Catkin knowing that she has you close by."

Urchin swallowed hard and nodded.

"Yes, Your Majesty," he said. "I'll guard her, and I'll guard the bay, and thank you, Your Majesty, for trusting me. Only—only I have to say this, sir—I'd imagined myself fighting beside you, and I want you to know that I'd give anything to do that, and die, if I had to."

"I know, Urchin," said Crispin gravely. "Are you grieved that I'm keeping you safe? Listen. You're right, I don't want you in the tower if the ravens take it. I need good Circle animals in safe places so they can continue the fight if I fall. We've sent Oakleaf and Almondflower to the Mole Palace. Oakleaf wanted to stay and fight, but he's young, Urchin. I want him to live, and I want you to live so that my son will have someone to look up to. Away you go."

Urchin shook his paw firmly, and Padra's, and kissed the queen's paw before going to find his cloak. He could still feel the press of Crispin's paws on his shoulders as he knelt to receive Juniper's blessing, and left by the tower stair, glancing up at the sky.

Padra and Crispin left the Throne Room together.

"Where's Prince Crown?" asked Padra.

"He hasn't been seen since he came to warn us of the ships," said Crispin.

"I'd hoped that he'd stay by us," said Padra.

"We don't know his reasons for leaving," said Crispin. "We mustn't blame him. And that little squirrel, Pitter, who brought us the mendingmoss, there's no sign of her, either. She told Cedar something about mendingmoss, and nobody has seen her since, so I suspect he's taken her home. So, there you are. He's looking after one of his own squirrels. May the Heart carry them safely past the ravens."

"You're a good king, Crispin," said Padra.

It was the greatest thing Crispin had heard that day. There were times when he hated being king, especially at times like this, when he had to take risks with the lives of brave animals who were dear to him. But if he were to die today, it would not be a scrap of a life that was laid down. It would be the life of a king of Mistmantle, offered to the Heart in a cry for the island.

One squirrel ignored the instructions to hide underground. That one was Gleaner. Long ago, she had been the devoted servant of Lady Aspen, Lord Husk's wife. *So Lady Aspen was dead. So she had done terrible things and planned worse ones.* Gleaner had long ago decided that none of it was Lady Aspen's fault, and anyway, she still loved her ladyship. Now that she could no longer look after Lady Aspen and her beautiful robes and jewels and her chamber, she looked after her grave.

Lady Aspen had been buried in a clearing in the Tangletwigs, a wood so overgrown with thornbushes that few animals lived there. As Gleaner visited the little cairn of stones every other day, she had learned to get there and back without a scratch. The flowers on that cairn were always fresh; Lady Aspen's silver bracelet was always polished.

Gleaner had heard about the threat of ravens. *Typical. Stupid Crispin can't even go and kill a few birds without putting the whole island in danger. What's Swan Isle to do with us?* Muttering her way through the Tangletwigs, she took an old cloak to drape over the cairn. It must be hidden from the eyes of the ravens. They had no right to see it.

Dragging the cloak through the Tangletwigs was proving almost impossible. At every step it snagged on the thorns. Gleaner muttered at it and heaved it free again.

"Want any help?" asked a husky voice behind her.

Gleaner turned sharply, ready to snap that she could manage perfectly well, thank you. But really, she would be glad for a helpful pair of paws with this—she heaved again—*this stupid cloak, it's doing it on purpose.* The gray mole was so close beside her that she jumped, then tried to pretend that she hadn't.

"Let me give you a paw with that," said the mole. His voice rasped as if he had a cough. "Are you Gleaner?"

Gleaner put her head to one side and twitched her mouth to mean, "What if I am?" The mole lifted a corner of the cloak to release it from a hawthorn twig.

"I'm only here to help," he said. "My name's Grith. Let's get this moved, shall we? Is this for Lady Aspen's grave?"

Gleaner glowered at him. Lady Aspen's grave was nobody's business but hers.

"What if it is?" she demanded, and bundled up the cloak, wincing as a thorn tore at her paw. "This island has too many busybodies."

"But not you," said Grith. "You just mind your own business and look after Lady Aspen's grave, after all this time. She made her mis-

104

takes, but wasn't she magnificent! My brother had the great honor of serving her. Loyalty's a fine thing, Gleaner. Let me help."

At dawn, animals in the tower rose from their prayers, shook each other's paws, kissed sword blades and bowstrings, put on helmets, and took their places by the boarded-up windows, at doors, gates, and battlements. Strong-smelling lotions were rubbed into fur. All over the island, warriors stood ready. If weapons failed, they would fight with claws and teeth to protect their young and their families from the tearing talons and beaks of the ravens. Crispin patrolled the battlements, giving encouragement, watching the skies. Mistmantle was ready.

"Caw! Caw!" On the far side of the mists, raven cries tore the dawn.

The Taloness cried out first—*Kill and devour!* The Silver Prince echoed her. The sails of the ravens' ships were furled, and the birds stood in rows, claw by claw, tail by tail, beak by beak, lined on the riggings and on the decks. Every clan and every tribe of ravens had rallied to the demand of the Taloness and the name of the Silver Prince, and each of the High Ravens, the heads of clans and captains of ships, had sharpened and silvered their talons.

The Taloness tipped her head left, right. They must find the tree-rat leaders and kill them, find their young, eat them. They would prefer to eat carrion, but if they must do the killing themselves, so be it.

With her brother dead and the prince unable to make plans for himself, all depended on her. She had done well to rally and lead the ravens, and she bristled her neck feathers in confidence. She considered whether to keep this island, but wreck and ruin would be more satisfying. She could lay it waste and leave it so that no creature again would ever talk of Mistmantle, the little secret island, the enchanted land in the mists. It would be Mistmantle of Destruction, Mistmantle of the Slaughter. There would be battles first, but when victory was won, the ravens would feast. The revenge of the Taloness and the Silver Prince on Mistmantle would be known by the world. The tree-rat they called king, the one who had killed the Archraven, would be forced to his knees before her. Stretching her wings and screeching out her battle cry, she soared over the mists.

Corr looked out from Fingal's chamber by the Spring Gate. He had been taken there to rest and get warm, but the constant calling out of orders and running of paws sent him padding to the door to see what was going on.

He wasn't a tower animal. He didn't know anything about bows, arrows, or swords, and he certainly wasn't running to safety with the little ones. There must be something he could do. All I can do is swim, he thought. What could he do by swimming?

He had swum beneath the raven boats before, so he could do it again. To do them any damage he'd need a sword, but he didn't know where to find one, so, after getting lost once or twice, he found the kitchens and chose a large, sharp knife from the racks on the wall. There was already an empty place next to it. Somebody else must have had the same idea. With a kitchen knife, he could do considerable damage to a ship.

Juniper had lit every single candle in the chamber, and they glowed, a soft and pale gold light, on ledges, on the floor, on tables. He had spent the night in prayer, sometimes alone, sometimes with the animals who came to him. Now he held Brother Fir's paw in his, sharing the voiceless prayers of the old priest, knowing that a strong spirit still glowed in the feeble body. It was as if something in the surrounding presence of the ravens came thickly, darkly, between himself and the sun. Swords and arrows could only do so much. There was a terrible evil in the hearts of these ravens, and only the Heart could overpower it.

On the battlements with archers and warriors, Crispin watched the great black birds sweep like screaming specters from the mists. *They're only birds. It's only a noise.* He held out his sword, ready to give the signal to the archers.

Not yet. Not close enough. Not yet . . . not yet . . .

NOW! With a high singing, arrows poured into the sky.

As the first rank of ravens spun from the sky around the tower, Urchin pressed his hind paws into the dunes above Curlingshell Bay and put both front paws to his sword. Crispin had sent archers and a small fighting band, as well as Heath of the Circle. Every animal stood close to the tunnel that would give the best cover from striking beaks.

Wide-winged ravens thronged the sky and filled the air with screaming. Urchin had learned to control his breathing and his thinking, but the racing of his heart was something he could do nothing about. The huge size of the ravens awed and horrified him. Heath shouted an order, and the first flight of arrows whizzed into the air, thudding into raven chests as the birds bore down. Urchin took his stance firmly, curling his claws into the sandy earth, feeling the press of another squirrel back against his. Raising his sword, he watched to see which bird would come at him first.

The hideous cawing grew louder. Urchin swirled the sword at the open beak that came for him, slashing for the throat, ducking to avoid the outstretched talons. A wing swept him off balance, and he stabbed upward, springing up again—stab, slash, swerve, and a hot splash and smell of blood. The heap of dead ravens mounted, the reek of blood and death rose around him, but still the ravens came on.

There was a cry at his back. He felt the sudden cold and change of balance. The squirrel at his back had fallen. A mole fighting beside him grabbed for the dropped sword and leaped to the empty place.

"With you, Urchin!" rasped the mole, and grunted as he brought another raven down.

The pale gold-and-pink stone of Mistmantle Tower became black with flapping wings and streaked with blood. Dead ravens littered the rocks. Swords clashed on beaks with a dull ring. Russet, Crispin, and Cedar fought on the battlements, Padra and Arran at the Spring Gate. Docken's band of hedgehogs and Fingal's otters defended the steps to the main door. Every gate was defended. Whenever a wounded Mistmantle animal fell, the defenders would fight around him until a healer could dart from cover to lift him to the safety of the tower, where every spare room was to be used for healing. Juniper left Fir in the care of Hope and Sepia and limped from one wounded animal to another, cleaning and dressing wounds, listening to the words of a dying squirrel.

"Down!" yelled Heath. "To the tunnel!"

"Tunnel!" shouted Urchin. A glance showed him that all the animals under his command had heard him and were slipping into the tunnels. He slashed down his sword on the neck of a raven that was biting his ankle, dropped into the cool darkness of a tunnel, wriggled into the burrow underneath, and leaned gratefully against the earth-smelling wall, gasping for breath. He could no longer hear the screeching ravens, but only the labored breathing of the animals around him.

The sandy earth was wonderfully cool. With a soft pattering of paws, the defenders of the bay hurried down through the network of tunnels to gather in the burrow. Urchin found he was shaking with effort.

Always clean your sword. He remembered Padra telling him that, long ago when he had been a page. Heath was a good commander, but at that moment he felt he'd give his right paw to have his old captain in command. He found a heap of leaves—all these burrows had been equipped for a siege—and was rubbing the blade clean when Heath said, "All here? Casualties?"

There were injuries to be washed and weapons to clean. Nobody wanted to eat, but the mouthful of water after battle was welcome and delicious. Heath was already moving from one animal to another, praising and encouraging, and hearing what they had to say. Urchin remembered that, as a Circle animal, he should do the same. He was examining a mole's swollen wrist when he realized Heath was beside him.

"Let me bind that up for you," said Heath. "If we had more moles like this, we'd see the whole flock of them away." Then he drew Urchin aside, to a tunnel where nobody else could hear them, and whispered to him in the darkness.

"We can't hold them," said Heath. "They just keep coming. The ships must be crammed with them."

Urchin tried to think of the possible things to do. There weren't many.

"We could do with reinforcements," he thought aloud, "but we can't spare animals from anywhere else."

"We could fall back to the tower," said Heath. "They must need all the help they can get, but we should wait for orders from the king. We could have defended this bay against the sort of numbers we fought against on Swan Isle, but not this. They must have gathered every raven from all the islands in all the seas. So long as animals stay underground, they're safe for the meantime. Let's just lie low for a while, get our breath back, and stop wasting arrows. I only hope the tower holds. It might."

Urchin thought he may have misunderstood. "Say that again, please?" he said.

"The tower might hold," said Heath.

"Might?"

"Yes," said Heath. "Only 'might.' Didn't the king talk to you about the possibility of the ravens taking the tower?"

"Well, yes," admitted Urchin. But it had seemed as realistic as the sky falling.

"He's got it well defended," said Heath. "But we can't be sure of anything, not against such hordes of them. In the meantime, we keep everybody's spirits strong, so don't look worried. Here's Brindle!"

Brindle was working his way through the other animals to find them. There was blood on his shoulder.

"I just looked to see what's happening out there," he said. "Nearly lost my arm. Those birds have gathered on the rocks and beaches, and I reckon more of them have gone inland. What could we do against them?"

"Animals in tunnels and trees can jump out and pick off the odd one," said Heath. "But there must be thousands of them."

"Is Lapwing still safe?" asked Urchin quietly.

"Should be exactly where I left her," he said. "But I'm just going to—"

He stopped dead, staring at something. Urchin hopped forward to see what he was looking at. In a corner of the burrow, a small cloaked squirrel was taking off a helmet. When she saw Brindle, Urchin, and Heath all watching her she quickly jammed it back on her head, but it was too late. Brindle seized her by the paw so violently that she squeaked, and dragged her into the tunnel beside them.

"Ca . . . Lapwing!" he whispered furiously, pulling off the helmet. "You were ordered to stay put!"

Catkin tilted up her chin.

"I was fighting for Mistmantle," she said. "How could I leave it to everyone else? I'm only doing what my father does. And my mother, too."

"Your father came up from being a page like the rest of us," said Brindle sternly. "He learned to obey orders, and it's time you did the same."

She'd asked for that, thought Urchin. She seemed to think this was all an exciting game, and she had to be at the center of it—but in the dim light he caught the glint of tears in her eyes, and the tightness of her face as she fought them.

"Brindle's thinking how upset your parents would be if you were hurt," he said.

"No, I'm not," said Brindle. "I'm thinking of having to face them and tell them I've lost their daughter. You were brought here to find out about living in the outside world, not to play the heroine and die in it. I'm supposed to keep you safe, and you're not making it easy."

"But you have been brave," Urchin said to her.

"And you'll have to be a lot braver before we're through," said Heath. "We all will. Rest now; prepare for whatever happens next. The Heart knows what that will be."

CHAPTER TEN

ORR SWAM STEADILY ON, rising for air when he needed to, twisting to look over his shoulder at how far he had come. He must take care. He'd have to swim right into the edges of the mist, but it seemed that he could do that safely, so long as he didn't swim *beyond* them. The day before, it had been hard to tell mist from fog, but he had worked out that the raven ships must have been just inside the mists, because he'd come home safely. So if the ships hadn't withdrawn—and there was no reason why they should—he'd be safe this time, too.

He swam fast and straight under water, smooth and strong. It was a long, long, and longer swim, making shoulders and limbs ache, but the need to defend the island urged him on. Every time he rose to the surface he turned his face to the sky, ready to gulp the air and plunge back under water if a wide-winged raven flew above him. At last, the air had a touch of mist on it. He dove down, gliding on until the dark hull loomed above him. The sinister croaking of ravens came from inside it.

Appalling pictures filled his mind, pictures of what the ravens would do to Mistmantle if they could. His home overturned, the nets slashed, the pots and pans buckled, the boats smashed to pieces, and his family—he couldn't bear to think of that. The king and queen, Urchin, Fingal, all of them would be slaughtered or forced into slavery. And Brother Fir—what would happen to old Brother Fir?

Above him, the raven ship smothered out light and air. His fur chilled. Corr muttered something to the Heart and rose so straight and fast through the water that the ship seemed to lurch toward him. Gripping the kitchen knife in both paws, gathering his strength, he sliced into the hull, once, twice, three times. Once more. The wood creaked, complained, and began to splinter.

Out of the way, fast, before she sinks. He twisted and swished forward, rising up out of the water to gasp for breath. He had struck his first blow for the island.

King Crispin made one last furious slash that sent a raven spinning to the ground, and leaped down the trapdoor from the battlements, pulling it shut with a bang. Cedar and Burr ran to catch him as he landed. He had given the order to fall back into the tower, but they had waited, knowing he would be the last to leave.

He wished they hadn't caught him. He needed a few seconds just to rest on all four paws, his head down, catching his breath and waiting for the stinging pain of his wound to subside. Burr took the sword from his paw and darted away to clean it. Cedar was still holding on to him, as if she were afraid he'd fall.

"I'm all right," he said. The chamber was full of exhausted animals, and he couldn't let them see that he was in pain. The air was thick with the smell of blood, sweat, and hot fur.

"Where's Whittle?" he asked. "He must commit the names of the dead to memory." He knelt to take the shaking paws of a young sword-hedgehog. "Well done, Hedgen, well done." He and the queen worked their way around the chamber, from one animal to the next. —*Go down to the healers, get that wound bathed.* —*Young hero, you've done enough for one day, go back to your burrow.* —*Tipp, Todd, your grandfather would be boasting of you.* Finally, the senior animals gathered in the Throne Room.

The fire, lamps, and candles were unlit. Burr slipped quietly about with a taper to lighten the room, but it didn't seem to make much difference. Padra and Arran sat side by side facing Crispin and Cedar. Docken was beside them, and Juniper arrived, his eyes hollow with exhaustion, then Moth the mole, rubbing her paws on her apron. Fingal and Needle slipped in quietly.

"How's Fir?" asked Crispin.

"Just the same," said Juniper. "Hope's with him."

Crispin nodded briskly. "Here it is, then," he said. "Every animal who fought today is a hero. There should be Threadings for every single one. Our losses are few, but they are terrible. Grubb and Hew, two moles from Anemone Wood, were killed, and Hazel the squirrel, and there are a lot more injured. We're all quicker on the move than the ravens are, and we fought well. But there are so many of them!"

"Why have they stopped?" asked Arran. "I thought at first that they'd left the tower to attack the rest of the island, but I just went up to Fir's turret to look. They're still here, but they're settling."

"They're regrouping," said Crispin. "And planning their next moves, I should think. Or trying to tempt us out into the open."

"The tower will hold, Your Majesty," said Docken. "Won't it?"

Needle squeezed her eyes shut against tears. The thought of the ravens taking over Mistmantle Tower was almost too much to bear. Fingal took her paw.

"They'll break their beaks on the rocks before they get in here," he said, and hugged her. "Ouch."

Crispin almost smiled. "What are the most important things on the island?" he asked.

Some said, "The animals," some said, "The young." Some said both.

"But not the tower," said Crispin. "If they take the tower, they do. It's just a place. We get as many animals as possible out of it first, and underground. The Mole Palace is being reinforced and guarded as thoroughly as possible. Ravens are too big to get into it underground, but I wouldn't put it past them to dig their way through from the

117

surface. There is a chain of moles in tunnels across the island, ready to pass the word along if we have to empty it quickly, and the young can be spread out into new burrows and tunnels, deeper underground, to keep them safe."

"There's something else we should think of," said Queen Cedar, rubbing her aching sword arm. "I was born on a fire island, and when the fire mountain exploded, all the animals fled to other islands. Some of us settled on Whitewings, and I don't know where the others went, though I think at least one family settled on Swan Isle. What I mean is— if you can't stay on your own island, you have to go somewhere else."

Silence fell on the Throne Room. Needle felt cold, and wished the queen hadn't said that.

"It's a last resort," said Cedar. "But do we know exactly what the ravens want? We've heard them screeching 'kill and devour,' but they don't seem to be devouring us yet."

"Beg your pardon, Your Majesty," said Docken, "but they don't want a snack. They'll wait until they've killed enough for a feast."

"Then what?" asked the queen. "They could keep some of us alive, as they did on Swan Isle, to be slaves. But they're not rational. They're like King Silverbirch on Whitewings—come to think of it, he liked shiny things, too. Obsessed with getting what they want when they want it. I don't think they really want us for food or slavery. I think they want to destroy the island and every living thing on it. Lay it all to waste."

"I'm afraid you may be right," said Crispin. "If the worst happens, we must have well-provisioned boats ready. Priority is to the very young, the very old, and those who look after them."

Arran said what they were all thinking. "We could never come home to Mistmantle," she said.

"If the ravens do what they're capable of," said Cedar, "there won't be any Mistmantle to come home to. Whitewings isn't as beautiful as this, but Queen Larch would make you welcome."

"Well, Your Majesties," said Padra cheerfully, "all this makes me even more determined to fight for Mistmantle. Stick your spines out, Needle."

"I'd love to have a go at that Silver Prince," said Fingal. "Has anyone actually seen him? Is he real, or have they just made him up?"

"They must be guarding him very closely," said Crispin. "We saw him on Swan Isle. He's real, but I'd say he's gray, not silver, and he doesn't look much of a prince."

"What a disappointment!" said Fingal. "All the same, I'll kiss whoever finishes him off. Unless it's you, Padra."

"Boats to be prepared, then," said Crispin. "And Heart grant that we don't need them. All of you, have a bag packed with emergency rations and a cloak, in case you have to get out of the tower quickly. Juni—"

A blaring of caws and screeches filled the air. All of them leaped to their paws.

"Plagues and fire, they're back!" muttered Padra, reaching for his helmet.

"To your places!" yelled Crispin. "Where do they all come from?"

Swords and shields were wielded by shoulders that already ached. To Crispin, every blow seemed to use the last strength he could find, but he struck again and again, the noise of battle clanging in his ears until Docken's voice rose above the rest.

"Your Majesty!" roared Docken. "They want to parley!"

Crispin shook sweat from his fur. The ravens were settling on the shore, finally falling silent. On a flagpole perched a great, glossy raven, her beak and talons sharpened and silvered, with more ravens circling her. Another came to perch near her, but he was so well guarded that Crispin could hardly see him. The female raven threw back her head.

"We will speak with the king!" she screamed. "And if any creature attempts to harm us or any of our ravens, and if any animal seeks to approach the Silver Prince, we will tear it apart."

Fingal, who had been fighting beside Padra at the gate, leaned on his sword and strained to hear her. "Who does she mean by 'we'?" he asked.

"Speak, raven," said Crispin.

"We are the Taloness," she announced. "You killed our brother, the Archraven. For this we will lay your island to waste. The name of Mistmantle will be a curse."

Crispin said nothing, so she continued.

"You sent water vermin to attack our ships," she said. "It was a bad

120

move. The birds in the hull were reinforcements. We could take this island without them, but they were ready for battle. When our ship was sunk, they flew to join the fight."

"Sunk one of the boats?" whispered Fingal to Padra. "Beyond the mists?"

"Shush," said Padra. "Listen."

"There are many more ships," called the Taloness. "All filled with ravens who long to feast on tree-rats. Will you surrender this tower now? Or shall we disturb your rest in the morning?"

To the watching animals, Crispin appeared as calm and strong as the beech trees in Anemone Wood. His voice carried through the evening air.

"We will take no rest," he said, "until every savage beak and claw is swept from this island. Our shores are already littered with your dead. Do not add to their number. Go, and we will not pursue. But if you stay, Taloness, your ranks will fall around you. By staying here, you put all your lives in danger."

The Taloness raised her head and gave such a long, rasping croak that she seemed to be choking. But it was a terrible laughter, echoed by the ravens around her, growing as all the armies of ravens took up the cackling, so loud and coarse that it hurt the ears. Even more were still flying to join them.

"Don't cover your ears," said Crispin to whoever was near enough to hear him. "That's what they want."

The Taloness stopped laughing and tipped her head to look about her. As she stopped, her armies instantly did the same. Her silvered talons flexed.

"We will inspect this island tonight," she announced, "and choose where we shall settle. This island is ours already, and is forfeit to the Silver Prince. We only require your tower for our stronghold and your bodies for our feast. In the morning, we will have both. We have warned you. You have all night to be afraid."

"Go, bird of vermin," said Crispin.

The Taloness raised her head. "Kill and devour!" she screamed.

"Kill and devour!" shrieked the ravens about her as they flew across the island.

Fingal and Padra looked up at the wheeling, croaking birds.

"If she devours me, I'll poison her," said Fingal. "They're disgusting, Padra, they make a mess everywhere, even when they're flying. If we have to be invaded, can't it be by something house-trained?"

"We'll send you out with a bucket and mop when all this is over," said Padra, and pointed. "Do you see that one?"

A large raven with a gray sheen to his feathers circled the tower. Another five surrounded him.

"That must be the Silver Prince," said Padra.

"Do you think so?" said Fingal. "That's not silver! That's gray. He's just a great fat gray lump of a bird. Why is he swerving like that?"

"Probably showing off," said Padra.

"So he's conceited as well as everything else," said Fingal. "And no more silver than I am. I'm disappointed."

122

Arran came to join them. "Yes, that's him," she said. "Apparently he does look silver in strong sunlight from the right direction."

"So does a wet otter!" said Fingal. "Oh, here's Crackle. Crackle, I'm the Silver Otter."

"No you're not!" Crackle giggled.

"I will be after a swim in a good light," said Fingal.

"Don't hang around chatting," said Padra. "We need to send otter parties out to prepare our boats, as Crispin said. Go by water as much as possible—I doubt that the ravens will attack you there—and put some bitter stuff on your fur. You too, Crackle."

"That's what I came for," said Crackle. She glanced nervously up at the sky, and they retreated to the shelter of the tower walls, where she fished a dusty old bottle from the pocket of her apron. "We found this in the cellar, and it's old and very strong. It's had pickled walnuts in it for years."

"Fingal, put that on," ordered Padra. "And before you make any clever remarks, I don't care if you'd rather be eaten by ravens than smell like a pickled walnut; just use it."

"Only if there's enough for the littlies in the Mole Palace," said Fingal.

"And," said Crackle, "have you seen Scatter? I'm worried about her. I haven't seen her since the ravens first came."

The otters glanced at each other. Arran shook her head.

"She's probably been sent to look after the young," said Padra. "Don't worry about her, Crackle."

Fingal, Arran, and Padra were among the animals who worked through the night, sending out orders for boats to be made ready, setting guards, strengthening the defenses and narrowing doorways and entrances. Fingal, thinking it might be useful, explored the underground waters and passageways he had discovered by accident long before. He and Padra made one last patrol of the shore and stopped when a sleek dark head bobbed up from the waves.

"Heart help us!" cried Fingal. "Him again! Padra, let's get him out!"

Corr could hardly swim. His fur was so heavy with seawater that it was all he could do to hold his head high enough to breathe. But when Padra and Fingal swam out to him, drew him to the shore, and hugged the warmth into him, he wanted to lie on the sand and die of wretchedness.

He tried to speak, to say that he was sorry and he was only trying to help, and how he'd expected all the ravens to drown when he sank the boat. It had never occurred to him that they'd fly straight over the mists to join the attack on Mistmantle. He had only seen that as he swam back and saw them darkening the sky above him.

CHAPTER ELEVEN

URCHIN HAD FALLEN INTO a light sleep with his sword still in his paw, half waking now and again. He dreamed he was in a cell on the Isle of Whitewings and had to escape from King Silverbirch, but when Brindle shook him awake he knew exactly where he was, and fought the urge to close his eyes again.

"Message from the king," said Brindle. "There's a mole here called Grith, carrying a king's token."

"Urgent business of the king," said a hoarse mole voice. "Is Urchin here?"

Urchin remembered the voice of the mole who had fought bravely at his back the day before. The crumpled leaf he held up to the lamplight bore the clear scar of Crispin's clawmark.

"I'm Urchin," he said, and smothered a yawn. "Where did you get that?" He was losing track of time, but it seemed impossible that even a fast mole could get to the tower and back so soon.

"Mole called Swish," said Grith, and passed the token to Heath, who had just woken. "She was trying to reach you, but the ravens attacked her. She got under cover, but she's in a bad way."

"Have you sent for a healer?" asked Heath.

"There's one with her now," said Grith.

"What on all the island was she doing aboveground?" demanded Brindle.

"Trying to rescue someone," said Grith. "Typical. I don't know if she'll come through. And I'm not here to talk about her. She said" —he lowered his voice—"that there's a young animal in here under special protection. She needs moving. Sharpish."

"Where to?" asked Brindle.

"Burrow," said Grith. "Underground, between the Tangletwigs and Anemone Wood. Urchin, you're to escort her."

"I should come too," said Brindle.

"You'll be needed here," said Grith.

"Excuse me," said Brindle, "but it won't do. As far as I'm concerned, I'm still under orders to look after her. I'll take her to safety, then come straight back, Heath."

"I know you will," said Heath. "Wake her up, give her a cloak and a flask of water. Heart keep you all."

"They're altering tunnels all over the island," muttered Grith. "And now we need one big enough for a full-grown hedgehog. I'll find the quickest way through. No time to lose."

Catkin appeared, her eyes wide. She had splashed cold water on her face to make herself wake up properly, and realized that the situation was serious. She slipped into place behind Brindle and Grith with Urchin following, his sword in his paw.

Corr sat by the fire in the tower kitchen with a blanket around his shoulders. The blur of memories from the last half hour began to settle themselves into order. Fingal had half carried him up the beach and dragged him into this kitchen with his fur still full of sand. He had been introduced to another otter, Padra's son, Tide, who was keeping tower supplies of wood and water. Then a pastry cook called Crackle had taken one look at his soaked fur and chattering teeth, ranted at Fingal for not taking better care of him, and seated him by the fire with a bowl of soup.

"I remember you!" she said. "You were half drowned last time you came here, too! You told us about the raven ships, didn't you! And you brought that lovely seaweed for Brother Fir!"

Still shivering, Corr nodded.

"I haven't forgotten about it," she reassured him. "It's beautiful seaweed, I just haven't had time to do anything with it, so I've dried it out. It'll keep. It's all drinks and quick meals for the warriors just now, but I'll make that seaweed cake as soon as I get the chance."

"Please, Master Fingal," said Corr, his voice low and shaking with cold, "there's no need to stay with me. I've caused enough trouble, and you've got important work to do."

"What important work?" asked Fingal. "Shoving stuff into boats? Any animal with paws and half a brain can do that. Somebody has to sit in the kitchen keeping you company, eating toast, and getting under Crackle's paws, and it's me. What have you done that was so terrible?"

Corr swallowed hard. It would be hard to tell, but at least it would be honest. Fingal wouldn't go on thinking he was a decent, sensible otter. He'd know how stupid he'd been, and how he deserved to be sent straight back home to stay there and do no more damage. So Corr put down his empty bowl and told Fingal about his journey, his hopes, his plans, and his meeting with Lapwing. Finally, looking down at his crinkled paws because he couldn't look Fingal in the face, he told how he'd taken the knife, swum out to the raven ship, and sunk it.

"Oh, was that you?" said Fingal. "Well done!" Crackle glanced with a frown at the knife rack.

"But it wasn't well done, sir!" cried Corr. "I didn't know there were so many of them, and I never thought they'd escape—I thought they'd just drown! Then I saw them all croaking and cawing and flocking inland, and it was my fault and there wasn't a thing I could do about it. I couldn't"—he gulped and tried again—"I couldn't warn you! I tried, but I couldn't get here in time! They all flew to the tower!"

"Mm," said Fingal. "They did, it was entertaining."

"Entertaining!" cried Crackle.

"Oh, yes," said Fingal. "We got a croaking-to from the Taloness. She seems to think there's more than one of her."

"Fingal!" said Crackle. "It isn't funny." Fingal looked at Crackle, and she giggled.

"But, sir, it was a stupid thing to do," said Corr bitterly. "I just wanted to do something to help, and I knew I could sink their boat, so I did. I thought I'd done something really great, but it was bound to be stupid if I thought of it."

"Oh, I don't know," said Fingal. "Sounds like the sort of thing I would have done myself, if I could have swum that far. It was very brave of you! I just wish I understood how you managed it. You must have lungs like bellows. And it did some good."

"Did it?" Corr felt a bit better.

"You must have drowned some of the vermin," said Fingal. "You've done far more than I have today, I should think. And the ones who came and attacked us—they probably would have done it anyway, sooner or later. Crackle, is there any more soup? Not for me, for him." He held out Corr's bowl. "And because you did this, if we make a calculated guess about the number of boats, and assume there's a hull full of ravens in all of them, we can more or less work out their numbers. It's like this, Corr. There are some animals, like my brother and the king and queen, who always manage to think one step ahead; they work out what somebody else will do next. The rest of us just muddle through. You've done well, Corr." He glanced toward a spider swinging gently from the fireplace. "Get this soup down you before something drowns in it." He patted Corr's shoulder and slipped over to Crackle. "I'll see if Fir is awake," he whispered. "If he is, Corr can go and see him."

He hurried through the passageways to the chamber, where the soft light and air of holiness subdued even him. Fir was awake, with life still sparkling and dancing in his deep dark eyes, but the king was at his bedside. It was no time to interrupt. Fingal slipped quietly away. Corr would have to wait a little longer to meet Brother Fir.

"Dear Crispin," Fir was saying, "we have faced worse than this. Be strong. All the island prays to the Heart, and the Heart hears us. Don't you feel it?"

Crispin wished he could rest his head on the bed and sleep it all away. Brother Fir hadn't seen the flocks of ravens darkening the sky, or heard their voices scarring through the daylight. But Crispin knew what he meant. They had faced darkness and treachery from within Mistmantle in the past. Now the enemy was from outside. It could be seen, measured, and touched. But what an enemy!

"Prevail, Crispin, by the strength of the Heart," he said. "Are the young safe?"

"Yes, Brother Fir."

"And you will die for the island if it is required of you," said Fir. "I know, I know. Hm. You can offer nothing more, but"—he took a deep, slow breath—"I think you will have to live for the island, and that may be harder."

Presently, Fir drifted into sleep. Crispin slipped away to Juniper's side as Hope tiptoed about, filling up beakers and water jugs.

"Of course I'll die for the island—I mean, for the islanders—if I have to," said Crispin. "But, Heart forgive me, Juniper, I don't want it to be yet. I want to put the island together again after this. Catkin isn't ready to be queen; she's only a child. I want to stay alive with Cedar and my children. I want to be a good king, and it could all be destroyed by petty, spiteful birds, just because there are so many of them."

Juniper remained quiet and thoughtful for a while. Then he said, "We will win, King Crispin, because it's impossible."

Crispin rubbed his face with his paws. "I'm too tired for riddles, Juniper," he said.

"It's not a riddle," said Juniper. "It's obvious. We are being called to fight beyond all that our strength and numbers can do. It's not only *their* strength and *their* numbers that we're up against. It's that powerful, poisonous evil that drives them from inside. It's beyond us. But it's not beyond the Heart. Nothing is—so we call upon the Heart to fight our battle for us, and the Heart will."

He gave a sudden gasp, as if pain had struck him. Crispin caught him as he reeled.

"Juniper, are you ill?"

Juniper's fur stood out stiffly. He stared, then shuddered violently again.

"Where's Urchin?" he demanded.

"Curlingshell Bay," said Crispin. "Why?"

"He's not!" said Juniper. "He's in danger! Somebody has to find him!"

131

In the workrooms, the windows had been boarded up to keep out the ravens. The most ancient and precious Threadings had been taken down and hidden, but the unfinished ones remained in their frames. Needle took a lamp to examine them and came to Myrtle's work.

No. Heart have mercy, please, no. If only I hadn't looked.

She turned her head and closed her eyes, then looked again. It was still there. A yellow poppy, its petals turned back to show the tall black stamens.

The death of royalty.

Oh, Heart, no.

CHAPTER TWELVE

FILBERT THE SQUIRREL was not exactly lost. He just didn't know where he was.

It had been very pleasant chatting with the young folks on the shore. That young hedgehog, Brindle, was a thoroughly nice chap, and they'd even done a bit of fishing together. But there was no time for all that now, dear me, no, not with all this bother. He'd done his bit in the battle by hiding in the hollow of a tree with a bow and arrow and leaning out to shoot. He wasn't sure if he'd killed any of those birds, but there were so many of them, he must have winged a few. He'd got a nasty knock on the head, too, from jumping out of his hiding place and banging his head on the tree trunk. Those knotholes were harder than they were when he was a lad. In fact, he'd had such a bang on the head that he felt a bit dizzy now, and couldn't quite remember where he was meant to be. He'd had some notion of going to the tower. *Tower. Tower.* Which way was that again?

In these days of attack, animals were supposed to stay belowground as much as possible. *Tunnels?* Filbert had looked but couldn't find one big enough. *Never cared for them anyway.* By the time he had trudged and stumbled his way to the edges of Anemone Wood, his head was spinning and he had forgotten all about tunnels. He had almost forgotten about the ravens.

The Silver Prince was perched in a tree with his escort. He preened his feathers and tossed his head. Everyone feared and honored him; everyone admired him. Quite right. He was born to be their idol. It was time they saw what the Silver Prince could do.

Tipping and tilting his head, he surveyed the ground. He was lucky. A tree-rat was traipsing through the wood. Slow, for a tree-rat. Stupid animal. He could take that one easily. Too easily. He'd have some fun with it first.

"Watch this!" he shouted to his escort. He spread his wings and wheeled down. The escort followed close behind.

"Leave me alone!" he cawed. "Watch me!" He tossed his head, flew down, and landed rather heavily in front of the traveler.

With a puzzled grunt, Filbert jumped back. He scrabbled clumsily for a stick that lay on the ground, but stumbled. The Silver Prince grabbed the stick in his beak and smashed it on a tree trunk. Filbert struggled to his paws and turned to run, but found the Silver Prince had flown over his head and was grinning at him.

He tried to dodge around a tree, but the raven was leering down at him. He backed away. A powerful wing knocked him over. Whichever way he ran, or tried to run, the raven was ahead of him, cawing and sneering. Talons flexed in front of his eyes so that he blinked and flinched. The black wings were ready to fold him . . . That beak!

"Ow!" The Silver Prince had pecked cruelly at his ear. "Get off, you! Get off!"

The Silver Prince was enjoying this. He pecked at the top of the squirrel's head; then as it ducked, he snatched a tuft of fur out of its tail. This was fun. He'd go on tormenting the tree-rat until it cried, groveled, and begged for its life.

Filbert thrashed out to beat the raven away, but the cruel beak pecked at his paws. The bird cackled and pecked Filbert's head again as he ducked and covered his face. Dazed and staggering, Filbert pulled off his cloak to flap it in the bird's face—but the raven caught it and tugged it from his paws.

"Vermin!" yelled Filbert. Clinging to the cloak, he found himself sprawled on the ground. He was still trying to crawl—if he could only grab the vermin's foot, he'd give it a good biting—when a powerful female squirrel voice rose from the ground.

"Leave him alone, you evil gray bat! Pick on someone your own size!"

Filbert tried to look around and see where the voice was coming from, but the raven flew down to peck at him again, dropping the cloak, which Filbert grabbed at and pulled over his head to protect himself—then he was sliding backward, sliding downward, someone was pulling him down—without understanding how he got there, he found he was half in and half out of a burrow with his cloak still over his head.

"Breathe in, can't you!" said the female squirrel behind him. "Just you squish yourself up a bit smaller, come on, make an effort, put your paws down and heave, get your head down—why can't that bird just go home and mind its own business, great big ugly thing. Now you push and I'll pull, it's a tight squeeze, but I got down here, I don't know how I managed it, but I did, and if I could do it so can you, one more push, come on, put your back into it!"

With an enormous effort, a grunt, and a mighty tug from beneath that made the earth walls crumble about him, Filbert thudded in the burrow. The cloak flopped on top of him. Amid the tangled tree roots stood a well-rounded female squirrel looking him up and down, her paws on her hips.

"Good thing I was here," she said. "The Heart must have sent me, for I don't usually live around here, but there's burrows all over the island going to be used that isn't usually, and we have to make sure they all got water and food, blankets, all the little necessaries, so I was along here with them little necessaries when I heard you shout. These birds, what will they do next, ooh, I don't know your name, Master Squirrel, I'm Apple, pleased to meet you."

"I'm Filbert," he said. His voice seemed to come from far away and was not quite under his control. He might have been imagining it, but there seemed to be a waft of something in the air, a smell that reminded him pleasantly of his childhood. "Most grateful to you, miss—madam—most grateful. Pardon me, madam, I've had a nasty bump on the head. And that business with that big bird. Bad. Horrible, horrible."

"Ooh, silly me!" cried the squirrel. "You're not well! Let's get you warmed up. What's that great bullying bird done to you?" She folded away the cloak and, in the feeble light, peered at his injuries. A bruise was swelling on his forehead, and there was blood on one ear and on the back of his head. A tuft of tail fur was missing.

"Let's get you cleaned up," said Apple. "I got some water and we'll clean up all those pecks, I'd peck him if I had the chance, see how he likes it. My little lad, my little foundling that I brung up, he's Urchin, they call him Urchin of the Riding Stars, he's in the Circle, they'll get all this sorted out, don't you worry."

Filbert sat down. His head throbbed and his injuries hurt, but it was rather nice to be fussed over like this. He hadn't had this much attention in a long time. The water, as she washed his wounds, was cool and soothing.

"Don't suppose you've eaten today?" asked Apple, dabbing at the cuts. "Mind you, just as well, hard enough getting you down into this burrow as it was, feed you too much and we'll never get you out again. Still, you have to eat something." She rubbed her hands on her fur. "Got some bread here."

"Pardon me, madam," slurred Filbert, his head spinning. "Don't feel much like eating."

"Course you don't, poor love," said Apple. "Ooh, I tell you what I've got! Just the thing for you!"

From her basket, she took a large green bottle and a wooden cup. Holding the cork in place, she shook the bottle vigorously.

"This is my apple-and-mint cordial," she said. "Famous, this. I gave some away for putting on fur, they say those ravens won't like the taste because they don't know what's good for them, put some on my own fur, but it does you more good inside than out. Pity to waste it. This'll put you right, puts everything right. I could mix it with water, but you look as if you need it neat." She poured a cupful. "Get that on the insides of you."

Filbert took the cup in both paws and drank while Apple shuffled things about in her basket again. She turned when she heard a sob.

Tears poured down Filbert's face. He put down the cup, covered his face with his paws, and wept.

"Oh, my dear!" cried Apple. "Oh, my dear, what's the matter? I know it's strong stuff, makes your eyes water, but it don't usually do *this* to anyone."

Filbert fought to overcome the sobbing. Finally, gulping, he wiped away his tears.

"My mother used to make cordial exactly like that," he said. "Nobody else could make it the same. I never tasted anything so good since she died. It takes me back to being a happy little lad of a squirrel . . . Oh, beg your pardon, Mistress Apple, but I never thought to have that taste in my mouth again. I'd forgotten how good it is."

Apple beamed with pleasure. "Good thing I brought plenty," she said, and refilled the cup.

Urchin whisked along tunnels, his drawn sword in his paw, ducking when the roof lowered. Nobody spoke. He heard the steady swish of paws on soft earth as they ran—Grith in front, Brindle next, his spines brushing on the wall. Catkin's paws made no sound at all, but her sword occasionally scraped. Urchin had no idea where she'd found it and suspected she could do more harm to herself than to an enemy, but she may as well keep it.

The tunnel twisted and led into another tunnel, newly dug, smelling of fresh earth. It led uphill, and he could tell from the scent of the air that a sandy burrow was to the left of them.

"Not that one," whispered Grith as Urchin raised his head to sniff the air. "Quick. Farther on, farther up."

It was too quiet. Urchin caught Catkin's paw in the dark and pulled her toward him.

"Quiet!" he whispered.

There was a sharp cry from Brindle, then nothing.

"Run, Catkin!" whispered Urchin—then he heard wings and the scratching of talons behind him.

Urchin flung Catkin against the wall, put his back against her, and lunged for the raven's throat, but even as the blow fell he felt the hard clench of talons on his sword paw, and his other arm was caught and held. There was a gasp from Catkin as she struck out with her sword, and a squawk from a raven.

"Well done!" yelled Urchin, remembering just in time not to say her name. "Keep fighting!" There was a clatter as the sword was knocked from her paw and a shriek as she was forced to the ground. That first sandy burrow must have been crammed with ravens. Strike, fight, struggle, twist, kick, bite—it was all he could do, and it was useless. There were wings in his face and talons on his arm as he was dragged behind Catkin to the higher burrow.

"It took six of you!" snarled Catkin—then she screamed. Urchin, pushed into the burrow after her, saw why.

Brindle lay on the floor. From the angle of his head, it seemed that his neck had been broken. A little line of blood trickled from his mouth. A ring of ravens stood around him, snarling and pecking as Urchin lunged forward and the guard ravens held him back.

Catkin squeaked tightly as if she were trying not to cry. Urchin twisted around to see her, but she was cloaked from sight by raven wings.

"Courage," he said. "You did well. Are you hurt, Lapwing?"

"Stop that," said a raven, stepping from the circle. "We know who she is. We know all about you."

The raven strutted forward. Urchin saw the figure crouching behind it, and fury turned him cold—fury at Grith the mole, who sat with a smile of malice on his face, and fury at himself for being tricked.

Grith lifted a paw. He still held the king's token.

"Pity about Swish," he said. "She put up a fight."

"Where is she now?" demanded Urchin.

Grith shrugged. "Who cares? I only killed her. How should I know which raven bellies she filled?"

The raven swung around and turned on him with such a glare that Grith shrank back. Then the raven advanced toward Urchin.

Urchin curled his claws and set his teeth. He forced himself not to back away from that great curved beak.

"How dare you talk to each other, you creatures, as if we were not here!" cried the raven. "We are the Taloness, Guardian of the Silver Prince, sister of the Archraven, most foully murdered by the tree-rat who calls himself king!"

There was a cry of protest from Catkin. The Taloness jumped forward and darted her beak at her.

"Silence, tree-rat!" She hopped closer. "You are his daughter. And you"—she tipped her head to look at Urchin—"are the pale one, the king's trusted friend. Grith has done well enough."

Grith pressed his face to the ground in thanks. He smiled up at the Taloness, but that spiteful leer was still on his face.

"Great Taloness," he said, "may I address the tree-rats? May I explain?"

"You have our permission," said the Taloness. "But be quick."

Grith crept up to Urchin and glared into his face. Cold, hard talons gripped Urchin.

"Do you remember Gloss?" asked Grith.

"I couldn't forget him," said Urchin. Gloss the mole had brought misery and tragedy to many animals in the past, but especially, in one act of evil and treachery, to Crispin.

"Gloss was my brother," said Grith in a low, accusing voice. "He served faithfully."

"He served Husk!" said Urchin.

"In his great courage," said Grith, his voice harsh as gravel, "he followed you to Swan Isle. He left Mistmantle, seeking Crispin the traitor."

"Crispin . . ." began Urchin, but a slap from the Taloness's beak silenced him.

"I never saw him again," said Grith. "For a long, long time, I did not know what had happened to him. I heard stories and rumors that he had hidden in your boat and sacrificed his life on Swan Isle. But I never knew for certain until the swans came here, begging for our help. They boasted! Lord Arcneck bragged that he had rid his island and this one of . . . I will not repeat what he called my brother." With a leap forward, he growled into Urchin's face. "Who killed my brother? Was it you? Crispin? Was it that swan?"

"Gloss murdered Whisper!" cried Urchin. "He meant to kill me and Crispin!"

"Shame he didn't," snarled Grith.

"Lady Whisper was lovely," said Urchin. "She was gentle and kind. She'd never done anyone any harm and he stabbed her, then he tried to kill Crispin. Crispin and Lord Arcneck were too quick and too strong for him."

"Two against one!" rasped Grith. "I knew it! I knew he would have no justice from Crispin. But he has justice from me. When the ravens came, I pledged loyalty to the Taloness and the Silver Prince. I offered them Crispin's daughter, and you."

"Enough," said the Taloness. "You have brought them to us. Now, little princess, what can we hope for from you?"

"Put my sword in my paw," said Catkin, "and I'll show you."

There was a harsh rasp of laughter from the Taloness.

"Take her away and tie her up," she said. "We need her. And this one"—she jerked her head at Urchin—"tie him up and keep him here for now. He'll be useful. Four of you—you four—stay with him. The rest, come with us."

"Madam Taloness?" said Grith.

The Taloness tipped her head to glare at him. Grith cowered.

"With us," she said, and Grith followed her slowly, almost crawling, as if he already regretted offering his service to the Taloness.

Urchin was surprised to find that he was sorry for Grith—but then his wrists and ankles were tied roughly, and he was pushed into a corner, still struggling with every ounce of strength. It wouldn't help, but it made him feel he was still fighting as he stretched and strained to see Catkin. Kicking and wriggling as they dragged her away, her claws drawing deep lines in the earth, she cast a last appealing glance at him over her shoulder. Then she disappeared into a tunnel behind Grith and the Taloness.

Urchin raged silently against himself as he slumped back against the wall. He had thought it strange that Grith held a king's token, but his explanation had seemed reasonable. Now Swish was dead, Brindle was dead, Catkin was a prisoner, and he . . .

. . . and he had failed them all. He squeezed his eyes shut at the shame of it. He hardly cared now what the ravens had in mind for him, and dared not think what they planned for Catkin.

CHAPTER THIRTEEN

GLEANER NEVER LEFT THE cairn now. She had made a nest and slept there at night. That mole had never appeared again. Typical of moles. But she didn't need anyone to help her defend Lady Aspen's grave. She had heard that during the battle on Swan Isle, they had a attacked a burial cairn, throwing the stones from the top. Let them just try it here. She had taken a knife from the kitchen and kept it in her paw even when she slept.

But she slept badly. This had always been her own place, hers and Lady Aspen's. Now animals were being moved from burrow to burrow to keep them safe. The whole point of the Tangletwigs was that it was hard to get in and out of, but for that very reason, animals were gathering there. Sepia had even had the nerve to ask if she'd seen Scatter. As if she'd notice, with all these strangers moving in, and as if she'd care! If nosey newcomers asked her what the cairn was for, she growled at them to mind their own business.

With his back against the earth wall of the burrow, Urchin listened and waited. He was still guarded by four ravens, all with the silvered talons that seemed to indicate the most important birds. He had tried, very subtly and gradually, to raise his wrists to his face and bite the ropes, but the ravens had been alert to every movement, and now his arms were pinioned to his sides. The best thing would be to stay very still and hope they would forget to watch him so carefully.

A rough squawking above made the guards look up. Wings flapped, loose earth showered down, followed by a big gray raven that dropped heavily into the burrow. The sight of tufts of red fur in his beak made Urchin's stomach contract.

"Kill and devour, Oh Silver Prince!" cried the guards, bowing their heads.

So this was the great Silver Prince. As far as Urchin could see, he wasn't silver and he wasn't much of a prince. With a look of conceited stupidity, the bird spat fur from its beak.

"A triumph!" he croaked. "Kill and devour! You missed my triumph. I will do something new now. Watch me!"

Urchin stayed very still and kept his gaze on the ground. If the Silver Prince wanted to impress them, he was in more danger than ever.

There was something Brother Fir used to say—*Think. Nobody is here to do your thinking for you.* Struggling had become pointless and there seemed no chance of rescue, but he could still think. What would Padra have told him?—*Know the territory.* Not just the land, but every-thing—the creatures around him and the circumstances. And what could he tell himself? Had he learned anything when he had been a prisoner on Whitewings?

Now that he came to think of it, those animals on Whitewings had done a lot of bickering among themselves, and it had always come as a relief when they did that. When they were fighting among them-selves, they had left him alone.

He listened carefully to the harsh raven voices. Why should the Mistmantle animals fight them, if he could make them fight each other?

The Silver Prince cackled and turned on Urchin. "I am hungry!" he croaked. "Where are the young?"

"You don't expect me to know that, do you?" said Urchin calmly.

With a shriek of rage the Silver Prince lurched at him, but the two guards pulled him away.

"The Taloness wants him kept," they said.

"Kill and devour," muttered the Silver Prince crossly, like a bad-tempered child.

"We should get up to ground," said one of the ravens. "Need orders. Find food."

"Any orders from the Taloness?" asked another.

Two things were becoming clear to Urchin. One was that the Silver

Prince was so stupid it was almost a shame to trick him. The other was that he could use the prince's pride and stupidity against him. It was a terrible risk, when the ravens could so easily kill him just for speaking; but for the sake of the island, it was worth it.

"Excuse me," he said, "who gives your orders?"

"Taloness," said the birds—but the Silver Prince leered over them in a way that made them twitch their heads and rustle their feathers.

"The Taloness does my orders!" he snapped.

"Does she?" asked Urchin quietly. And now he'll decide to give his own orders, he thought. And the first one will be my execution. But I have to take the risk.

"I don't understand," he said. "Do you like being belowground, in tunnels? You are the Great Silver Prince of Destiny. How can anyone give *you* orders?"

The Silver Prince spread his wings, blinked, and planted his feet apart, looking to Urchin like a fat indignant pigeon. The other ravens stood absolutely still and silent, their heads bowed. Slowly, lifting his talons very carefully and deliberately, he strutted to Urchin.

Urchin lowered his gaze and hoped death would be quick. If he had encouraged the ravens to fight against each other, Mistmantle might have a chance. *Heart receive me.*

Caw, crraaw, craaaw! A searing croak of triumph filled the burrow as the Silver Prince turned to the other ravens. In a moment of wonderful joy, Urchin found he was still alive and unhurt, and could breathe freely again.

"I am the Silver Prince of Destiny!" cawed the raven. "I will show you what I can do! I am the one you waited for! I am the son of the Archraven! Come with me!"

A raven stepped forward. "Two of us will come with you, sir," it said. "In your wisdom, please permit two to guard the captive."

"Two of you!" he cried, "Guard the tree-rat! The rest, come with me! And do not speak to me of the Taloness!"

The Silver Prince inclined his head and led the way from the tunnel. Urchin leaned back against the earth wall and sighed quietly with relief. The Silver Prince had halved the guard for him, and the ravens had been awake all night. That was better—but what had he done in encouraging the Silver Prince to fly free? Sent him in search of some defenseless little animal to bully? But if the ravens could be encouraged to attack each other, they wouldn't be hurting Mistmantle animals at the same time.

He wriggled his arm to see the bracelet, true and clear on his wrist. Somewhere, stored in his heart, were all the bright days he had ever known, all the love ever shown to him, all the joy he had ever felt. It was all there, still inside him. And he knew that somewhere in and beyond the beating of his own heart was the Heart that broke with love for Mistmantle, and was beating still, and always would.

He didn't know whether he would survive this. But he knew that the power that gives life and freedom would live, and the power to kill and devour would destroy itself.

The Gathering Chamber was darkened by the boarded-up windows. Crispin gave final orders to the animals of the Circle, who stood about him, bloodstained, disheveled, and keen-eyed. From all parts of the tower came the steady tapping of hammers as carpenters narrowed doorways.

"Beg Your Majesty's pardon," said Docken, "but the ravens will tear down the woodwork."

"Eventually they will," said Crispin. "But it'll hold them off for a while. We'll make it as hard for them as we possibly can. Twigg has some exceptionally solid wood, so with any luck they'll break their beaks on it."

They laughed nervously. Crispin smiled and went on.

"If the tower falls, you are to leave it by any tunnel, any window, any way that you can find to escape safely. Just go. Get to the coves and shores, ready to evacuate the island if you have to. If you can't get out, move underground."

The animals glanced sideways at each other. Nobody liked to ask the question. Finally, Mother Huggen did.

"And if we are all running away through tunnels, Your Majesty—and I personally don't expect to run fast, and there's not so many tunnels I can get through these days—where will you be?"

Crispin smiled. "I will be here, Mother Huggen," he said.

"Then so should we be, sir," said Russet.

"You animals are what matters," said Crispin. "Not the tower, and not me. Get out, continue your fight for the animals of Mistmantle. The tower can fall, I can die, but as long as Mistmantle has animals like you, it will go on. We will all groom our fur with anything—vinegar, mustard, ginger, lemon—anything that they won't like. If we die, at least we won't feed them. Animals of the Circle, spend this evening with those you love the best. If your children are in the Mole Palace, Arran will escort you there."

"I thought we were moving the children out of there, sir," said Russet.

"Little by little, yes," said Crispin. "But only as soon as the other burrows are made ready and safe. And it will be guarded. Heart keep you all."

The animals bowed and seemed reluctant to leave. Then Moth took Crispin's paw. "Heart keep you, Your Majesty," she said, and slipped over to Cedar. "And *Your* Majesty."

Each animal bowed and shook paws with the king and queen, each with a blessing or a promise of great efforts in the battle to come. When everyone else had left, Padra stepped forward, bowed, and, ignoring Crispin's outstretched paws, knelt before him.

"You're my king," he said, "and you're my oldest friend. That doesn't give me the right to disobey orders, but I can ask you to reconsider." He looked up into Crispin's face. "Don't order me to leave the tower. I'll get Arran and Fingal out, but let me stay."

"We need captains of your caliber," said Crispin, "and I mean alive, not dead in the tower. Get up off the floor, Padra."

Padra rose, smiling as usual, but sorrow was in his eyes. "Fingal's shaping up," he said, "and I trained Urchin. I think he's managed to

151

learn a few things. Oh, and," he added innocently, "I suppose the queen will leave the tower too?"

Cedar laughed.

"Nice to hear you laughing again, Cedar," said Padra.

"I stay," said Cedar. "I don't suppose the king will lock me in a cell for disobeying orders."

"Would you put me in a cell, Crispin?" asked Padra. "Shall I disobey orders and find out?"

"Oh, stay if you must, Padra," said Crispin, and his heart felt lighter for it. "Sharpen your sword."

"I intended to stay anyway"—Padra smiled—"but it's good to have permission."

The taunting began first. The Taloness and her armies circled the island, screeching their battle cry. They wheeled in toward the tower and swerved away, swooped, ripped at the turf and the island's crops, and rose again.

"Stand firm," said Crispin on the battlements.

"Stand firm," said Padra and Fingal inside the Spring Gate.

"Stand firm," said Captain Docken at the main gate.

"Stand firm," said rows of moles to each other.

Oh, Heart help us, thought Queen Cedar as the birds wheeled nearer. They were close enough now for her to see their beaks. They had been sharpened like daggers and carved to be jagged.

The birds ringed the island. The Taloness threw back her head and cawed. Then the circle of birds drew in, blacker and tighter, rushing toward the tower, so many and so fast that there would be no point in trying to fight from outside. There was one burst of arrows from the walls, then Crispin, Cedar, and the archers dived under trapdoors for cover.

"Every window!" yelled Crispin. "Every door, every corridor, every tunnel!"

In the dark Gathering Chamber, the walls were bare. Precious Threadings had been taken down, rolled up, and hidden.

"Russet!" Crispin called. "Arran! Set archers at their places!"

The ravens would attempt to break the glass and tear down the wood. Archers would be ready to shoot at anything that broke through. Defenders ran to the Gathering Chamber, and Crispin put a paw across the shoulder of a young mole.

"It's a bad year for vermin," he said. "Ready to show them what we can do?"

In the workrooms, Thripple and Needle had invented their own defenses and set them in place. Heaving enormous skeins and cones of wool, they had crisscrossed a web around door handles, looms, hooks, anything that could be used to trap the birds, if they were to break through the windows. The workrooms should, they agreed, be as safe as anywhere. The windows where animals would sit to sew in a good light had been boarded up and protected with more woven mesh. The storerooms where threads and clothes were stored were windowless, because light would fade them. Needle had asked Crackle to take refuge with them, but Crackle would not leave her kitchen.

Sepia tucked the blanket over Fir's paws to keep them warm, watching his sleeping face and wishing she could share his peacefulness. Even as she prayed, she felt sick with fear. Before the Heart she named the warriors fighting across the island, facing those cruel beaks and talons: *Longpaw, Crispin, Cedar, Padra, Arran, Docken, Russet, Heath . . . Urchin, Urchin.*

The Gathering Chamber windows were holding against the furious blows of raven beaks, so the birds had picked up stones to beat at them. Shattered glass flew from the tower. Breaking through the wood came next, and Crispin and the defenders stood ready. The curtains had been drawn—"something for them to get tangled in," suggested the queen.

"The waiting gets to you, doesn't it, Your Majesty," said Docken quietly. Talons rasped and squeaked against the wood, and he flinched. "Sorry, Your Majesty, but it's like scratching on glass, that noise."

"I know," said Crispin. "You'd think they could just get on with it, wouldn't you? I could go and brew us all a cordial, but I don't suppose we'll have time."

The shredding of wood came again, harsh enough to jangle the nerves. A shock of pain ran through Crispin's old wound.

"Horrible noise," he said, and raised his voice. "Shall we drown them out? Sing!"

"While the stars rise and set . . ." began Russet—it was a favorite old Mistmantle song that they had all learned in their infancy, and voice by voice they joined in—

> *"And the waves ebb and flow,*
> *While the mists rise above us and the earth holds below,"*

The panels of wood were tearing apart now. The defenders sang louder, their singing spreading through the tower. Archers heard it and took up the song at the windows. Some sang flat or out of tune, some only remembered a few lines, but they sang out loud and kept singing until the vicious beaks and claws finally splintered the wood. Beaks slashed the curtains. Crispin kissed his sword blade and speared it into the throat of the first raven to emerge. Then the clashing of swords, beaks, and talons began.

All over the tower, ravens wrenched the boards from the windows. When the defenders fought them off and sent them tumbling down the walls, more flew in to take their places. If the ravens found a window too small or too hard to break through, they joined the attack on another one. They poured through the workroom windows and into Needle and Thripple's web, where they squawked and struggled—but before Needle had time to cheer, they had shredded their way through.

"Run!" cried Thripple.

Swords clashed, voices rang, ravens screeched, wood splintered. Arrows flew from the remaining windows. In the Gathering Chamber, Crispin and his troops fought furiously on—one more, one more, one more—but there were always more ravens, flying in to take the places of the fallen. Crispin struck out with every ounce of heart and mind and will, of paw and shoulder, of skill and instinct, knowing it was only a matter of time, and the Heart must do the rest.

CHAPTER FOURTEEN

LITTLE BY LITTLE, EVERY move so tiny that even raven eyes would not notice, Urchin was working his paw free. Blood smeared the floor where Brindle's body had been dragged away. Catkin. *Catkin, Catkin, I'm sorry, Catkin.* But sorry was not enough, and what would he say when he stood before Crispin? He couldn't even hold Curlingshell Bay. He could at least get out of this captivity, tell Crispin what had happened, and be another useful warrior. At least he could still fight ravens.

A raven twitched and turned its head. Crispin froze. But the raven was not attending to him. It cawed to its companion and they tipped their beaks, listening. Urchin listened too, resisting the instinct to twitch his ears, not wanting to draw their attention.

"Tunnels 'round here?" said one. "Tunnels?"

"There's the one he came down," said the other.

157

Urchin strained to hear over their harsh voices. Something was moving, close to the tunnel he had come through. It was behind him, the softest brush of paws. More than one animal, but he couldn't tell which kind. If Mistmantle animals were close by, they should be warned of the presence of ravens, and the best way to do that was to make the birds speak up or caw. He yawned loudly.

"Silence, tree-rat!" rasped a raven, as the other bird poked its beak into tunnels and prodded at the earth roof. "Tunnels! Where are they?"

"I don't know," said Urchin. "This isn't my part of the island."

"I'll search," said the other raven. It flattened its wings against its body and stalked along the tunnel. Only one now, thought Urchin.

"Insolent tree-rat!" rasped the raven. "Tell me! Tunnels!"

"Moles are the ones who know about tunnels," said Urchin. "I'm a squirrel."

There was a caw of rage, and silvered talons whipped out toward his face. He closed his eyes and ducked, but at the same moment he pulled his paw free. Better not to let the ravens see that. The raven's claw clutched his ear.

"Tunnels, tree-rat," it said, cawing into his face. Urchin pressed his head back against the earth wall. The bird was so close that he could see into its throat. It tried to speak again, but this time all that came out was a harsh rattle, as if it were choking; and as Urchin turned his head away, the raven thudded backward onto the ground.

"Urchin!" whispered a low voice. Urchin looked up. Loose earth crumbled from the wall opposite him. Sword in paw, a squat little mole dropped into the chamber.

"Todd!" whispered Urchin, and laughed for joy. "Todd!"

"That's me," said Todd, and turned as the other raven, alerted by its companion's sudden silence, ran from the tunnel. Todd's sword was waiting for it.

"Blooming spuggies," he said, wiping the blade clean. "Big noisy spuggies. Any more of 'em about?"

"Not that I know of," said Urchin. "But we need to get out."

Todd was already kneeling at Urchin's side, slicing through the ropes. "You've nearly done this for yourself, sir," he remarked.

"I would have looked silly without you," said Urchin. His sword had been propped against a wall, and now he felt its familiar shape in his paw again. "Well done, Todd!" He didn't hug the mole, as he didn't want to upset Todd's dignity, but he clapped him on the shoulder.

"Your grandfather Lugg used to do this," he said. "Turn up just when he was needed."

"Must run in the family," said Todd. "Are you injured? Bit of blood on your arm."

"I'm all right," said Urchin. "But they've got Catkin. They went along that tunnel, the broad one. They must be well ahead of us now. We need to get word to the king, and alert the Circle. If they imprison her underground, the moles might be able to find her."

"Best move, then," said Todd. There was the soft thud of a curled-up

159

hedgehog landing behind him. "Oh, here come the troops."

"Hello, Urchin," said Hope politely as he uncurled.

"Hope!" said Urchin. "You brave hedgehog! Shouldn't you be in the tower?"

Hope trundled happily toward him and stopped just as Urchin thought he'd bump into him. "I'm a diversion," he said. "So was Needle."

"Needle!" Urchin looked up to see her peering from the hole Todd had made. "Shouldn't you be in the tower?"

"I was," she said. She wriggled out and shook out her spines as if she were ready for a fight. "Thripple and I got out—we had orders to—so at least we didn't have to watch what those vermin were doing to our workrooms. And they were coming to find you, so . . ."

"Catkin's missing," said Urchin.

Urchin had known Needle all his life, and had never seen such horror on her face. She looked as if her worst nightmares were coming true before her eyes.

"Needle, what . . ." he began.

"We have to find her!" she cried. "Now! Split up. Urchin, come with me. We'll—"

"Hold on," said Urchin. "She could be anywhere. They know who she is. We were betrayed. They'll have a whole pack of ravens guarding her."

"Then it's no good," said Needle bleakly. "She'll be dead by now."

Hope scurried to her and took her paws. "Don't say that," he said.

"I think we should go back to the tower and tell the king and queen. They ought to know."

"The tower could fall at any minute," said Todd. "And the king's given orders to leave it."

"He hasn't ordered me," said Urchin. "I wasn't there."

"True enough," said Todd.

"I left," said Needle. "He never said I mustn't go back."

"And I should go back and help Brother Juniper, and look after Brother Fir," said Hope, "because that's what I do. Is Mum safe?"

"She went underground to a burrow," said Needle. "She was going to join your sister."

"So we go to the defense of the tower," said Urchin. "Report to the king. He'll want to send search parties for Catkin."

"I'll lead the way, if you don't mind, Urchin," said Todd. "I know the networks at least as well as anyone just now. There's animals being shunted around all over the place, so it's important not to block the tunnels."

"It'll be all right, Urchin," said Hope, as if he could sense Urchin's disquiet. But for Urchin, ready to thrash his way through to the tower however he could, it would be a wretched arrival.

Against the first wave of birds to fly through the tower windows, Crispin, Russet, and the rest of the defenders battled on. But three by three, then four by four the birds flew in, wheeling about them. Cedar had run to the help of the warriors in the Throne Room, where they fought desperately, seeing no end to the flapping black wings. The strongest of the doors were barricaded, and at the Spring Gate Padra and Fingal fought back-to-back, yelling encouragement to each other and defiance to the ravens.

"Fly, all of you!" cried the queen, but perhaps the warriors around her didn't hear her because the ravens seized her by the neck and pinned her to the ground. As the sword was dashed from her paw, she shrieked.

"Fly!" yelled Padra as he and Fingal fought their way backward through the entrance, slamming doors behind them, kicking over water jars, pushing stones into tunnels, anything that would make the entrances too narrow for the ravens. "Did you hear, Fingal? Fly!"

Fingal caught his breath. He tried to say that he wasn't leaving Padra, but as long as he wielded his sword, there was no strength left for speech.

"When you're told!" said Padra. They reached the solid door leading from the otter quarters to the main tower, heaved it shut, and barred it. A channel had been dug out at this point, carrying spring-water and finally joining an underground stream.

"They won't get through that door," Padra panted. "Fingal, run when you're told. It's the king's orders, not mine, so do as you're told."

Fingal tried again to speak. This time he could have managed the words, but Padra kicked him into the stream and, with a final "Heart keep you!" ran up the stairs. Crispin would need him.

Another otter was swimming ahead of Fingal.

"Corr," called Fingal, "is that you?"

Corr twisted in the water and waited for Fingal to catch up.

"Crackle said there was a way to underground waters from beneath the kitchens," he said. "She pointed me in the right direction, and I was about to say I wanted to stay when she . . . sort of . . ."

". . . kicked you through a trapdoor?" said Fingal.

Corr shook his whiskers. "I think her paw slipped," he said.

"I doubt it," said Fingal. "Stick with me. There's a lake, if you go far enough, with caves around it. I found it by accident a long time ago, and I've been back since to explore. We can make a place of safety there for anyone who needs one. Keep listening. If there are any of these vermin about, we could do a bit of useful spying."

The battle for the Gathering Chamber had been lost. Broken glass littered the floor. Protesting, making every last sword blow count, the defenders had obeyed the king's orders to leave, determined to regroup and be ready to fight again. Ravens perched on ledges and on the windowsill. Crispin stood disarmed and surrounded.

Heart forgive me, he thought. *I have failed Mistmantle.* And as the ravens dragged Cedar, bloodstained and exhausted, from the Throne Room, two things became very clear to Crispin. One was that more sorrow could be heaped upon sorrow, more heartbreak upon heartbreak. The other was that there were still things worth fighting for.

Urchin followed Todd and Hope, ducking where the tunnels were low, slithering down when they sloped downhill. It was a harder journey than they had expected, and slower than they'd hoped. They had to stop and squash against the wall as animals scurried past—infants being moved to safety and tower animals hurrying out, their eyes wide as they muttered and raged about ravens. At a crossing place, Todd stopped so suddenly that they ran into each other.

"Sorry," said Urchin as he ran into Hope, and, "Ow!" as Needle ran into him.

"That's all right," said Hope.

"Mind where you're going!" said Todd. "Tipp, what are you doing here?"

Tipp, Todd's brother, stepped into the light of a tunnel lantern. With a sword at his hip, he stood out dramatically in the lamplight. Behind him, a young squirrel moved into view.

"Prince Oakleaf!" said Urchin.

"I'm helping to move the little ones," said Prince Oakleaf. "I couldn't just stay in hiding."

There was no arguing with that. At the prince's age, Urchin would have felt the same. Hope was sniffing about, putting his ear against walls, and scrabbling.

"We're going to the tower," said Needle. "And don't tell us the tower is being emptied, because there isn't time to explain."

"Quickest way," said Tipp, "will be—"

"This way," said Hope confidently. He disappeared down a flight of steps cut into the earth, and bobbed up again. "Excuse me interrupting, but we should go this way."

"You'll end up in the underground lake if you do," said Tipp.

"No, *on* it," said Hope, "I've been there with Fingal; he's got little boats and things down there. It'll be faster to go that way, in a boat across the underground lake."

"I'll stay with my brother," said Todd. "But if you want to . . ."

Needle and Urchin were already pattering down the steps after Hope.

CHAPTER FIFTEEN

A T THE KITCHEN TABLE, Crackle cried into her arms until her face hurt. Around her, other kitchen animals who had stayed in the tower dried their tears on aprons and tea towels. Finally, when there were no more tears to cry, Crackle dried her eyes and found a broom.

Flour, nuts, and dried fruit lay among the broken glass and pottery on the floor. The ravens had eaten what they wanted and scattered the rest, tearing open flour sacks, knocking over bottles, throwing berries on the floor and stamping on them until Crackle could not bear to watch for another moment. She had hidden in the cellar until the sound of cawing and tearing was over, and then crept up to see her ransacked kitchen.

She was still shaking. She clutched the broom with both paws to steady herself.

"We'll need hot soapy water," said a hedgehog. "They've spilled honey and most of the syrup. Everything's sticky."

"It's this way," said Hope. In the high arched caves, his voice echoed.

"You sure?" asked Urchin, and then realized what a silly question it was. He'd never known anyone like Hope for navigating underground. The sound of water was nearer.

"Is this really bringing us near to the tower?" said Needle.

"I've been here with Fingal," said Hope. "We came by accident the first time, you know, when I fell down the water thing, and on purpose after that, but he's been here more than I have." He sniffed at the air, sneezed, and apologized. "This way. Needle, can you swim?"

"A bit," she said. "It depends on how far."

"Well," said Hope, considering, "it's only across a very little river. But I suppose I could find Fingal and ask him to carry you."

"I'll swim," said Needle.

Hope turned so sharply that Urchin lost sight of him altogether for a few seconds, and had to follow the scuffling of his paws. The cave Hope led them to became so narrow that it was more like a tunnel; but as it widened again, Urchin saw an underground river running so slowly and gently that it made only a few soft ripples.

"There's a cave to go through on the other side," said Hope. "I can't see it very well, but I know it's there."

"I can see it," said Urchin, peering at the black cave mouth ahead of them. "Shall I go first?"

The water felt fresh and cool, and Urchin had never swum underground before. He found it silent and mysterious, and if things had been different, he might have enjoyed it. He could have listened to the smooth, soft splash of water and turned on his back to watch the reflections of rippling waves on the cave roof. But he couldn't enjoy anything just now. The thought of Catkin weighed like a gray stone in his heart. He scrambled to the shore, shook himself dry, and dried his sword as well as he could on the sandy earth. Hope scurried confidently past him.

"Want a paw?" said Urchin as Needle climbed to the shore, but she glanced fiercely at him. "Sorry."

"Keep up!" called Hope, and trundled ahead of them into the cave. Urchin followed him through the soaring corridor of rock. Without warning the cave widened out, and he gasped. In the dimness they stood at the edge of an underground lake: wide, still, and silent as moonlight. The soaring stones made their voices echo.

"It's vast!" whispered Urchin, and knelt beside Hope, placing a paw on his back. Straining his eyes, he could just see the shore at the other side.

"Boats," said Hope. "We've been busy down here, making it nice." He paused, lifting his right paw and then his left and turning a few degrees to each side to get his bearings. "Right," he said. "In the cove."

In a dry cove, pulled well away from the water's edge, was a long, light boat with neatly shipped paddles. A lantern hung on the stern, with dry flints waiting in the boat. Urchin and Hope carried it to the water. When they had lit the lantern, it glowed with a halo that cast a glow on the dark water and showed Needle and Urchin the tension in each other's faces. Hope seemed completely unperturbed.

"Will it carry three?" asked Urchin doubtfully.

"I don't think so," said Hope.

"Then I'll take you across one at a time," said Urchin. "Needle, you first?"

"Yes, please!" said Needle, with a frown of anxiety on her face, and snapped, "I don't need help!" as he offered her a paw. Urchin settled himself in the front of the boat. At least she hadn't asked him if he'd ever handled this sort of boat before. To his relief, he found it was easy. The little boat skimmed through the water, cleaving a clear wake behind it, almost like flying. It would be so good to forget ravens, forget Catkin and the last yearning look over her shoulder, to forget everything except the smooth rush of the boat to the opposite shore—but it wasn't like that.

"What is it, Needle?" he asked. "You're all cross and edgy."

"Oh, nothing!" she snapped. "We're only being attacked by ravens!" Then she flicked at the water with her paw. "Sorry, Urchin. It's . . ."

The boat sheared softly into sand. Needle stepped out. A shallow stairway led into the sandstone rocks.

"Somebody's going to die," she muttered. "Somebody important."

"How do you know?" asked Urchin, but Needle shook her head.

Urchin had discovered before that he could be strong and calm when he really needed to, even when he hadn't felt remotely strong and calm before. It worked now.

"Needle," he said, "we all know that. We're all important, and this is a war. Some of us are going to die."

With pain and horror in her eyes, she swung around to face him. "Don't say 'us'!" she cried. "You mustn't say 'us'!" She turned and ran for the stair.

At the top of the stair she stopped to dry her tears, take a deep breath, pull herself together, and wish Urchin hadn't said that. It was bad enough knowing that one of the royal family would die, without thinking that Urchin might, too.

Urchin used the paddle to push the boat out again. He would have explained to Needle that by "us" he meant all the islanders, not just the two of them, but she had run up those stairs before he could say another word. Hope was waiting patiently at the other side. There wasn't much to say as they crossed the lake. But when they pulled the boat to shore, a slapping of otter paws and tail and the bright, torchlit face that appeared made everything feel better.

"That's what I said," said Hope, and blew out the lantern. "Fingal's made it nice here."

"Fingal!" cried Urchin.

"Hello, Urchin and Hope!" said Fingal. "Needle just flew up here like a squirrel up a tree, wanting to know the quickest way back to the

tower. I showed her the way through the cellar and the kitchens—
Oh, that's a secret route, so I haven't told you that—and she was off.
Come and join us in the ottery!"

"I have to get to the king," said Urchin, but as Fingal was lolloping
up the stairs and around the corner, there wasn't much chance to
argue. Following him, he found a pleasant, comfortable cave with a
sandy floor, lanterns casting a warm light on the pale gold rock, and a
fire burning. ("Makes it look cheerful!" said Fingal.) With another
staircase leading upward out of the cave, it was almost like being on a
tower landing.

"Tide and Swanfeather!" said Urchin. Seeing Padra and Arran's son
and daughter safe was such a relief that, for a moment, everything
looked better. "Oh, and . . . are you Corr? I've heard all about you. I'm
Urchin."

He wondered why Corr was staring at him in that wide-eyed way.
Was he covered in blood, or was he just a mess? Then he realized that
Corr was looking at him the way he used to look at Crispin and Padra.

"Good to see you're safe, Corr," he said.

Warmth and joy flowed through Corr. He had dreamed of meeting
Urchin of the Riding Stars, but never of meeting him like this. *Glad to
see you're safe, Corr.* As if they'd known each other for years.

Fingal held out a cup of water, and Urchin gulped it down gladly.
There hadn't been time to feel tired or hungry, but he knew he
was desperately thirsty. It didn't take long to tell Fingal all that had
happened, while Corr looked from one to the other and tried to

make sense of it all. When Urchin reached the part about Brindle, Corr gasped.

"He can't be dead!" cried Corr. "Brindle was my friend!"

Fingal put a paw around his shoulders. "I'm so sorry, Corr," he said. "He must have been a very good friend."

"He was," said Corr.

"I've been finding out about Corr," said Fingal, looking past him at Urchin. "He has a great-aunt Kerrera and a boat that needs to go to Twigg. He had a great time at Curlingshell Bay; he made friends with a squirrel called Lapwing." He raised an eyebrow.

"Please, Master Urchin, sir," asked Corr, "what happened to Lapwing? You keep talking about Catkin . . . the only Catkin I know about is the princess, and she wasn't at Curlingshell Bay, but Lapwing was. . . ."

He stopped. Urchin saw the question on his face.

Fingal patted his shoulder. "You're not supposed to know about this, Corr," he said. "But everything's different now, and we may as well put you in the picture. One—Lapwing is Princess Catkin. Two—we know the ravens have caught her, but not where they've taken her. Three—we have to pound it into Urchin's thick skull that it *isn't his fault.*"

"Don't bother," said Urchin.

"But we're still *talking!*" cried Corr. "We should be finding her! I mean"—he added, embarrassed by his own outburst—"with respect . . . sorry."

"Respect, plague," said Fingal. "You're right. But there's no sighting of her and no clue as to where to start looking."

"I've listened everywhere I've gone," said Hope. "You learn to listen with paws and prickles as well as ears, and there hasn't been a trace of her."

"Corr and I can go for a swim and see if we can find anything out," said Fingal. "Does anyone know if it's day or night?"

Hope raised his head and twitched his nose. "Needle will know," he said.

Urchin began to say that Needle wasn't there, but a moment later she appeared from the upward stairway. She still looked anxious, but this time she had the air of a female hedgehog with a task on her paws.

"The kitchens!" she said, and licked stickiness from her paws. "They're doing their best to clean up, but it's such a mess."

"Any news of Catkin?" asked Urchin.

"None," said Needle. "Listen, everyone. There are ravens all over the tower. I heard that Crispin and Cedar are still alive, but nobody seems to know anything about them. They're almost certainly in the Gathering Chamber. I've worked out what we can do. We need a few slim, nippy animals who know every back stair of the tower, animals who can wriggle behind skirting boards and come and go without the ravens knowing anything about it." She looked hopefully at Urchin.

"I was a tower page," he said. He removed a spider that was swinging by a thread from Needle's prickles and transferred it to a lamp bracket, where it began to spin a web. "Pages know all the secret ways and the back stairs."

"And I found a new one whenever I went exploring and got lost," said Hope. "I did a lot of that when I was small, and I've remembered them all."

"And there's Sepia," said Needle.

"Where is she?" asked Urchin.

"She stayed in the tower, helping Juniper look after Brother Fir," she told him. "She wasn't supposed to, but she did. She doesn't know the tower as well as you two, but she learns quickly. If you three—Urchin, Hope, and Sepia—are hidden in the tower, you can listen and spy, find out who's safe and who isn't, then we can decide what to do about it. You might learn something about where Catkin is."

"Trust Needle to be sensible," said Fingal. "Make her a captain at once. Urchin, Hope, you go and do your spying in the tower. Corr and I will have a swim around and find out what we can."

"Can we come?" piped up Swanfeather.

"If anything happened to you," said Fingal, "your father would bite my head off, run me through with his sword, and keep me locked up in a barrel for a week. Then he'd give me to your mum, and I'm really, really scared of her. Ready, Corr!"

Corr jumped to his paws. Then he stared at the lamp bracket.

"That spider," he said. "Catching things in webs. Like fishing nets."

"What?" said Swanfeather.

"There could be something in that," said Fingal.

174

"Sorry," said Needle. "I know what you're thinking, but it doesn't work. Thripple and I tried it in the workrooms. We thought we could trap the ravens by weaving meshes and webs all over the place, but the ravens just ripped them to bits. Good idea, though, Corr."

Corr was still gazing at the spider. "But spiders have *sticky* webs," he said. "That's how they catch things."

"So if spiders can catch flies in sticky webs . . ." said Needle.

". . . and if we can make sticky meshes . . ." said Urchin.

"Sticky fishing nets!" cried Corr.

"Brilliant!" exclaimed Fingal.

"Where can we find some rope?" asked Tide.

"And there are workroom animals," said Urchin, warming to the idea. "They'll be really good at that. They must be scattered all over the island, but we can get messages out to them. . . . Apple and her friends all knit. . . . We need fast animals who know the tunnels, to get the message out. Teams of them to relay it all over Mistmantle. Get the whole island making raven traps. Needle, what time is it?"

"Early evening," she said. "Still light."

"The ravens should be slowing down," said Fingal. "But they're bound to attack in full force in the morning. We'll have to work all night. Tide, Swanfeather, there's rope in the boat coves. You'll have to tease it out to make it finer. Corr, let's go for that swim."

Corr slipped into the water beside Fingal, still reminding himself that this was really him, young Corr, who had never counted for anything much, swimming alongside Fingal of the Floods as if they had

175

grown up together. He glanced sideways at Fingal, who turned his head and grinned.

The underground lake lead to a twisting waterway between the rocks. Corr gazed about as he swam. He had heard of places like this, high-roofed, rocky tunnels where reflections of the water danced all around. Weeds drifted about them and tangled gently in his paws. They swam on in magical silence until Fingal said, "This comes out near the tower rocks. There's a good view of the jetty, but since we're more useful alive than dead, we have to stay well hidden. We'll just scan the shore, see where the birds are, slip a word to anyone we see, make sticky nets, look out for Catkin, and get out of the way sharpish, away from the tower. It's a bit of a tight squeeze here, but we'll manage it. There's nothing like being besieged by plaguing ravens for keeping us thin."

The tunnel became so tight that Corr feared he'd get stuck and have to ask Fingal to take his paws and heave him through—but by squeezing his shoulders in and his head down, and scrabbling with his paws, he pulled himself out and scrambled up the rocks. Harsh raven voices cawed above and around him.

"They're making a lot of noise around the jetty," whispered Fingal. "Don't shake yourself!"

The warning came just in time to stop Corr from instinctively shaking himself dry. It was the most natural thing in the world to do, and not doing it was uncomfortable; but a spray of water in the evening sun could have caught the ravens' eyes. He let the cold water seep through his fur and chill on his skin; and, as they clambered onto the rocks and looked cautiously over, he forgot everything but the sight before him.

From their hiding place, they had a clear view of the jetty. When he saw what the ravens had done, he knew he had never in his life before been truly angry.

"Lapwing!" he whispered.

"Get down!" whispered Fingal.

CHAPTER SIXTEEN

NEEDLE PICKED HER WAY over tangled wool, silk, and ribbon. She held her spines as tightly flattened as she could, but fragments of frayed silk and tufts of wool still snagged in them.

Her nose twitched. Why was there a smell of ginger? Something moved in a corner, and she whirled around.

"Myrtle!" she whispered. "You were supposed to run away!"

"I ran a little bit," said Myrtle, her eyes huge as she looked up at Needle. "Then I ran back and hid in the cupboard."

"Whyever did you do that?" demanded Needle.

"I don't know," she said. "I put gingery stuff all over me so they can't eat me." She opened her paw, in which a few small beetles wriggled. "I found these. Would you like one?"

Needle ate the smallest one to please Myrtle. Searching for undamaged skeins of wool, she felt those large eyes following her.

Myrtle, nervously popping beetles into her mouth, must be wondering what to do next.

"You can help me, Myrtle," she said. "We need to make a web. Shall I show you how to do that?"

They worked steadily together, side by side, Myrtle singing softly to herself and rocking with the rhythm of looping and knotting the wool. When there was a scuffling sound in the skirting board, and Needle lay on the floor and whispered something into it, she hardly seemed bothered. They worked on so busily that neither of them noticed the ravens approaching until the sky darkened.

Myrtle glanced up, shrieked, and cowered as huge black wings rustled. A raven flew in through the window, knocked the torch bracket from the wall with a swing of its beak, and tipped over a lamp stand. Two more followed it.

"This is our place," cawed the first raven, flexing silver claws and tipping its head sideways. "We will sleep here tonight." He pecked at a piece of lace so fine that Needle couldn't help wincing as he tossed it about and dropped it. "This rubbish will do to nest in. Shred it!" His eyes fell on a tapestry frame leaning against the wall, almost the only unbroken thing left in the room, with a barely started Threading across it, and he tilted his head. "What is this?"

Needle slipped in front of the frame. She knelt to adjust it—it had been knocked off balance—and, as she did so, made a decision so vital that she dared not think about it too much. She turned and knelt before the raven.

"Great raven," she said. "What can we do? A power such as yours has never been seen on this island. We cannot stand against you. This frame is for making the pictures that honor our leaders, whoever they are."

She bowed so low to the floor that her forehead was almost on the raven's claw.

"Let me search these cupboards," she said. "I will gather the finest gold and silver threads we have left. You are the lords of the island now, and you are the ones we must honor in our work. Please, please, I would speak with the Taloness."

The Taloness stood on the dais in the Gathering Chamber with King Crispin and Queen Cedar before her. About them were the largest and strongest of the ravens. She nodded at two of them, then at Cedar.

"Stand her against the wall," she said.

Crispin caught Cedar's wrist, but the ravens wrenched her from him and pushed her to the wall. Raven beaks held all four of Crispin's paws. When a raven appeared in the doorway, the Taloness cawed sharply at it.

"Kill and devour, Great Taloness!" it said.

"We shall kill and devour you, craven wreck-beak, if you interrupt us for no good reason," croaked the Taloness. "What is this?"

"Great Taloness," said the raven, bowing its head in submission, "there are creatures here who wish to surrender to you."

The Taloness cawed deeply. It was almost a growl.

"They will be part of the feast," she said. "We have a great entertainment prepared." She looked sideways at Crispin. "A great entertainment. But the Silver Prince has not yet come. While we wait, bring us these vermin."

With a twitch of her neck, she strutted to Crispin and glared down at him.

"Do you think you have seen the full strength of our armies yet?" she demanded. "Behind the foul fogs of this island, our ships are crammed. Your final humiliation and death will wait until all the island is ours. By then you will have watched your creatures grovel before us and before the Silver Prince, and watched us devour them, one by one." She made a rattling noise in her throat. "You consider yourself a king. You are soft on your creatures." She leaned closer. Her voice became a growling whisper. "You will suffer for it. Let us claim your darlings."

She hopped across the floor, coarse black wings flapping. "Let them in!" she snarled.

Crispin watched steadily. Whatever happened, he must show no anger. It would be like the raging of a helpless child. He must keep his heart centerd in the Heart that cared for Mistmantle, however hard that seemed. All his energy must be focused on this—keeping his senses alert, his mind sharp, and his heart in the Heart.

There was a teaching he had learned from childhood—*The Heart that gave us the mists broke with love for Mistmantle, but it still beats.* He

181

had never quite understood it. Sometimes he had thought he did, and then realized that he hadn't gotten it at all. He still didn't understand it, but now he *felt* it. It was real and true for him now as he stood surrounded by smashed furniture and broken windows with his own heart breaking for Mistmantle, as loyal Needle and little Myrtle—oh, she looked so very little—were ushered in, struggling to carry canvas, paints, pencils, wools, and a Threadings frame.

Needle stood with her head bowed. Once, shyly, she raised her eyes to look up at the Taloness as she knelt before her.

"Great Taloness," she said, "here is all that is dear to us, the means of our work. Now that the island is yours, our work is yours. We are the makers of Threadings, and the Threadings are more important than anything on all the island. Grant us to make the picture of your triumph, for you are now our rulers. We will make a tribute that will last forever."

"Spine-slug," spat the Taloness. "Turn. Look over there. Who's that?"

Needle stood and turned. She met Crispin's eyes.

"Crispin the squirrel," she said calmly.

"Squirrel?" rasped the Taloness in a low, warning voice.

"The tree-rat," said Needle.

"Your king?" said the Taloness. "Look at us!"

"If he were truly a king," said Needle, turning to face her, "he would never have brought down your anger against us. I have given my life to making these Threadings, but he has let them be destroyed.

Permit me to tell your story, madam. It is the greatest story of all."

A triumphant light was in the Taloness's eyes. "You will make our picture?" she said. "You will glorify the Silver Prince?"

"I must," said Needle. "The Threadings must always tell the truth. The victory is yours, and they will show it."

"You treacherous little vermin!" spat the Taloness, but she cackled in triumph.

"I never had any loyalty to him," said Needle. "Only to the Threadings."

Caw! The Taloness sprang. Needle ducked and curled up against that terrible sharp beak and the sharpened talons.

"Uncurl yourself, spine-slug!" shrieked the Taloness. "Your loyalty is to us! And to the Silver Prince! Repeat it! Hail to the Silver Prince!"

"Hail to the Silver Prince!" said Needle.

"Hail to the Taloness!"

"Hail to the Taloness!" cried Needle.

"And death to the tree-rat!" said the Taloness.

"Death to the tree-rat!" shouted Needle, and the air grew coarse and cracked with raven laughter. It stopped abruptly.

"Work by the window," she ordered. "Make your picture where the tree-rat can see it."

"Please, mighty Taloness," said Needle, "may I have a torch to work by?"

"Oh, we must all see well tonight," said the Taloness. "No sleep! Make your picture, spine-slug. If we dislike it, you will watch as

183

we tear it apart, and then we will tear *you* apart, and that little servant. And may all you sniveling, shuffling, earthbound animals betray this tree-rat so readily."

Needle and Myrtle scurried to the window to set up the frame. They laid out pencils, paints, wool, and needles. The Taloness perched on the jagged edge of a windowpane, looked down, and raised her left foot as if she were giving a signal. She craned her neck, stretching her beak forward, searching.

"Where is the Silver Prince?" she croaked. "Can they not find him?"

A dark shape wheeled through the sky toward them. A raven settled on the sill.

"Kill and devour, Taloness!" it said. "The Silver Prince has urgent business of his own. He will attend you in time."

All through the long silence that followed, Needle dared not look up. At last, the Taloness spoke.

"In time?" she repeated.

Crispin had heard that tone of voice before. She had used it when she had told him he would suffer. Mind in heart, he thought. Mind in heart. Hold on. What on all the island is Needle up to? His guards dragged him to the window and, at a jerk of the Taloness's head, stood him with his back to it.

"Our plan for our feast," she said, "is that we will eat the young first. But we have seen no young on this island. Where are they?"

"Would I tell you," said Crispin quietly, "if I knew?"

184

Her hooded eyelids lowered and lifted again. "You are the king," she said. "You must know."

Crispin looked steadily back at her. "Our animals are free," he said. "They make their own decisions."

She gave something between a twitch and a shrug. "No matter," she said. "We will kill and devour them soon enough. Young tree-rat tastes good."

She threw back her head. From the open beak came a screech of triumph that made Crispin's ears ring and his old wound prickle with shock. Needle and Myrtle pressed their paws to their ears.

"Turn him to the window!" she screeched.

"No!" screamed Cedar. For a moment of cold terror, Needle. thought that the ravens would fling him down. But they held him at the shattered window and dragged the queen to his side.

By the power of the evening sun they saw the sea, the shore, and the mooring posts to the west of the jetty. And when he looked down, Crispin saw something worse than nightmares.

There were ravens on the jetty, more in a boat, and four on guard on the shore. In the sea, tied to a mooring post with the water up to her waist, stood Catkin. Stranded in the steadily rising sea, she stood alone, vulnerable, and unbearably young.

"The tide is rising," remarked the Taloness. "That whole post will be under water before morning. She certainly will. She's very small."

Crispin did not have to look at Cedar to feel her pain. He knew she was shaking.

"Mother," said the Taloness, "can you see your baby? Perhaps you can remember where the other babies are? One drowned tree-rat will not feed us all."

Catkin looked out to the mists. The ravens in the boat in front of her could see her face clearly, so she must not show fear.

There was always hope, she told herself as the surface of the water lapped coldly around her. Something might happen. She might be rescued. She might rescue herself if she could only wriggle free; but there were so many cords, and so tight! The ravens might become sorry for her and let her go. No, there was no hope in that. What else? Lightning might hit the post and set her free! You never knew! The tide might not rise high enough to drown her. But if she died, she would die magnificently, with her chin up and her eyes on the stars, crying, "Heart keep Mistmantle!" and "Heart keep King Crispin and Queen Cedar!"

Oh, no. She shouldn't have thought of them. She mustn't do that again, because thinking of her parents made her want to cry, and she must not cry. *I will not cry. Don't think of them. Don't think of Oakleaf and Almondflower. But I wish I'd been nicer to Oakleaf.*

She wriggled her claws and moved her ankles as much as she could. She couldn't save herself from drowning, but at least she didn't have to get a cramp.

From the waist down she had acclimatized to the water, but every wave that lapped higher was cold. Her fur was fluffed up, and her arms and shoulders were freezing. If only she had something to look at! But there was only mist, sky, and sea, and the occasional shape of a raven flying past.

She must think of something strong, something good to die with, just in case nothing wonderful happened to save her. *Heart help me. Please. I'll be really, really nice to Oakleaf. I'll never again tell him he's too young to play. I'll listen when he tries to tell me things, even if I know them already. And if I become queen I'll be a really good one; but to do that I have to stay alive, so please help me.*

She looked up into the sky. Gold flew across it, turning to flares of red. A fiery sky that gilded the waves for her. That was what she needed. Her parents and Sepia had taught her to think of something nice before she went to sleep. If she were to die, she must die with that sky in her eyes, reliving the best ever moments of her life. . . .

. . . Waking up on festival days to see a garlanded dais and animals practicing songs and acrobatics. Seeing her parents dressed for great occasions with gleaming crowns and robes. Singing with Sepia and the choir in the gallery of the Gathering Chamber. Running through flowers in summer. Learning to swim with Tide and Swanfeather, and Fingal would . . .

She bit her lip. She'd give anything to see Fingal now. Everything was better when he was about. *Don't think of Fingal. Think of frost patterns on the window in winter, the soft white enchantment of snow at night, the day she, Oakleaf, and the young otters had borrowed a tea tray from the kitchen and sledded down the hills. . . .*

A violent cawing at her ear made her jerk and shriek. "Leave me alone!" she snarled. They laughed, but she didn't care. It wasn't fair to startle her like that; it wasn't fair—none of this was fair! She shouldn't be here! She should be playing, running up and down the tower walls, staying out of the way in case anyone said it was her bedtime—bedtime would be lovely. A hot drink, a lamp, and her own warm bed . . .

Don't think of that. Don't cry—but it wasn't right, it wasn't fair! She struggled and wriggled, angry, not just for herself but for all the young animals who should be enjoying the summer and were now penned up in hiding places. They might never again be free, never again see their families. . . .

She squeezed her eyes shut and folded her lips tightly, but it was no good. Hot tears trickled down her face. At least the ravens weren't looking. They'd think she was crying for misery, cold, fear, or self-pity. She wasn't. She was crying with anger.

It was growing darker now, and colder. She thought back over the last summer. It had been all right until the swans arrived, but even then she had been proud of her father going to Swan Isle. It had been fun at Curlingshell Bay with Brindle—*Don't think of Brindle*—and her new otter friend, Corr. The battle had not been at all as she had imagined it—there was too much happening at once, and no time to think—but she had done her best, and at the end there had been a wave of pride in her heart because she had fought for Mistmantle at Urchin's side.

All her life she had admired Urchin, even when she had been jealous of him. That battle—she smiled when she thought of it—had been the most terrifying, most confusing, and most exciting moment of her life. But it had not brought her home to the tower. It had brought her here, with every wave lifting the water a little higher.

Never say, *"If only."* Juniper had taught her that. Never say, *"If only that hadn't happened."*

She wished she could know that Urchin was safe. *Heart, please keep Urchin safe.* She had tried to take one last look to say good-bye as they dragged her away.

That beautiful sky was darkening. She looked out at the mists, her eyes still blurring. That must be why the mists looked different. It was as if she could see a shape—vague and uncertain—but if she kept looking at it, it seemed more or less heart-shaped. The last of the red in the sunset must be giving it that pale peach-pink color, with maybe a thread of gold . . . It reminded her of something. . . .

She gasped.

It looked like the Heartstone!

CHAPTER SEVENTEEN

CRISPIN STILL STOOD AT THE window. Nothing could be worse than this. The tide came in, the light faded, and the water surrounding the little figure at the mooring post rose higher. The ravens at the jetty lit beacons. In the Gathering Chamber and on the walls outside, candles were placed around the window, and torches in the few unbroken lamp brackets were lit.

"A good view of your little tree-rat may help you to concentrate," said the Taloness, "on where we can find the young." She peered around to see Crispin's face. "Do you still not know where they are? There is time enough to remember before high tide. If you don't know where they are, tree-rat, perhaps you know where they *might* be? Have you put that bitter taste on them? We can wash it off! Your brat must taste only of salt water by now!"

Crispin said nothing. The Taloness had made it plain. She was offering to release Catkin if he told her where to find the rest of the young. Either Catkin drowned slowly, or the young of Mistmantle were massacred. Every minute of his silence lifted the waters higher around her shoulders. His heart reached out to her as if he could protect her—but he couldn't. He could not save his own child's life at the cost of all the rest.

He honestly didn't know where all the young were. He had given orders for them to be taken from the Mole Palace and spread around the island, underground, and as near to the shores as possible, so long as they were well hidden. If he could have sent the ravens in the wrong direction, he would have done so—but the young could be anywhere.

And—and this was, in a way, comforting—he couldn't trust the Taloness. If he told her where to find the young, she'd probably let Catkin die anyway. The ravens were like that. Without looking at her, he knew that Cedar felt the same, even as her heart broke for Catkin.

Beside him something clattered, making him jolt. Needle had dropped her pencil.

"Sorry," she whispered shyly as she picked it up. "Please, Madam Taloness, may I turn the frame to the lamp?"

The Taloness inclined her head. Needle and Myrtle turned the frame toward the light, and Crispin glanced at it as they went on drawing.

Needle had sketched in a coronation scene, with the Taloness and the Silver Prince enthroned and Mistmantle animals kneeling about them. A basket full of berries, shells, nuts, flowers, and leaves lay on the floor, as if the island's treasures were being offered as tribute to the ravens.

Were those almonds in the basket? And a sprig of hawthorn? Crispin looked away quickly. Nothing must show in his face, but he lifted his heart and gave thanks for the months, so long ago, when he had been a young tower squirrel with Tay and Brother Fir drilling the Threadings Code into his head.

Almonds for secrecy. Hawthorn for hope.

He dared not look again too soon. He gazed down on Catkin and wondered if she was crying. He glanced at Cedar and saw unbearable pain on her face.

Around the tower, behind skirting boards, above ceilings, and under stairs, Sepia, Hope, and Urchin ran on silent paws. Messages ran from beneath the workrooms to behind the Gathering Chamber, from the Chamber of Candles to the kitchen, from the cellars to the underground waterways. Networks spread across the island. Mole to mole to squirrel to squirrel to hedgehog to hedgehog to otter to otter, the messages were passed on, one to the next, to the next, to the next, running through tunnels, through waterways, from one burrow to another, to the caves on the shore. When they heard it, animals sprang to their paws to scrabble about for wool, reeds, ribbons, grasses, cottons, old cloaks to unravel, old fishing nets, resins, syrups, and sap.

"We should have tied her to the other side of the post," remarked the Taloness. "You could have seen her tears. She could have looked up into your face and watched as you let her drown. Where are the young?"

Crispin did not answer. He watched Catkin, reached out with all his mind and heart to her, and prayed for all the sons and daughters of Mistmantle.

The Taloness hopped to Cedar, rasping her challenge into the queen's face.

"Where are they?"

"Beyond your reach," said Cedar.

Needle was quietly giving Myrtle instructions. Crispin twitched an ear.

"That's good, Myrtle," said Needle. "Put one in here, in this corner."

Crispin glanced quickly at the picture. Spiderwebs? Why was she telling Myrtle to draw spiderwebs? They'd never meant anything in the Threadings Code, but it must be important. Needle had made sure he noticed it. With fine, quick lines she sketched in a small squirrel on the left, with a flower beside her.

A figure on the left, so probably female. The flower was a kingcup. That stood for royalty. Catkin? *My Catkin. The water must be so cold. If I could only die for you, my Catkin, my little girl.* The ravens were less watchful now. Their eyelids drooped. If the guards holding them fell asleep, could he and Cedar shake free and fight off the rest? Was it worth the risk?

"Kill and devour," cawed the Taloness. "Fetch the next guards."

A raven went to the door, croaking. More ravens marched into the chamber to replace the guard, but the ravens around Catkin remained the same.

"Myrtle," said Needle quietly, "do you have a very pale color there? Something about the color of the sand under the castle, that sort of shade, or honey. Very pale honey. Yes, that one."

The Taloness had stopped haranguing Crispin and Cedar. She was strutting before the new guards, briefing them, demanding news of the island.

"Where is the Silver Prince?" she asked.

For the first time since they had arrived on the island, the ravens seemed slow to obey. "He is guarding the island for you," they said.

A snarl rasped in her throat. "We have minions to do that!" she croaked. "Send him to me. Tell him he has only to wait until high tide to devour the princess! And you"—she pecked at Crispin's shoulder—"will watch him eat her! Go, ravens! Find him!"

The Taloness chased and pecked at her own guards. Crispin glanced again at the Threading. More spiderwebs? Another squirrel, but pale. *Urchin.* He stood between the Taloness and the Silver Prince, and it looked as if he was offering them swords—but swords were usually pointed up for victory or down for defeat. These were lying across Urchin's paws, one pointing from the Silver Prince to the Taloness, one from the Taloness to the Silver Prince. He looked away quickly. The Taloness was growing impatient waiting for the Silver Prince, who had still not come. Was Needle telling him that this was Urchin's doing? But it wasn't helping Catkin, as the night grew darker. His heart twisted. The water was around her shoulders.

Needle wriggled and shifted, and he glanced at the picture. The squirrel who might be Catkin held something in her paws.

All over the island, nets, webs, and meshes grew, and were shuffled along tunnels to be ready for use. They mustn't be stickied too soon, but the pots of syrup, sap, and resin were kept beside them. Old animals with wrinkled paws advised about how to weave with reeds and and grasses. Grandfathers triumphantly held up the balls of string that they had always said would come in useful. Otters compared their netting techniques, wide mesh or narrow, long pattern or short, locked-loop stitch or split and slot. Knitters worked furiously with huge needles—pass the stitch over, knit two together. In burrows full of grandmotherly hedgehogs, the knitting was becoming competitive.

The beacons hardly showed the shore. Crispin could just see the small figure, her head tilted. If he could throw off these guards, if Cedar could do the same, if they could seize a weapon—a bit of broken glass would do—they could run down the walls. But getting free of the guards was the impossible part.

"Move the lamp over here, Myrtle," said Needle. "I can't see what I'm doing."

What was Catkin in the picture holding? A bird? That didn't make sense. A bird meant freedom. There must be something in the code that he'd forgotten, some other meaning, or maybe Needle had drawn it badly—No, that was impossible. There was a click as Needle dropped her pencil. She crawled about looking for it, pressing her face to the ground as she searched.

"The water is up to her neck," rasped the Taloness.

"If we told you," said Cedar, and Crispin heard how she fought the tremor in her voice. "If we told you where our young are, you wouldn't release her. We know you well."

A long, chilling cackle came from deep in the Taloness's throat. "We might," she said. "You cannot tell. You do not know us so well, not at all."

Crispin strained to listen. He was sure he'd heard something scuffling under the floor, but he might be mistaken. The Taloness was talking, and Needle was still shuffling about. A raven flew to the window.

"There is something silver in the tower, mighty Taloness!" it said. "Something moving!"

"Where?" she demanded.

"Here and there, Mighty Taloness," it said. "At a window, then another window! It could be tree-rats with swords!"

"Then hunt them down and kill them," ordered the Taloness. "Kill and devour! And do not trouble us about it! If you find armed tree-rats and spine-slugs in our tower, bring back their bodies and weapons. Gather them for the Silver Prince." She turned to the window and shrieked.

Crispin gasped. Something silver swished through the air.

"Silver!" cried the Taloness. "Where from?" She rounded on the guards. "Stay with our prisoners!"

For a moment she perched on the broken glass. Then she flew out of the broken window, and Crispin saw her wheel into the darkness. Another star danced across the sky, and another, before she returned to perch on the jagged edge of the sill.

"This island rains silver!" she cried. "Ravens! Catch the silver from the sky! We will have it!" She turned on the guards holding Crispin and Cedar. "Not you! You stay!"

"The stars are riding!" cried Crispin, gazing into the sky. Did they ride tonight for good or for harm? If for good, that bird in Needle's Threading sang out the truth. If for harm, they announced Catkin's death, and he was the last king of an island that would fall and never rise again. He looked down to see an empty place where Catkin had been.

Catkin had decided to be as brave as she could for as long as she could, and looked into the sky. She could no longer see the Heartstone shape in the mist, but it had been there. She had seen it and was sure, holding it in her mind and heart as a treasure.

She hoped that nobody from the island could see her dying, because it would be so distressing for them. But how terrible to die with only ravens around her and nobody to care where she was, or what was happening! They probably thought she was still safe with Brindle. And what had happened to Urchin?

She took a deep breath and yawned, because yawning might keep her from crying. Then, deciding that she might as well sing her loudest and best, and sing for Mistmantle until the water filled her mouth, she lifted her head and took a deep breath.

"Come with me to the moss and the moor . . ."

Tears sprang to her eyes, and she cried out with joy. From the dark, secret sky a star twirled down to the sea, spinning, pausing as if it had changed its mind in midair, and twisting across the sky. Another swooped and rose with a dash of silver, and another.

"Riding stars!" she cried. *Heart, please, if you really care, let them be for good and not for harm. Let the stars be for the saving of Mistmantle. Let them help me to live and not to die—but even if I die, I can see them! The stars rode for me!*

A star swished down to the sea. A raven dodged, croaking with terror and greed. Catkin laughed. The ravens wouldn't understand riding stars, and didn't know whether to catch the stars or hide from them. The stars were wild and free, and Catkin, shivering, sang for them.

> *"Heart keep you*
> *Heart hold you*
> *Heart free you—"*

Ooh! The squeak was because something had just bitten her wrist. She wriggled and tried to kick. A soft splash in front of her made her look down. Two otter noses and just a little of their whiskery faces showed above the water.

"Shh!" said Fingal. "We'll have to swim under water, but we'll keep lifting you up so you can take a breath. Ready?"

The bands around her ankles and waist floated free. Her wrists could move.

"Take a deep breath," said Corr.

"Taloness!" cried a raven. "The stars are flying!"

"They fly for us!" cried the Taloness. "They salute the Silver Prince! Go, catch the stars for us!"

She strutted to the Threading, where Needle and Myrtle were carefully adding details. "Look! Even the spine-slugs know the greatness of the Taloness and the Silver Prince. Put stars in the drawing, spine-slug, or we rip you to pieces!"

Needle completed the circle she was drawing around the female squirrel. "Yes, Mighty Taloness," she said.

"Stars!" ordered the Taloness. She tilted her head to one side and her eyes fixed on Myrtle, who was drawing a sunflower in the corner.

"Stars, Myrtle," said Needle. "Draw a star."

The Taloness put her head to one side again. She examined the picture, then strutted to the window.

"The water has moved too quickly," she said. "Is that little tree-rat dead? Not even her ears showing? And we missed it!"

Crispin clung to hope. She couldn't have disappeared under water so quickly—one moment the water had barely reached her chin, the next she had vanished. Something had happened. Against the fierce pounding of his heart and the straining of his nerves, he held on to the hope in the Threading. Catkin with a bird for freedom, and a circle drawn around her for safety. Needle knew something. He had no idea what, or how, but she did. And Myrtle, who had no idea what she was doing, was drawing a sunflower.

Cedar hadn't needed to learn the Threadings Code, but she had chosen to. Crispin hoped she had seen, and understood.

"So it died with nobody to notice," spat the Taloness. "What a disappointment. We shall have to drown another one now." She nodded at Myrtle. "That spine-slug will do."

There was a harsh rustle of wings. Myrtle shrieked as the Taloness trapped her under her silver talons.

CHAPTER EIGHTEEN

I N A LAST FURIOUS STRUGGLE, Crispin twisted, strained, kicked, and thrashed. The Taloness raised her beak to stab. Then nobody knew what happened first: Needle with a long sewing needle in her paw leaping onto the Taloness's back, Crispin breaking free from his guards, or Urchin leaping through the broken window with one sword in his paw and another at his hip.

Crispin caught the sword Urchin threw to him. With a swing of the blade, Urchin hit the Taloness's feet, forcing her to drop Myrtle, then he and Crispin were back-to-back as they set about the ravens. Swords flashed, wings flapped and fell, talons tore. The door banged open and Padra ran in, a sword in each paw, throwing one to the queen. As a raven flew screeching through the window, fleeing from the riding stars, Padra sent it spinning back into the sky. One more landed on the sill, its beak open and its talons stretched with rage.

"Needle!" yelled Urchin.

Myrtle and Needle were bending over a pot of paint as if they were still in the workrooms. As the raven swooped, a burst of yellow paint met it in the face and sent it tumbling backward, and there was no more screeching, cawing, flapping. Dead ravens lay on the floor.

"Catkin's safe, Your Majesties," said Urchin, panting, because it was important to get that clear first.

"There'll be more of them," said Padra. "Out, quickly."

"This way," said Urchin. "To the back of this chamber, around that tight corner, and down to the Chamber of Candles."

"What happened to the Taloness?" asked Cedar. She was still shaking.

"She got away, I think," said Needle.

"Run, then," said Crispin, "before she brings a whole pack of them."

They ran across the Gathering Chamber, Padra and Cedar first with drawn swords to protect Needle and Myrtle, and Urchin and Crispin last. But already the cries of ravens were too close. A glance over his shoulder showed Urchin the wheeling, cawing birds weaving through the riding stars, fascinated and terrified, and one enormous, funeral-black, silver-clawed raven that flew into the chamber and swooped straight at them.

The doorway to the passage was well concealed and too small for ravens. Needle, Myrtle, Cedar, and Padra were through already as the raven screeched and darted down, and a push from Crispin sent Urchin sprawling through the entrance.

Scrambling to his paws, he looked back. Black wings hid Crispin from him. As he lunged forward, talons closed on Crispin's shoulders. Urchin struck out and felt the jarring in his arm as the raven caught his sword and wrenched it from his grasp. It fell with a clatter, far away across the floor.

With a squawk of pain and anger, the raven fell sideways. Crispin was on his paws again, and it seemed that they were all dragging each other through the tunnel entrance. Cedar wiped her sword on the ground.

"You owe that one to Cedar," said Padra. "She got to it first."

"Verminous claw-thugs," muttered Cedar. "Tell me about Catkin!"

"Fingal wasn't going to let her drown!" said Needle. "She's perfectly safe. Shouldn't we be running?"

"They can't follow us in here," said Padra. "I doubt they could even see the entrance. Crispin, are you all right?"

"I am," said Crispin. "Urchin?"

"I lost my sword," said Urchin. "Sorry."

"You nearly lost your paw," said Crispin. "Swords can be replaced. Straight to the Chamber of Candles, before anything else happens."

"Padra," said the king quietly as they filed through the long corridor, "where did you spring from?"

"Didn't do much springing," said Padra. "I held them off as long as I could when you gave orders to leave the tower, but the vermin overpowered me and left me trussed up in a cell. Your old cell, you'll be happy to know. However, for the last few hours the tower has been crawling with animals." He looked around at Urchin. "Especially that animal. What with him and Hope and Sepia all pattering about up and down behind skirting boards and stairways I never knew existed, all full of bits of useful information, how's a prisoner supposed to get a decent sleep? There was a lot of scrabbling under the window of my cell, then up popped Hope and untied me. I couldn't get out the way he got in, but with a bit of work I had the bars off the window, then I waited until the ravens were distracted, and ran for it. Crispin, your dungeons are useless."

"So those reports of flashes of silver from the tower . . ." said Crispin. "Was that you, Urchin?"

"It was all of us," said Urchin, holding his right wrist in his left paw.

"It was supposed to distract the ravens from Catkin," said Needle. "And from you too, but mostly from Catkin, so the otters could rescue her. We hadn't expected riding stars."

Pain grew in Urchin's wrist. It was beginning to throb where the raven had forced the sword from him. Their harsh cawing had gone on for so long, and so loudly, that it was as if he could still hear them as he stumbled on to the Chamber of Candles. Then the door was opened, the warm glow of candles met them, and Juniper's arm was across his shoulders.

"Urchin, are you all right?" Juniper drew him into the center of the chamber and went to welcome the others, leaving Urchin to stand wide-eyed in the soothing light, still holding his wrist. It was as if a door had slammed shut against ravens, croaking, talons, beaks, and broken glass. He stood in a different world, where Fir sat propped up on pillows, blankets and cushions were stacked neatly in a corner, a half-finished net lay on the floor, and a saucepan sat on a brazier, giving off a waft of spiced wine. But the best thing of all, that made Urchin's heart strong and took the edge from the pain, was the sight of Catkin kneeling by the warmth of the brazier with Sepia holding a blanket around her shoulders and hugging warmth into her. A cup of something steaming hot was in Catkin's paws, and Hope was piling pillows around her. There was a cry of joy as Cedar sprang forward, and a squeak of "Mummy!" from Catkin. Then Crispin, Cedar, and Catkin were all hugging each other in a tangle of red fur, paws, tails, and blanket. Myrtle, Needle, and Sepia slipped to the net and began busily knotting and twisting, as if they had only just left off.

"What happened to your wrist?" asked Juniper. Urchin looked and saw how puffed up his arm had become. It was swollen from paw to elbow. Kept still, it didn't hurt too much, but moving it made him catch his breath.

"Keep it raised," said Juniper. "I'll put a comfrey dressing on it and bind it up. You look as if you should rest."

"There's some comfrey distillation here," said Sepia, and hurried to look at Urchin's wrist.

Urchin had never felt so tired in his life. There hadn't been time for weariness before. But now Crispin was beside him, and the things he had dreaded to say still had to be said. Crispin's kindness, asking after the hurt wrist, was almost unbearable.

"It'll soon mend, sir," he said, not looking the king in the eyes.

"I'm sorry I didn't get to that raven sooner, Urchin," said Cedar.

The queen apologizing to him was a little more than Urchin could bear just now. It didn't help that Catkin was running to hug him, clinging to him with damp fur and small eager paws.

"I'm sorry I didn't rescue you, Urchin," she said. "I really tried! I really fought them!"

"I should have rescued you," he said, but she only hugged him again and told him not to be silly. "Fingal and Corr and all of them came as soon as they could," she gabbled to her parents. "They would have done it sooner, but they had to wait until it was dark and the ravens were distracted and Urchin and everyone were shining swords out of the windows to draw their attention away. They all came for me: Fingal, Corr, Tide . . ."

"Tide was there?" said Padra.

"Oh yes, and Swanfeather. They bit through the cords and we swam back to the cavern; they gave me a ride and I had to keep bobbing up to breathe, and they popped up sometimes too, a long way away from me, to distract the ravens. It was wonderful!"

"So," said Crispin, "Fingal, Corr, and the twins rescued you and took you back to the cavern. Where's that?"

"It's one of the caverns around the underground lake," said Needle. "The lake Fingal found years ago when we were all looking for the Heartstone. He's been exploring there a lot. He's made that cavern into a place of safety. A bit like the Mole Palace but a lot smaller and nearer."

"And wetter," said Hope.

"And not so comfortable," said Needle. "But it'll do."

"They took me back there," said Catkin, "and I was freezing. There was a fire, but only a little one. So they got me up here, in the warm."

"Where we could look after her," said Sepia.

"Sepia," said Crispin, "you seem to have a calling for drying off Catkin in a crisis."

Sepia raised Urchin's paw and wound the bandage around it. Urchin thanked her, but he didn't feel fit for Sepia's company just now. She'd never failed Catkin.

"We kept telling each other what was happening," said Needle. "And, sir, we sent messages all over the island. Everyone's making nets—like that one, but sticky—to catch ravens. We're really organized, Your Majesty, but we hadn't allowed for the riding stars."

"Riding stars!" said Padra. "And we missed them!"

"They weren't that good," said Catkin.

"So," said Needle, "I knew about Catkin and the rescue because I listened to Urchin through the floorboards. I tried to keep you informed by the Threading." Her mouth stretched, and her voice became higher as she fought against tears. "I hated pretending, sir, and all those things I had to say!"

"You were never a very convincing traitor," he said, and hugged her in spite of the prickles. "And it worked. I know the Threadings Code."

"Myrtle doesn't," she said. "Not yet. But she put in a sunflower."

207

"She couldn't have put in anything better,"Crispin said, and turned to Urchin, who hadn't spoken for a long time. "Urchin, have I told you to learn the Threadings Code?"

"No, Your Majesty," said Urchin quietly.

"You should!" said Crispin. "A bird for freedom, circle for safety. What was that bit about the swords between the ravens? They're not going to kill each other, are they?"

"They might!" said Sepia eagerly. "Urchin did that—Oh, sorry, Urchin, it's your tell."

Urchin turned to put more wood on the fire.

It was a great relief to Urchin when they were all busy making meshes, which Crispin seemed to think was a wonderful idea, and he could quietly ask the king for a word in private. Carrying a lamp, he followed Crispin into the corridor, where they could speak alone.

"I've let you down, Your Majesty," he said, "and not just in something small." He lowered his gaze. "I was with Catkin and she was caught, and that should never have happened. So"—he forced his voice to speak the words, finding it even harder than he had expected—"if I still had a sword I'd lay it down before you, but I couldn't even hold on to that. I ask . . . Your Majesty . . ."

One more effort. "I can't stay in the Circle after this," he said.

There was a pause, but not as if Crispin were angry, testing him, or thinking about what to say. It was more like a breathing space.

"Tell me exactly what happened, Urchin," said Crispin. "*Exactly*. Every detail. Take your time."

Urchin began from the defense of the bay and the discovery that Catkin was with them. Then there had been the message from Grith—"and I thought it was strange, I should have pressed him about the token . . . there wasn't time. . . ." And the ambush.

"I see," said Crispin. "Thank you, Urchin. Now imagine that you're the king. A young Circle animal has just told you the story you've told me. What would you do?"

Urchin tried imagining it. Then he tried to look at it in a few different ways, and ask himself questions. He opened his mouth to answer that perhaps the young squirrel shouldn't have trusted the king's token, but then realized it was a perfectly reasonable thing to do, so he shut his mouth and looked at the ground.

"Urchin?" said Crispin gently.

"I'd say . . ." Urchin found that his voice didn't want to do anything at all and could only manage a low mutter, "I'd say he hadn't done anything wrong, sir."

"And you'd be right," said Crispin.

"But she was still caught, sir!" cried Urchin. "She nearly died! Brindle died!"

"That's because, between you, you couldn't take on a whole flight of ravens," said Crispin. "If you thought you could, you have an exaggerated idea of your abilities."

"Yes, sir," said Urchin, feeling a little better.

"You will make mistakes," said Crispin. "We all do. At the time of Husk's rise to power, who was senior captain?"

Urchin knew the answer, but he didn't want to say it.

"Urchin?" said Crispin.

"You were, sir. But . . ."

"But nothing, Urchin. It's a poor excuse to say that Husk was too clever for me. I should have recognized what he was doing much sooner, and put a stop to it. That still comes back to haunt me."

"Sir!" said Urchin. "Don't! Don't talk about yourself like that!"

Crispin smiled a little. "I've made worse mistakes than yours," he said. "I just wish I knew where Grith is now. If you did still have a sword, Urchin, and laid it before me, I'd give it straight back to you and tell you not to be so silly. I've no intention of releasing you from the Circle. I need animals like you. And by the way, thank you for risking your life, losing your sword, and very nearly dying to save me from a raven. How's the wrist?"

"Hurts a bit, Your Majesty," said Urchin. "Better than it was. And Catkin was very brave."

"I'm pleased to hear it," said Crispin. "Now let's go back into the Chamber of Candles, and you can tell me what you've done to make the ravens fight each other. If you've achieved that, you've made very good use of your captivity." He looked past Urchin at somebody running toward them. "Crackle's in a hurry. Is that a honey pot she's carrying?"

He guided Crackle and Urchin into the Chamber of Candles. Myrtle and Needle were whispering together as they wove the net, while Hope and Sepia dragged a finished one across the floor and said something about taking it to Fingal. Fir appeared to be asleep, but his eyes opened a little as Crispin came back in. His voice was slow, wheezy, and low, but perfectly clear. He stretched out a trembling paw, and Crispin took it.

"You need do nothing much now, Crispin," he said. "Be still. The Heart will fight for you. The enemy have called for The Voyager."

"Juniper," asked Urchin quietly, "what's Brother Fir talking about? We don't have a Voyager, and if we did, why would the enemy call him?"

"Because they don't mean to," said Juniper, and before Urchin could ask him to stop talking in riddles, added, "You don't think an enemy would call a Voyager on purpose, do you?"

Brother Fir closed his eyes. "He has come," he said. "He is very near to us."

The fire made Urchin realize how tired he was, and how hungry; but he was too weary to eat, and certainly too weary to care about mysterious prophecies. Juniper put a cup of spiced wine into his good paw.

"I don't understand it," said Urchin. Even speaking was a huge effort. "I don't understand anything. The tower's a mess, the Heart alone knows where the Taloness and the stupid prince are. The ravens are supposed to be calling for our Voyager, and I didn't know we had one. We're still so outnumbered it's ridiculous, and Fir says Crispin doesn't have to fight. Myrtle and Needle—I never understood all that Threadings stuff. . . ."

"Shh!" said Juniper. "You should sleep while you can. It's going to be all right. I don't know how, but we don't have to. It will be, that's all we need to know." He brought a pillow from the heap of bedding. "Curl up by the fire and sleep."

"Juniper," said Urchin, "in the Threadings, what's a sunflower?"

"Joy and celebration," said Juniper, spreading a blanket over him.

That didn't make sense either. It occurred to him that he was glad it was his right paw the ravens had attacked, not his left, or his mother's bracelet might have been broken. It circled his wrist as safely as ever. He fell asleep dreaming of woven webs, woven Threadings, and woven bracelets, not knowing which was which.

As Urchin slept, animals all over the island—in trees, in burrows, on shores, and in tunnels—wove and webbed and knotted, whispered and prayed. Nets were hung from trees, over burrows, across cave mouths, and over the shattered windows of the tower. In the Chamber of Candles, Myrtle drew sunflowers on the floor before pulling a blanket over herself and sleeping with her head in Needle's lap. Hope was ordered by the king to stop working and sleep, so he did. Padra found a heap of thin rope nobody had started on yet, and twisted in into knots.

"It's been a long time since I did this," he remarked, and looked across at Urchin to make sure he really was asleep. "He's good, Crispin. He really is."

CHAPTER NINETEEN

T DAWN, THE MOST TERRIBLE sound woke the island. Harsh enough to shake the nerves, discordant enough to make claws curl and fur prickle, the crashing of raven voices ripped through Mistmantle. On shores and in tunnels under the woods, animals leaped to their paws and reached for their weapons. In the Chamber of Candles, hidden underground, they heard nothing, but Brother Fir stirred in his sleep and moaned, and Juniper suddenly shuddered and hobbled from the chamber. Urchin woke in time to see him run back in.

"They're gathering!" said Juniper. "Everyone wake up! Sepia, Hope, stay with Brother Fir. You too, Myrtle."

"To Fir's turret, the rest of us," said Crispin, fastening on his sword. "It gives the best view of the island, and last I knew it was still intact. As far as possible we'll go by the back stairs, but look out for ravens, all the same. If Urchin's got them fighting among themselves, we have a chance."

Crispin, Cedar, and Padra led the way from the chamber, with Urchin and Juniper following and Needle hurrying behind all the way up to Fir's turret. The fireplace was tidy, the windows were unbroken, and the cups and plates had been stacked neatly by the hearth.

"We can still do more to fortify the defenses," said Crispin. "Now that we have a reasonable chance, I can bring in help without throwing animals' lives away. Send a mole for Russet and Docken. Stockpile this turret with bows, arrows, and swords. The windows are small, that's an advantage. They can't attack more than one to a window. Padra, did you bring those nets? We'll put them out when I give the signal. Urchin, Needle! Is there any glue left in the tower?"

Urchin and Needle hurried down to the workrooms. It was like the days when they had first come to the tower, running up and down the stairs on errands. They even laughed as they struggled up the stairs heaving two heavy pots of glue, but it was different when they reached the turret room and looked out.

The island was edged with black, as if it wore mourning—rows of great black birds lined the treetops, the battlements, the shores, the jetty, the masts of the little boats. Urchin thought it was a good thing Fingal couldn't see his boat now, with ravens perched on the mast and clawing the paintwork.

The sight of the ravens was not the worst thing. The worst thing was the noise. They were all chanting in unison now, a rasp like the

sharpening of a thousand knives on stone, so loud that it was painful—
Kill and devour! Kill and devour! Alone on the battlements, her head
held high, one claw raised, talons flexed, her escorts around her, stood
the Taloness.

"Your Majesty," called Juniper, shouting over the noise, "she's not
joining in. Neither are her guards."

Crispin leaned cautiously from the narrow window. "You're right,"
he said. "Come and look, everyone! They're chanting at each other!"

"And mostly at the Taloness," said Padra.

Needle gasped and pointed. "What's that?"

Something was flying into sight. It could have been a flag. If the
children had been out playing, Needle would have taken it for a kite.

"It's him!" said Urchin.

The Silver Prince had prepared for battle. A cloak, bloodred,
streamed behind him, and above his beak rose a mask, silver and red,
flashing in the morning light.

"Show-off," said Padra. "Looks ridiculous."

The Silver Prince, too, settled on the battlements, his escorts
beside him. It was the escorts, not the Silver Prince, who croaked out
the challenge.

"The Taloness seeks power for herself! The Taloness seeks to give
orders to the Silver Prince! The Silver Prince is the Raven of Destiny
and the Son of the Archraven! He orders death to the Taloness! Kill
and devour!"

"The net, please," said Crispin, and opened the window. Struggling

215

with the weight of the net, Padra and Cedar hooked the edge over the brackets that held Fir's window boxes and shook it out to hang over the wall, covering the windows of the chamber beneath. Needle carefully tipped glue down it as the sky above them blackened with ravens.

The cacophony grew louder: high, screaming, and discordant, tearing at Urchin's ears, still louder, higher, and harsher, until every animal in the turret pressed paws over ears. Ravens rose into the air, their cries shrill and cruel, their talons stretched out. Screeching, they flew down on the Taloness and her defenders. Where she fled they followed her, flying into the claws of her escorts or into the nets hanging from tree to tree.

Urchin wanted to look away. It seemed indecent, like gloating, to watch the island's enemies destroy each other; but it was impossible not to watch. Bodies dropped from the sky, feathers rained. Ravens pursuing each other flew into the nets. Flapping to escape, they bit, tore, and struggled, and became more completely trapped. The Taloness flew toward the tower, saw just in time the net in which ravens were already struggling, and wheeled around to fly inland. Three, then four and five other ravens fell on her in the air.

"They're killing the Taloness!" cried Needle.

"They're all killing each other," said Crispin. Fighting to be free from the nets, angry and terrified, the ravens were turning on each other. Needle turned her face away as they pecked and clawed. Urchin didn't want to look either, as the nets reddened. He tried to focus his attention in his heart, as Brother Fir had taught him, because it helped to take his mind from the rising in his stomach. He must not be sick.

"You don't have to watch this, Urchin," said Crispin.

Urchin didn't answer. As long as Crispin stood steadily at that window, seeing the worst that the ravens could do to each other, he would watch, too. He knew that Crispin had to because he was the king, and would not turn his face away from what happened on the island. He himself had to watch because he was responsible for this. He had set the ravens against each other, and he must face what he had done. The Taloness lay dead on the battlements.

Crispin looked into the sky. "They're flying higher," he said. "They're learning to avoid the nets."

Padra joined him at the window. "That's good," he said. "They have to come down sooner or later. They might have the sense to fly back over the mists to their ships, and go."

"We're not safe yet," said Crispin. "We don't know whether there are still reinforcements on the ships."

"Surely not!" said Cedar. "There are so many here already, and so many killed!"

"They must have some birds still there, even just the crews," said Crispin. "Sooner or later, they're sure to fly in; and look at the numbers that escaped from the ship Corr sank. This is only a breathing space. Now that they've finished off the Taloness, they can concentrate on the island again."

"Let them try," said Padra. "We'll trap the lot of them. The whole island was making nets last night, so we must have plenty."

"We'll need them," said Crispin. "That fight among themselves has swung everything in our favor, but we haven't won yet. We have to be ready for the next wave, unless the Silver Prince calls it off."

"We can try to warn the island to be ready, Your Majesty," Urchin suggested. "Make sure they stay on their guard. We may not have a lot of time, but I'm not much use with a sword or a bow today, so I could do that. Please?"

"He could round up some help from Fingal and whoever else is in that cavern," said Padra. "They can send messages by water."

"Then go, Urchin. Don't be seen and don't take unnecessary risks," said Crispin.

"Shall I go too?" offered Cedar.

Crispin hesitated, but only for a moment. "Yes," he said. "Go with him. If . . ."

He leaned from the window, his sword in his paw. Urchin stepped to his side and looked out as Padra took his place at the next window and turned his face away in disgust.

"Plague and fire!" he said softly. "They're eating their own dead."

"Do you see what the Silver Prince is doing?" asked Crispin.

Urchin leaned out, shading his eyes against the sun. The Prince, still in his cloak and mask, stood far away in a tree with a cluster of ravens about him.

"He's giving orders," he said.

218

They watched. The Silver Prince tipped his head, raising a claw.

"He's seen where we are," said Crispin. "They can attack if they want to. They can't do much about these little ones. Leave two of them open, one for you, Padra, one for me. Needle, do we still have any nets to sticky up the other windows? No point in waiting until the Silver Prince works out what he wants to do next." He leaned sideways to get a good view of the Silver Prince. "He's pointing at the mists now."

With a cry of "Kill and devour!" the ravens rose into the air. Two flew to the open windows of the tower and were struck down by Padra and Crispin, but the rest, cawing out their battle cry, flew for the mists.

"Some are staying, some are going," said Padra. "And the Heart alone knows what's coming over the mists next. Plague and fire!"

"Go then, Urchin," said Crispin. "Get the word around the island to be ready for another attack. Get help to the tower, if it can be spared. Take a sword; you can use your left paw if you have to. Heart keep you." His eyes met Cedar's. "Heart keep you."

"Heart keep you," she replied, and smiled, as if it were any ordinary day. She picked up a bow and a quiver of arrows. "Ready, Urchin? We'll go by way of the kitchens and see if there's anything to eat on the way. I'm starving."

"Queen Cedar!" called Needle as they were nearly out the door. "Please, please, Your Majesty, please take care. Stay safe. And you too, Urchin."

"We'll be all right," said Urchin, and ran down the stairs after the queen.

"Needle," said Crispin, "get some more of that sticky stuff, will you, please?" He waited until they had all gone, and turned to Padra and Juniper.

"It'll take a while for the wretched birds to get there," he said, "and for the next wave to come. Hopefully we can get enough nets out to trap every one of them. Juniper, do what you do best. Pray. Padra, I wondered why there were no more ravens in the tower. I believe it's because they went to take sides with either the Taloness or the Silver Prince. If they try to get back through the windows, they'll be netted. Are the Spring Gate and the tunnels safe?"

"Nothing the size of a raven could get through," said Padra. "We narrowed the entrances."

"Then we stay here," said Crispin, "where we have the best viewpoint of the island. It will take them a while to get to the boats and back. We'll renew the nets at the windows. And if all fails, and they do get in . . ."

"We keep fighting," said Padra. "But not on empty stomachs. Breakfast?"

CHAPTER TWENTY

ORR HAD WOVEN NETS, smeared them with sap gathered from trees when the ravens hadn't been looking, and spread them over every cave entrance he could find. He had been sure he could find the way back to Fingal's cavern. But the way there wasn't as simple as he remembered. One turning in a tunnel looked much like another. Entrances that had been made too small for ravens were, in some cases, too small for otters, and sticky nets blocked the entrances he might have used. If he kept swimming, he'd be sure to come to the lake. Surely? Or the sea? He reminded himself yet again that he was playing an important part in the campaign to save Mistmantle. He had helped to rescue Princess Catkin, and he was looking forward to telling them at home about that; but it was better not to think about home. He mustn't think too much about being lost, either, and having been lost for a long time, and whether he'd ever find his way back. Sooner or later he'd meet an animal who could tell him where he was. But not here. He'd just reached another dead end. Go back and try again.

In the kitchens, Crackle had tidied, polished, washed, and scrubbed. She felt better for that. It kept her mind from ravens and battles, and besides, she couldn't bear a messy kitchen. If the ravens managed to break in and wreck it again, they'd have to kill her first. And if the king and queen, Heart love them, and Padra and the rest of them saved the island and sent those big noisy birds back to where they belonged, they would find the kitchen swept, cleaned, and ready for supper.

Urchin and the queen had come hurrying into the kitchen, but they'd only stopped to say "so far, so good," and ask for water and bread to eat on their way to goodness only knew where. Crackle had stuffed walnut bread and raisins into a bag. Working in the kitchens, she knew what every animal liked. Then Needle had come down asking for bread, fish, and water she could take to the turret. Crackle had sent her back with seed bread, smoked trout, apricots, apple juice, and a bottle of wine she fetched from the cellar. (There were strange noises from beneath the cellar, which Crackle decided to ignore.) It was a pity, though, that Needle was in a hurry to get back to the turret. It was lonely in the big, quiet kitchen.

Now what? The floors were scrubbed, the depleted nut, berry, and grain stores had been locked away, the few jars and bottles that had not been smashed were in a gleaming row on their shelves. She needed something to concentrate on. She worked mostly as a pastry cook, but she had been well taught and could turn her paw to cooking anything. Even with the kitchen plundered, she could put some sort of meal together for whoever was left to eat it. Cooking would calm her down and give her something to do.

Under the floor, something scuttled. Crackle froze, listening. The scuffling was nearer, but she couldn't be sure what sort of creature it was. Could there still be ravens in the tower? She took the poker in both paws and set her teeth. She was not going to be bullied by a big bird with dirty habits and no manners.

The scuffling stopped. Crackle relaxed her grip on the poker but kept it on the table beside her, just in case.

That special seaweed was still there, washed, dried, and ready to use. Kingsmantle, or Queen's something-or-other. When Corr had first brought it she had asked around the kitchens about how to cook it. Everyone had a different idea. But in these last few days, when messages had been buzzing all over the island through the tunnels, Crackle had asked the departing tower animals to find a recipe for kingsmantle seaweed and send word of it to her. She had memorized a few and forgotten the rest. (One had been offered by a squirrel called Filbert who said it was the way his mother used to make it, but the quantity of black pepper and cloves had horrified Crackle.) Then a message had come from Longpaw and Sepia's mum to say her friend used to make kingsmantle cake just the way Brother Fir liked it: soft and light on the inside and crisp on the outside, with nutmeg, cinnamon, cassia, and just a little lemon rind. Crackle had the spices, and a shriveled old lemon lay in the bottom of a basket. Making this cake would require skill and careful attention. Good. That would keep her mind from—

There was that sound again. She gathered all her ingredients, placed the poker within easy reach, and got to work.

In the Chamber of Candles, Sepia held Brother Fir's right paw lightly in hers. He was more like himself today, though sometimes Sepia couldn't tell whether he was talking to her or to someone who wasn't there. Sometimes he got her name right, and sometimes he called her "Linnet."

"They sent me to Watchtop Hill," he was saying, and Sepia wasn't sure whether he was looking at her or through her. "That was the year of those wasps, you remember, and we were to set honey traps for them. I didn't want you to do it because I didn't want you to get stung. I stood on the hill, and that was when I knew there would be riding stars. The way the air felt and smelled, the feeling of the sky, that told me. I knew they were ready to dance. And when I counted, I knew when to stop. Four. And I told you, didn't I? I did, didn't I, Linnet?"

"Yes," said Sepia, "you did."

"And the riding stars came, after four days," said Fir. "And I told you, didn't I, that I had known. And I asked why an ordinary guard squirrel should be able to tell when there would be riding stars, and you said, 'What ordinary guard squirrel?' Do you remember?"

"Yes," said Sepia gently. "I remember it."

He slept for a while, then woke again and was ready to sit up. He asked for a drink, this time remembering that she was Sepia, not Linnet. Hope poured the cup of warm wine and elderberry, and then lay on the floor with his ear against it. Myrtle looked up from the net she was making.

"That's funny," said Hope. "It's not there."

"What's not where?" asked Sepia.

"Otter," he said, and turned around a few times.

"Please, Master Hope," whispered Myrtle shyly, "if the otter isn't there, why are you trying to find it?"

Hope stopped turning around and looked in her direction. "It's there somewhere," he said. "I meant, it wasn't *there*, where I was listening. Shh! It's . . . there!" He ran to the door and pulled it open with both paws.

"Hello!" he said. "Are you a lost otter? You can come in with us if you like."

Corr didn't usually hug hedgehogs, but he was so relieved at the sound of a kind voice that he wanted to hug this one. But he didn't want anyone to think he'd been at all lost, or a bit worried about it, so he just said, "Oh, thanks! I think I took a wrong turn. Aren't you the hedgehog from Fingal's cavern?"

"Yes, I'm Hope," he said. "Sepia's here—"

"Sepia of the Songs?" gasped Corr.

". . . Yes, and a hedgehog called Myrtle, and . . ." He ushered Corr into the chamber.

Corr stood astonished. Creamy white candles stood on the floor, on ledges, and in alcoves. Ribbons of wax trickled down their sides and settled around them as the flames flickered in the doorway's draft. Soft light and stillness and something else—he didn't know what it was, but he knew it was there—hallowed the air.

That sweet-faced squirrel beside the bed must be Sepia. She was singing very softly, turning to smile up at him in her song. The little hedgehog steadily wove her web. Propped on pillows on a small neat bed against the wall, with a blanket the color of oatmeal around his shoulders, his eyes closed, lay a very old squirrel.

The song had finished, but it seemed to hang in the air like incense. Nothing Corr had ever done seemed important anymore. He realized that Sepia was watching him, still smiling gently, knowing that the atmosphere of the chamber had entranced him, and it would take him a little time to become accustomed to it.

"It's Brother Fir!" whispered Corr.

"Did you want to meet him?" whispered Sepia. "You're very welcome to stay with us until he wakes up again. I think I've sung him to sleep."

"My dear Sepia," said Fir, without opening his eyes, "you have done nothing of the sort. Hm. I would not have missed a note of it."

"There's a young otter here to see you, Brother Fir," said Sepia. "His name is . . ." She looked up at him.

"Corr," he said.

Fir was already smiling before he opened his eyes and looked along the bed at Corr. He stretched out both paws and, without help, sat up straight as Corr stood warmed and transfixed by the depth, the love, and the sparkle in those immensely deep dark eyes.

"I knew you would come!" said Brother Fir. "Corr!" He chuckled softly. "Corr! I am so glad! Come and sit by me!"

Crackle hovered a paw over the kingsmantle cake. It was cool now. What a pity there was nobody here to admire it except for a couple of hedgehog cooks. It really was a very beautiful cake, with its crisp layers of seaweed, the gold fringe showing around the edges. But she hadn't made it to be admired, she had made it for Brother Fir, and it wouldn't do him any good sitting in all its glory on the kitchen table. Straight to the Chamber of Candles. She took a few false turns, but just as she wondered if she might be going in completely the wrong direction, Hope came out to meet her.

"I heard you coming," he said. "Were you looking for us? We're all here, come in."

"Ooh!" said Crackle. She had never before been in the Chamber of Candles, and was wide-eyed at its beauty. Then she said "Ooh" again, because there was that otter, the one who had brought the seaweed in the first place, and she nearly said "Ooh" once more because Brother Fir looked so well, sitting up, bright-eyed and chatting eagerly to the otter—but she didn't like to repeat herself, so she only curtsied, and said, "Kingsmantle cake for you, Brother Fir, and that's the otter who brought the seaweed."

"Kingsmantle cake!" cried Brother Fir, and joy danced in his eyes and in his lopsided smile. "How can all be so good? How many are we? Does anyone have a knife?" And then he laughed again, as if there were a joke that nobody else had understood. "Corr! Kingsmantle seaweed!"

"More nets!" shouted Urchin and Cedar as they ran from one tunnel to another. "More nets, ready for the next attack!" At a turning, Urchin nearly ran into Tipp and Todd.

"Steady on!" said Todd.

"What happened to your sword arm?" asked Tipp.

"It'll mend," said Urchin. "We need more nets."

"More blooming knitting!" said Todd. "We're running out of things to knit down here!"

"Where are we?" asked Cedar.

"Under the Tangletwigs, Your Majesty," said Tipp with a deep bow.

"Plenty of stuff up there to knit with, but it shreds you to bits getting hold of it," said Todd. "Gleaner's got this blanket thing that's pretty well shredded already, but she only uses it to keep that shrine safe."

"Is she still guarding it?" asked Cedar.

"She's taken blooming root, I should think, Your Majesty," said Todd.

"Your Majesty," said Tipp, "we have urged her to stay belowground. She won't, but she can hide in the cover of the Tangletwigs when she needs to."

"The cover's good there," said Cedar. "It may be a good place to fall back to, or defend from. Tipp, Todd, carry the message across the island. The nets are working, but we need more."

"Your Majesty!" Tipp bowed and was soon heard shouting the order down a tunnel. He returned, bowing again, as the echo of mole voices, growing fainter, carried the message around the island.

Todd stamped off in a different direction. "More nets!" he shouted. "Stand by for more blooming big spuggies!" Plodding back again, he too bowed to the queen. "Sorted, Your Majesty."

A ragged chorus of screeching sounded above them.

"They're at it again, ma'am," said Todd.

"They're going for the Tangletwigs," said Cedar.

"I can feel it in the air," said Juniper. "The next attack is coming."

"Glad to hear it," said Padra.

"Yes," said Crispin. "Let's get it over with."

Docken, Russet, and Heath had been sent for. Needle, without speaking a word, had made it quite clear that she was staying. The small chamber was filled with sheaves of arrows, bows leaning against walls, swords propped up against the door. Nobody liked to see Fir's peaceful turret used like this. *But it's not as if we have a choice,* Crispin had said.

From the turret windows they watched the birds gather. It was as if a band were around the island, growing tighter. Ravens after ravens after ravens thronged to the island.

"They're organized," muttered Padra. "They're flying in ranks."

"Hold back from the arrows for now," ordered Crispin. "Let the nets do the work for us first. When the nets are too full to trap any more, or if any of the vermin manage to get out of them, we shoot. If they keep coming and we run out of arrows, we fight with our swords, and keep on fighting." I'd rather set fire to the tower myself, he thought, than let these vermin have it.

The ravens came on, so thick and heavy that Needle, who had never handled a bow in her life, picked one up and strung it as she had seen the archers do. If she watched how the other defenders did it, she could at least get the arrow to fly from the bow, and it was bound to hit something.

The great black wings were nearer. Needle heard the screeching as ravens flew into the netted windows on the floor below, and the caws of indignation as they became trapped. Screeches of rage echoed from all around the island, tearing into the ears of the islanders, but still, the ravens came on.

"There has to be a limit to them!" shouted Crispin. "They have to stop, sooner or later!"

"The nets are filling up!" yelled Padra.

"Let me see what's happening in the tower," said Juniper.

"Needle," called Crispin, "go with him!"

Needle snatched up a bow and a quiver of arrows and ran down the stairs. Each window was darkened by nets of screaming ravens, dead ravens, flapping ravens, ravens turning beaks and talons on each other. Outside the shattered windows of the Gathering Chamber, the whole net writhed like a screeching black beast with the weight of the birds. But from the very top of the window, a ray of light fell onto the floor.

Needle shrieked, seized Juniper's paw, and pointed. Weighed down with ravens, the net was pulling away from the top of the broken window. Soon there would be a gap big enough for the next wave of birds to fly through. They dashed back, banging the doors shut.

"Tell the king!" she said. "I have to find Crackle!"

Juniper hurried limping for the stairs, banging doors shut after him. Powered with anger, Needle ran for the kitchens, flinging her bow and arrows into a corner.

"Crackle!" she yelled.

Crackle appeared, her eyes bright. She began to say something about Brother Fir, but Needle wasn't listening.

"We need oil!" she shouted. "Cooking oil—butter—soapy water might do—anything slippery!"

Juniper stumbled into the turret, barring the door behind him. Crispin leaned from the tower and swept his sword through the neck of a raven as it swooped down on him.

"The nets are tearing!" cried Juniper.

"Ready to fire!" called the king.

The defenders stood ready at the windows. Fire, and fire, and fire. Arrows flew, sang, and hit. Ravens thudded to the ground.

"There are fewer of them!" shouted Docken. "Every one's a hit, Your Majesty!"

There were fewer arrows, too. Soon, hardly any were left rattling in the quivers. The ravens came on. Crispin fired again into the raven clouds.

"What in the island is that!" shouted Docken, squinting up at the sky.

"Oh, it's just him," said Padra.

Cloaked and masked, the Silver Prince wheeled above the island, his escorts surrounding him, keeping him out of range of the arrows. He flew slowly, as if he had all the leisure in the world. He was flying as if he had won, making a lap of honor around Mistmantle.

Below them, ravens poured into the Gathering Chamber.

CHAPTER TWENTY-ONE

IN THE UNDERGROWTH of the Tangletwigs, Urchin lay flat under a sprawling hawthorn and passed arrows to Cedar. He had tried to fire a bow, fighting the pain in his injured wrist, but there wasn't the strength in that arm now. All he could do was be ready with the arrows, and there weren't many left. From their hiding place near a tunnel entrance he could see the cairn over Lady Aspen's grave. He could see Gleaner huddled in the brambles at the edge of the clearing.

On the other side of the clearing, covered with leaves and keeping very still, lay Grith. He had done his part. He had given Catkin and Urchin to the ravens. He had no idea what had happened to Catkin—he hoped she was dead, but there were rumors that she had been rescued by interfering otters, and, to his great disappointment, Urchin had escaped. That was the ravens' fault, not his. Grith snarled softly in his throat when he thought of Urchin. To have the favor of the Silver

Prince, he must deliver Urchin to him. This time the Silver Prince would personally devour Urchin, preferably where the king could see it.

He had come here to the Tangletwigs to ask for Gleaner's help. Gleaner hated Crispin and everyone who had ever helped him. But she had growled, snarled, ordered Grith out of the Tangletwigs, and even brandished her kitchen knife at him. To spite her, he had snatched away that rag she used to cover the burial mound. Now, under the cover of the Tangletwigs, he searched for a tunnel way to the tower. That's where Urchin would be.

Another raven fell spinning from the sky to the thornbushes. The queen was already fitting the next arrow.

"Gleaner should be farther in!" yelled Urchin. "She's hardly under cover!"

Cedar fired again. Another raven fell. "We can't do anything about it!" she yelled.

Grith raised his head. Urchin was here! Some dark power must be at work for Urchin to be delivered to him so easily! The Silver Prince, circling the island, would come this way soon. If Grith could have Urchin waiting for him . . .

But Urchin was at a distance, under cover, too far to reach in the thorns of the Tangletwigs. The queen was with him, and armed. Grith probably couldn't get the better of Urchin in a fight, and certainly couldn't take on both of them, but he could show the Silver Prince where they were. The bodyguard would wrench away the thorns for him.

If he begged, the Silver Prince might let him kill the queen. Ravens liked carrion. He would be happy to execute Queen Cedar for the Silver Prince to eat. His brother Gloss had murdered Crispin's first wife, and he would be proud to kill the second. *Patience, patience.* He had Urchin and the Silver Prince so close. He only had to bring them together and watch the prince do his worst.

The Silver Prince was spiraling, the circles smaller and smaller, his escorts following. Cedar stopped firing and shaded her eyes at the sky.

"He's closing in on the Tangletwigs," she said. "If he gets near enough, I might get a shot at him."

The Silver Prince squinted through the eyeholes of his mask. The island was his. Must be. The sky was still full of his ravens. Awed and admiring, his troops watched him. He had brought down the Taloness, and now he would have the tree-rats at his mercy in spite of their pathetic fishing nets. He would take appalling revenges on them for those nets.

It was a hot day for flying, and the cloak grew heavy. The mask restricted his vision. Let his troops and his victims see his glorious silver plumage! He clawed the cloak from his neck, threw off the mask, and, as they fell to earth, he soared.

Grith saw the cloak and the mask fall to the ground as the Silver Prince rose. Eager and triumphant, he rushed forward.

"Great Silver Prince!" he cried.

"Who's that mole?" whispered Cedar. "What does he think he's doing?"

Urchin twisted to look through the undergrowth. Rage stabbed through him.

"It's Grith!" he said. "Grith, who betrayed us!"

"Keep still!" ordered the queen, and lowered her voice to a whisper. "I've only two arrows left, we can't take risks. What's he up to?"

On the open ground of the clearing, Grith fell to his knees on the discarded cloak. He stretched out his arms.

"I have delivered them to your talons, Great Silver Prince!" he called. "Urchin the tree-rat and the tree-rat queen! They are here! They are yours!" But the Silver Prince rose higher and could not hear him.

"It is shouting defiance at me!" said the Silver Prince.

"I think it is surrendering to you," said one of his escorts, and the prince laughed.

"So it should," he said. "Kill it!"

Three of them fell upon Grith. Urchin closed his eyes against the sight of the sharp talons attacking Grith. There was still blood on the ravens' beaks as they rose again.

The Silver Prince circled in triumph again, but as he did, his eyes were caught by a gleam of silver. Something flashed in the sunlight. He wheeled a little lower, his eyes on the silver. It was some piece of jewelry lying on a pile of stones. What were those stones, a throne? Or maybe a holy place! He would destroy their sanctuary, and that silver thing would become his trophy! With a cry of "Kill and devour," strident enough to make sure his troops

236

would be watching, he soared, wheeled once more, and struck.

The rush of wings made Gleaner shudder and jump. The gleaming black beak, fierce and open, snatched up Lady Aspen's bracelet and raised it high. The Silver Prince was throwing up his head in triumph and spreading his wings even at the moment when Gleaner plunged the knife into his throat.

His beak fell open. The twisted silver bracelet tumbled down and Gleaner caught it, hugging it as the Silver Prince fell, pressing it to her fur like a crying baby, shielding it from the blood spurting from the Silver Prince's neck. Ravens hurtled down on her.

Two fell with Cedar's arrows in them. Tipp and Todd darted from a tunnel to finish off another as it landed, and Urchin, keeping as low as he could, crawled under the scratching thornbushes. His left paw was not as strong as his right, nor so accurate, but he'd just have to try harder than ever to make every stroke count. Two ravens were on top of Gleaner now.

Slash against the legs of the raven holding her, and *slash* again with the back of the same stroke. He stabbed up at the beak of the raven gripping Gleaner's neck, and ducked as another beak darted at his ear. A hot pain stung his arm, but he had hardly seen the raven clawing him before it fell back with Cedar's arrow in its heart, and he was able to drag Gleaner, bleeding and barely conscious, deep into the thorny cover of the Tangletwigs.

"Gleaner?" he said. Her eyes opened a little and closed again, and she curled up her knees as if wrapping herself around the silver bracelet. Above them, the ravens cried out, but it was not their usual war cry. They were croaking a lament.

From a deep wound in her neck, blood stained Gleaner's fur. One leg was twisted and swollen, and the other badly gashed. He looked for something to stem the bleeding, but the leaves here were too small, so he pressed the cold flat of his sword-hilt against her neck as he peered out through the undergrowth.

The body of the Silver Prince lay sprawled on the ground. Ravens gathered around it, wailing in despair.

"You killed him, Gleaner," Urchin said. "You killed the Silver Prince!" There was no response.

Urchin knew that there was only one person Gleaner really cared about. He knew, too, better than she did, the terrible things Lady Aspen had done and tried to do. But Gleaner had adored her.

"You saved Lady Aspen's bracelet. Can you hear me, Gleaner? You saved Lady Aspen's bracelet." *Lady Aspen, who had wanted me dead when I was only a young tower page.* "She would have been very pleased with you."

Weakly, Gleaner smiled.

"You'll be all right, Gleaner," he said, and licked away blood as it trickled from a wound on his left arm. He wore his mother's bracelet on that side, and it mustn't get stained. He felt nauseous and suddenly sleepy. As he rubbed his eyes, he wondered where all that blood was coming from—but he was so sleepy.

"What are they doing?" said Crispin. With his sword still in his paw, he leaned from the window. "They seem to have lost all sense of strategy. They're just swooping about."

"They seem to be gathering at the Tangletwigs, sir," observed Russet. "It's quieter than it was."

"There are voices from inside the tower, Your Majesty," said Juniper.

"They're all under control, Your Majesty," said Needle. "Don't worry about them; I've sorted them out."

"Are there any more coming over the mists?" asked Padra, and leaned from the window to answer his own question. There were still ravens flying in, but not so many.

"And some of those ravens from the Tangletwigs seem to be flying away," said Crispin. "Are they retreating or just regrouping?"

He stepped from one window to the next, taking his time. The last arrows had been fired. As far as he could see, the island was dotted with crawling black nets. For a long time, he looked out at the mists, narrowing his eyes.

"Padra," he said at last, very softly, "come and see this. I may be imagining it."

Padra came to his side and looked.

"What do you think?" asked Crispin. "Is it—"

"Yes," said Padra. "Yes, it is." He put a paw on the king's shoulder and swallowed hard, turning his face away. It wouldn't do for a captain to cry, even for joy.

Pitter felt she had never really lived before this moment, leaning forward on the back of Prince Crown as he carried her through the sky. The sparkling mesh was folded tightly in her paw. She wanted to laugh, she wanted to dance, she wanted to catch this moment in a shaft of sunlight and keep it forever! Swans flew ahead of her, their wings white and powerful, their long necks outstretched, squirrels on their backs with the meshes in their paws. More flew around them. Pitter pressed her paws into Prince Crown's soft, gleaming feathers. There was nothing so beautiful as a swan.

Pitter looked ahead at Queen Larch, the small, slender hedgehog riding at the front of the flock, and then at Scatter, who was flying alongside her. Their long, dangerous escape from Mistmantle to Whitewings seemed far away now, in a different world. She was so absorbed with the joy of all this that she only just noticed the steep climb, and held on tightly as Crown rose higher, following the swan in front. Queen Larch's swan soared over the mists. Small in the distance, but coming closer with every wing beat, the island of Mistmantle was in sight.

★

"Swans!" said Crispin.

"And squirrels!" said Padra. "Doing what you did!"

"And"—Crispin shaded his eyes— "they're carrying something."

240

"Your Majesty!" cried Russet. "What are the ravens doing now?"

As disorganized, panicking ravens flew back to their ships, the reinforcements had flown over the mists. Meeting in the air, getting in each other's way, confused and panicked, they pecked, clawed, and fought in the sky. Mistmantle defenders aboveground peered up, shaded their eyes with their paws, and began to believe that it might be coming to an end.

"On to the battlements!" ordered Crispin. "We need to see this properly! No ravens close, are there?"

For the squirrels, it was a matter of a spring from the window to the gutter and two more leaps to the battlements. Padra and Docken, muttering something about rodents, followed by running down the stairs, along a passageway, and through a door to stand beside them and watch the sweep of silver meshes across the skies. Needle hastily said something about looking in on her prisoners, and ran down the stairs.

Pitter watched Queen Larch. The timing must be perfect, and they had not expected to find ravens fighting among themselves—but some, the last from the boats, flew around and above the fights, still trying to reach Mistmantle. Only seconds now, and Queen Larch would give the signal to throw the mesh they had brought from Whitewings.

Pitter was shaking so much she was afraid she would fall off the swan. She pressed her knees against his feathers and held on as

Queen Larch lifted her right paw high in the air. The swans rose higher. Pitter glanced across at Scatter and caught a smile of joy as they cast the mesh forward.

It floated down, a delicate shimmering thing, so light that surely it couldn't be of any use at all against strong beaks and sharp, hard talons—but as it settled over the ravens, Pitter saw what it could do. Though beaks struck and struck again, wings flapped and talons grabbed, the ravens could do nothing about the mesh that held and trapped them.

But I'm glad they won't drown, thought Pitter. Even though they're ravens. The next flight of swans skimmed behind, catching the net and towing it to land between them, ignoring the screeching and cawing of the ravens.

Needle ran up to the turret, found it empty, and caught the flash of silver from the battlements. She rushed to the king's side and saw the astonished joy on the defenders' faces that kept them from cheering. Speechless, breathless, exhausted, every animal raised its sword high to salute the swans and their riders.

The leading swan, carrying a small female hedgehog, swerved toward the battlements.

"Who's that?" wondered Crispin.

"I remember her," said Juniper. "Queen Larch of Whitewings. And there—Your Majesty—there's Scatter! She went to fetch help from Whitewings!"

"And little Pitter!" said Crispin. "And Prince Crown! Heart forgive me, I thought he'd deserted us!"

The leading swan settled on the battlements. The hedgehog stepped down as the king and the defenders bowed, and Juniper offered his paw.

"Your Majesties," he said. "Queen Larch of Whitewings, King Crispin of Mistmantle."

Queen Larch wobbled a little as she took Crispin's paw. "So sorry," she said. "I'm not used to flying. We got here as quickly as we could, though I regret it wasn't sooner."

"Your Majesty," said Crispin. "You come at exactly the right time, and Mistmantle will honor and thank you forever." He looked up and stepped back to make room for Prince Crown to land. "Prince Crown! Noblest of swans! You flew to Whitewings for help!"

"It was Scatter's idea," said Prince Crown, his eyes bright with joy, "and Pitter came too. We took rides on boats when we could. The rearguard swans are carrying nets, Your Majesty, in case there are any more ravens out there beyond the mists. And we'll sink their boats, sir."

Crispin realized that sweat had soaked through his fur. This was no way to meet a queen. But there was still work to do, and he turned to the animals behind him.

"May I introduce Padra the otter, the senior captain of Mistmantle; Docken the hedgehog, captain of Mistmantle; Russet and Heath of the Circle; Needle of the Threadings. Needle, Juniper, did you find any ravens in the tower?"

Needle and Juniper looked at each other. "Yes, Your Majesty," said Needle, struggling hard not to laugh. A Circle hedgehog shouldn't giggle, especially at a time like this.

"Padra," Crispin said, "go with Needle and see what she's found. Russet, Heath, send messengers out. Where's Longpaw? Our creatures can come out of hiding. Mistmantle"—he swallowed hard, and fought the catch in his voice—"Mistmantle is free and at peace. May the Heart be thanked. Juniper, is there wine in this turret? Our rescuers need refreshment. Prince Crown, you have flown far—can you fly a little farther, a very little?"

"I'll be glad to!" said Prince Crown. "My wings have scarcely stretched!"

"Then," said Crispin, "will you take me over the Tangletwigs? Something there has disturbed the ravens, and I need to know what."

Juniper suddenly realized that a long held-dream could just about come true. It might happen. He could almost taste it.

"Perhaps I should come with you, Your Majesty," he said. "You may need a priest. I still have a scrap of mendingmoss, though it's not much, and you might need a healer. And"—it seemed childish to say it, but he had to be honest—"I've always wanted—"

"To ride on a swan," said Crispin. "I know. Madam, excuse us. The Circle animals will look after you. Our priest and I have a little more work to do."

244

Needle led Padra to the doors of the Gathering Chamber.

"Stand well back, Captain Padra," she said. The floor's slippery."

He drew his sword. Needle unbolted the door and opened it just a little, enough for him to catch a glimpse. The ravens had given up. They flapped, floundered, and struggled to rise, only to slither to the floor again. Here and there, a talon waved in the air.

"*Caark*," croaked a voice.

"What on all the island have you done?" said Padra.

Needle shut and bolted the door.

"We had to stop them somehow," said Needle, laughter spilling out of her. "They were getting in wherever the nets were tearing, and it wasn't enough to shut them in, because they'd tear through the woodwork eventually. But there wouldn't be room for many of them to fly indoors—they'd have to land—so Crackle and I made it slippery. We used cooking oil on this bit, I think. Soapy water in the lower corridor; they were getting in there too."

From behind the door came a slither, a bump, and a croak.

"Needle," said Padra as something hit the door, "never laugh at—"

"Never laugh at what, Captain Padra?" asked Needle, as he seemed to be finding it difficult to speak.

"Never laugh at a defeated—"

Slither, bump. Croak.

Cedar had crawled through the Tangletwigs and crouched there, looking up at the skies, then down at Urchin. She had seen the ravens fly away in terror. Something had happened in the skies, but she had no idea what. The important thing was to get Urchin and Gleaner back to the tower. Gleaner was badly injured, but she would live. She wasn't at all sure about Urchin.

Mendingmoss would have helped, but it had become scarce, and she had none in her healer's satchel. All she could do was fold the satchel strap tightly around Urchin's wrist and hold it in place, but already it was stained deep crimson. Blood was on his fur and on her own paws as she pressed the bandage.

She scanned the Tangletwigs, desperate for a sign of help. Nobody was near. At least there were no more ravens, though she had heard their raucous voices so long that they still rang in her head.

"Stay, Urchin," she said. "Stay with me. Stay for Mistmantle. Stay for Crispin, for Juniper, for Needle, for all of us. Think of—" *Is he in love with anyone? Take a guess.* "Stay for Sepia. Stay for your friends. Stay for Oakleaf and Catkin, and Almondflower, stay, Urchin!"

She pressed harder on the wound to stop the bleeding. She was the only animal on Mistmantle who had known Urchin's parents. She had seen his father's body brought back to the Fortress at Whitewings; and his mother, Almond, had been her dearest friend and her heroine. She couldn't do anything for them now, but she could give every ounce of her strength and skill to save their son. Blood had soaked the bracelet on his wrist, and the sight of it brought tears to her eyes.

"Stay, Urchin of the Riding Stars," she said. "What would Apple do without you? I lost your mother and I'm not going to lose you. I should have insisted on staying with her. Well, I'm staying with you, so you stay with me, Urchin. Fight." What could she talk about to keep him alive? "Do you remember, we saved Juniper's life? He survived all that time in the sea, and you can survive this. What will Crispin say if I don't bring you back safely?"

Urchin was drifting away on waves of dreaming. A voice reached him, but he had no idea whose it was.

"Heart keep him," said Cedar. "Heart help him." She raised a paw to dry her eyes. She had sent moles for help, but it might take too long. Had the bleeding slowed down? Or was he just slowly bleeding to death?

Above her was a wing beat. *And I could do without you, you filthy verminous ravens*—but even as she reached for her sword she heard the strong, steady beat and knew that these were not raven wings. They were swans.

"Here!" she shouted, raising her sword. "Here!"

At last, Juniper knew what it felt like to ride a swan and knew, too, why Urchin could never describe it. Joy and exhilaration poured through him. Then they were wheeling over the Tangletwigs and Crispin was calling out, "It's Cedar! She's there!" In a moment of terrifying joy the swans plunged to earth, then Juniper was tumbling

247

from his swan and scrambling to Urchin's side, reaching into his satchel for mendingmoss.

"Here, let me do it, Your Majesty," he said. Deep dark blood was everywhere, on the ground, on Cedar's paws, covering Urchin's fur. It seeped steadily from the tear in his arm, so deep that Juniper, examining it, felt as if a claw tore through his own arm. He pressed the mendingmoss into place, wrapping it about with a bandage that grew red even before it was fastened. *Heart hold him, Heart give him strength. Can he have any more blood to lose?*

"There's Gleaner, too," said Cedar. "She's terribly injured, but she'll live."

There was a gasp from Crispin as he saw the big gray bird lying on its back, the blood drying from a wound in its throat. Its talons curled toward the sky. "That's the Silver Prince!" he said. "He's dead! Cedar, was that you? Urchin?"

"Neither of us," she said. It hardly seemed important now. "Gleaner. Get them onto the swans. Can any of you carry two? Someone has to hold him and keep pressing on that wound. And," she whispered, "we should send for Apple."

She squeezed her eyes shut. *Almond, Candle, you who live beyond me in the Heart's keeping, can you see your son? I will look after him. Help him, help him, help me. Heart help him. Hold on, Urchin, hold on.*

CHAPTER TWENTY-TWO

B ROTHER FIR SANK BACK against the pillows. Hope washed the stickiness from his wrinkled paws.

"That," said Fir contentedly, "was the most excellent kingsmantle cake I have ever tasted. My dear Crackle, you are a queen among pastry cooks. Corr, however did you find such seaweed?"

"It was a very long way out," said Corr. "But I think I can find it again, if you'd like me to look."

But he knew that the offer was pointless, even as Fir said, "Thank you, Corr, but that would mean a long journey for you, and I would rather have your company."

Corr wanted to tell Brother Fir that there was plenty of time to fetch seaweed, and talk, and eat cake, and talk some more. He wanted to tell him that they had all the time in the world. But it wouldn't be true, and he couldn't lie to Brother Fir.

Sepia slipped into the chamber. Her eyes looked very large, and her voice was unsteady.

"The victory is ours," she said. "The Taloness and the Silver Prince are dead."

"And yet you, little daughter," said Fir, "are distressed."

"What happened?" asked Corr.

"Urchin . . ." she said, and ran from the chamber.

As darkness gathered over the island, members of the Circle and guards strode with drawn swords to the nets of ravens. Their orders were to take prisoners and show mercy to the wounded, but the ravens had turned on each other so fiercely that few remained alive. Those who did survive were so badly injured that they died minutes after the Circle animals had cut them free and given them water.

In the night, the rushing of high winds over the island woke Corr at the Spring Gate and Catkin in the tower. Corr slipped into the stream to swim to the shore; Catkin pattered to the window. All through the tower, animals looked out. The wind caught up the smoke and reek of burning, carried it away, and swept it beyond the mists. In the morning, the island felt clean.

Animals emerged from hiding, blinking in the light, running into the sunlight, shaking soil from their ears and dashing away to find out if their friends were safe. Every tunnel, every burrow, and every hollow tree was inspected. Not a single raven remained on the island.

The Mistmantle dead were laid to rest with tears and with honor.

Scrambling out of burrows, animals raged against the wrecked burrows and ruined nests, then set to work sweeping, scrubbing, and mending. It would take a long time. Crops must be salvaged as much as possible, and another planting put in.

As tower animals wound their way back, parents and children hugged each other. Mother Huggen placed baby animals back into the arms of their mothers, then dried her tears and set to tidying up the Mole Palace. Young animals who had been sheltered below-ground raced over shores, tumbled in and out of trees, swam, splashed, danced, hugged, and laughed.

In the workrooms Thripple, Needle, and the other needle animals heaved their ancient and most treasured Threadings from their hiding places. These, at least, were undamaged. Then they examined the shreds of the rest. Nearly all their remaining wool and silk had been used to make nets. This autumn there would be plant fibers to spin, and perhaps a boat would bring wool. They still had paint.

"And there are always pebbles and shells on the shore," said Thripple. "We can make pictures with those. And fish bones."

"Fish bones!" said Needle.

"Why ever not?" asked Thripple, and Needle couldn't think of a good answer.

In the Tangletwigs, Needle's mother and little brother found a tattered length of red fabric that looked a lot like a torn bit of old curtain from the tower, and a broken mask like the ones children might use in their plays. The mask was too damaged to be of any use, but the curtain would tear up to make a nest.

In the castle, tower animals made up beds and nests. Moth the mole brought Princess Almondflower back to the tower. The small princess rolled on her swansdown quilt with little squeaks of delight before falling asleep on it.

"That's her settled, at least," said Cedar. "And Gleaner's family has been sent for. But not all the animals have been restored to their proper places. Brother Fir wanted to go back to his turret, and I've sent maids to sweep and clean it and make it ready. There may not be much time."

"So I've heard," said Moth. "But for some reason that I haven't yet got hold of, those corridors farther down the tower are very slippery, and Juniper says it wouldn't be safe to carry him up there."

"Can they get him to a window?" asked Cedar.

"I'm not sure," said Moth. "I can find out."

"Because if he can be moved to an open window, big enough to pass him through," said Cedar, "he can be flown to the turret."

Later that evening, as a warm golden sunset flamed over Mistmantle, four swans hovered at the Gathering Chamber windows, carrying a plain wood-and-canvas stretcher in their beaks. With great gentleness, Juniper lifted Brother Fir onto it, and the swans rose into the air, solemn and dignified, carrying Brother Fir back home to his turret, where Arran leaned from a window to receive him, and Hope turned down the covers on the plain little bed, one last time.

At the Spring Gate, Sepia sat by Urchin's bed, holding his paw. He was still unconscious, his head on one side, both wrists bandaged. His whiskers were limp and his ears drooped. Juniper felt for his pulse.

"Talk to him, Sepia," he said.

"I'll stay with him," she said, "if you want to go to Fir."

"It isn't only Fir," said Juniper. "I have to go to the rest of the wounded." He prayed a blessing over Urchin and hovered at the door. "There's a guard outside. Send for me if anything happens. Talk to him, sing to him, do anything to help him stay alive." Still looking over his shoulder, he left.

Sepia talked. She talked of the Spring Festival when she had first met Urchin, Needle, and the other tower animals. She talked of the search for the Heartstone and the rescue of the Heir of Mistmantle. When she ran out of things to talk to him about, she sang.

Urchin felt he was drifting out to sea. He shouldn't be drifting away like this. He'd be carried away through the mist, and this time there'd be no returning, ever, ever, ever . . . But he had no strength to fight it. He could only float out on the tide. It didn't matter anymore.

He could hear a voice, clear, sweet, and beautiful: singing, like Sepia's voice. It made him want to stay with his friends on Mistmantle. But Mistmantle was such a long way back! He was in the boat that had carried him away to Whitewings. . . . He was a prisoner . . . He was about to be killed. He caught a glimpse of a smiling mole in a blue cloak . . . and then of a pale squirrel with a face he thought he should know, and nothing mattered but that he should go to her. The tide carried him to her, and all he had to do was drift.

The door opened. Sepia stopped singing, jumped up and curtsied, because Crispin was there, his arm across Apple's shoulders as he ushered her into the chamber. Apple's eyes and nose were pink from crying, and Sepia's heart hurt for her. They were followed by a stout and rather shy-looking male squirrel Sepia had never met before, carrying Apple's basket.

"Hold his right paw, Mistress Apple, not his left," said Sepia as Apple settled herself beside the bed. "His left paw mustn't be moved."

Apple wrapped both her wrinkled paws around Urchin's.

"Heart love you, look at you!" she said. "This is no way to be when the king needs you, Urchin, you need to get better, get up on your paws, we're all right proud of you, aren't we, Your Majesty, we want you up and about so we can all give you a pat on the back and that, and besides, I got something to tell you, or, like, ask you about, in a manner of speaking, or at least, Master Filbert does. Now here's Sepia and Fingal waiting for you to get better, and Juniper. You press my paw if you can hear me, Urchin."

Urchin's eyes were still closed. His paw in Apple's did not move.

"Now, I tell you, Urchin," said Apple. For the first time, Sepia heard tears in her voice. "I tell you, you and me go back a long way, don't we, to all that long ago when I got you out of the water, Heart love the scrappy lttle thing you were, or you would have drownded. And I did-n't get you out of that water and bring you up all these years just so some great bullying ugly bird can pick you off, and if I had them birds, here, ooh, I'd make short work of 'em for you. Spuggies, young Todd calls 'em, big greedy spuggies. So you just live, Urchin, because you're not dying for some big spuggy. And I tell you what else, Urchin. I brought you this, this is a real good batch from two years back, this is the best, I brought it to you to help you along."

From the basket, Filbert passed her a small, tightly stoppered bottle. When Apple pulled out the cork, a bitter tang of old apple, strong mint, and vinegar prickled through the little chamber.

"Just a moment, Mistress Apple," said Crispin. "We should ask Brother Juniper if it's all right to give Urchin anything." He called to the page. "Fetch Brother Juniper, please!"

Juniper soon came limping hastily, frowning a little in anxiety, with Fingal slipping in behind him. He exchanged a few words with Apple.

"Oh, yes!" he said, and held out his paw for the cork. "We should try this!" With a keen new light in his face, he raised Urchin's head and waved the cork before his face.

"Urchin!" he said.

Urchin's right ear twitched. His eyelids flickered, just once.

"Pour out a teaspoonful, Apple," said Juniper. "That's all. Thanks. Let me just put a drop or two on his tongue."

His paws shook a little with nervous hope. He trickled a few drops of cordial between Urchin's lips.

Urchin's mouth twitched. His eyes flickered open and shut. There was a jerk of his head and, in a low and very quiet voice, he whispered a single word. With a look of triumph, Apple turned to the rest of them.

"You see!" she said. "Trust my old cordial, it's doing him good already."

"Wonderful stuff, that!" agreed Filbert.

"It's certainly made him fight," said Crispin.

"Funny thing to say," said Apple as she pressed the cork back into place. "He said, 'vial.' Least, I think that's what he said. That's a tower word, I mean, a posh word, isn't it, for a bottle? Isn't that what he said? Vial?"

"I'm sure it is," said Fingal, feeling the subtle prod of the king's elbow in his ribs. Apple leaned over Urchin and raised her voice.

"Can you hear me?" she bellowed. "It comes in bottles in Anemone Wood, not vials, that's you talking like a proper tower squirrel, so you just buck up and start tower squirreling again!"

Fingal's whiskers twitched. Urchin murmured again.

"That's right, our Urchin," said Apple.

"He's asking for water," said Juniper, and lifted a cup to Urchin's lips.

Fingal knelt to kiss Apple's paw and give Sepia a quick pat on the shoulder, then bowed to the king and left the chamber. Juniper followed him soon after, and they darted into Padra's chamber to share the news. It had been a long time since they had laughed this much.

Juniper had stopped laughing when he climbed the many, many stairs to Fir's turret. Urchin was still in danger, windows all over the tower were still broken, the smell of burning feathers was everywhere, Brother Fir could not last much longer, and how long since he had slept? Too long. He found he was dragging his paws with exhaustion as he reached the turret, where the lamps were low and gentle around Fir's bed. Someone had placed lavender and roses in a vase by the bed, and the air was sweet with them.

Hope was quietly sorting out blankets and pillows in a corner. Brother Fir turned his head toward Juniper, and his paw lifted a little, shaking, in a blessing.

"Urchin opened his eyes for a second," he said. "He tried to speak."

"Juniper?"

Fir's voice was so weak that Juniper had to bend close to hear him. The words were painfully slow.

"Corr."

"Yes, Brother Fir?"

"The ravens and Corr."

"I understand, Brother Fir. The ravens called his name."

"And . . ." He smiled faintly. "The seaweed."

"Kingsmantle," said Juniper. "The robes of a king. Yes, I worked that one out too."

"The king . . ."

"King Crispin must be told? Yes, of course. Are you comfortable?"

In the soft light it seemed that Brother Fir's shriveled body grew even smaller, and his dark eyes with their depth of love, suffering, and joy grew even deeper and larger, as if all of him were in his eyes. His smile was the most beautiful Juniper had ever seen.

"I am happier now," said Fir, "than I have ever been."

Presently, he fell asleep. Juniper tried to suppress a series of enormous yawns, and couldn't.

"Brother Juniper," said Hope.

"Yes, Hope?"

"I've made up a bed for you," he said. "I'll watch with Brother Fir. And Captain Lady Arran says she'll take a turn with him, and so will Scatter, now she's home, and the queen. So you can sleep, Brother Juniper."

"We still need healers," said Juniper, and again pretended not to yawn.

"There are lots of healers," said Hope, "and they're all very good. And if you're really, really tired, you might make mistakes." He smoothed the blanket on a mattress on the floor.

"Hope," said Juniper, limping wearily to the makeshift bed, "where would the island be without you?"

"Thank you, Brother Juniper, but I think it would stay put," said Hope.

Juniper raised his paw. "Heart keep you, Hope," he said.

"Heart keep you too, Brother Juniper," said Hope, and trotted to take his place at Fir's bedside.

All the next day, quiet paws pattered around the tower. Everyone knew that Urchin of the Riding Stars and Gleaner were badly wounded, and Fir was dying. They all wanted to help and to show that they cared, but nobody liked to intrude.

Very early in the morning, Prince Crown carried Crispin around the island. He visited animals, heard about their injuries and the damage to their homes and crops, and stopped to talk to Corr's family before flying back to survey the damage to the tower. Queen Larch and Queen Cedar joined them, standing on the rocks outside the tower, shading their eyes as they looked up at broken windows.

"We'll need new glass made," said Crispin. "Fortunately it's summer, so it can wait. We need to get the rest of the broken glass taken out. It'll give our glaziers a chance to show their skill; it's a long time since the glass kilns were reopened. The main thing they need is sand, and we have plenty of that; but just now it's more important that every animal has a home and a food supply."

"Please, King Crispin," said Prince Crown, "on my father's island, when the ravens had gone, the royal quarters were to be cleaned first. If he were king here, the tower would be repaired first, then the ordinary homes."

"Your father and I have different ways of doing things," said Crispin. "He believes that the animals are there for the king, and I believe that the king is there for the animals. I don't want animals to die for me, but because I'm king—if necessary—I'd die for the animals. That's being king. At least, it is here."

There was a silence as Crown's eyes met his.

"When I'm king," said Crown quietly, and sounding a little embarrassed, "I want to be a king like you."

Crispin laid his paw on the ring of dark feathers on the top of Crown's head. "You'll be a good king," he said. Then he turned to Queen Larch, who was picking up a scrap of honey-colored wool from the floor. "You must have thought of using nets and meshes as soon as Prince Crown came to you," he said. "That was brilliant."

Larch looked uneasy, and fidgeted with the scrap of wool. "It's been done before on Whitewings," she said, "and it's not part of our history to be proud of. When Urchin first came to our island, the swans were all captives with chains and collars. That was because King Silverbirch and Smokewreath the Sorcerer had used fine meshes to catch them and imprison them in the first place. The Whitewings swans still talk of Urchin as the one who won their freedom for them. So, when Scatter and her friends arrived, we knew that what had worked on the swans would work on the ravens. And when we told the swans we needed them to free Urchin and Cedar and their friends, we couldn't hold them back."

"And I must fly over the mists again," said Prince Crown. "Shall I take Pitter home to Swan Isle?"

"Does she want to go back?" asked Queen Cedar. "I don't think she had much of a life there. From what she told Sepia and me, she doesn't have much to go back to."

"I'm sorry about that," said Crown. "I'd take her under my protection and make sure she was happy."

"All the same," said the queen. "I think she'd love to stay, at least for a while longer."

"She can stay as long as she likes," said Crispin. "In the brief time we've known her, she's saved my life and the Heart alone knows how many others." He inclined his head to listen. "I can hear singing."

"Sepia's rehearsing the choristers," said Cedar. "The little ones seemed to think there was something very important to rehearse for. You know how secretive they are."

Corr, not sure what to do next, wandered down to the jetty. He was glad to see Fingal twirling idly about in the water with Tide and Swanfeather, and slipped into the sea to join them.

"I suppose I ought to go home now," said Corr.

"Home?" said Fingal. "You mean, fishing-nets home? Do you think so? Do you miss them?"

Corr turned a somersault to give himself thinking time.

"I sort of—I've missed them more than I thought I would. Especially when, you know, when it got very tough. When I was . . ." He didn't like to admit that he'd been afraid.

"Scared?" said Fingal. "We all get scared. I get scared. Even my brother does. But he's a captain, and captains aren't allowed to show it."

"Being lost was worst," said Corr.

"Sorry, my fault," said Fingal. "I should have taken better care of you. So you just want to patch up your boat and go home, then?"

"No!" said Corr. He turned another somersault. "I miss them. I really, really want to tell them about everything I've been doing and who I've met, and it's not to show off, it's just, I want to share it with them. But I think I've changed—I mean, I'm the same otter, but I've done a lot, and I can't pretend I haven't. I don't think I could just go back to mending fishing nets as if none of it had happened."

"Good," said Fingal. "Because the king might have something to say. I mean, you only warned him of the ravens . . ."

"Yes, but—"

" . . . rescued Princess Catwing or whatever she's called these days . . ."

" . . . that was all of us—"

" . . . and done all that net-making stuff. I think King Crispin will want a word with you. Stay around a bit longer. I've been repairing my boat. I came in here to get the sawdust out of my fur. Those vermin were using my boat! It was due a coat of paint anyway. Do you want to give me a paw? We'll take it to Twigg and ask him to do something with yours too."

The idea of staying here, messing about in boats with Fingal, was completely wonderful. "Sounds like the best thing ever," said Corr, and rolled over to look at the sky.

In the evening, as Juniper kept watch by Brother Fir, and Needle sat beside Urchin at the Spring Gate, the singing began. Sepia had gathered her choir to rehearse on the shore, and their sweet silvery voices rose and fell, weaving and layering their harmonies until every animal stopped what it was doing to listen. Otters heard them and lolloped from the water. Arran heard it and felt tears in her eyes. Needle, holding Urchin's paw, heard it and saw Urchin turn his head and, briefly, open his eyes. Then, hushing them gently, Sepia ushered them to the battlements, where they sang for the Whitewings creatures who had helped them, and for the king and queen. The queen opened a window so that Gleaner would hear them, and for the first time since the attack, Gleaner slept without nightmares of the Silver Prince. But most of all they sang for Brother Fir, who smiled in his sleep, as if their song could carry him to the Heart.

In the morning, Urchin knew before he opened his eyes that the tide had carried him home to Mistmantle again. He felt stronger, as if he could sit up. As he slowly blinked awake he saw Sepia smiling down at him, but the voice he heard was Needle's.

"You had us really worried!" she scolded. "Don't you ever do that again!" She was about to hug him, but decided it would be safer for him if she didn't. "I know I said to you before that somebody was going to die. Well, it wasn't you, so you're not allowed to. And anyway, you're not royalty."

"Pardon?" said Urchin, his eyes still on Sepia's smile.

"I saw it in a Threading," she said. "Myrtle drew the death of royalty. But all the time it wasn't one of our royalty; it was that stupid bird. I never thought of that. I really don't like Myrtle's gift."

Urchin closed his eyes again. He was tired already.

CHAPTER TWENTY-THREE

GLEANER HAD NEVER LIKED Queen Cedar. She had no right to be on the island at all, never mind being queen. She would never have a trace of Lady Aspen's beauty and elegance. But even Gleaner conceded that she was a decent enough healer, and the rest of the nurses who looked after her were reasonable.

Several times a day they helped to move her, because she could no longer move herself. They plumped pillows and turned her bed to the light. Still having some use of her forepaws, she could feed herself, but only with difficulty. Her legs seemed to have nothing to do with her anymore.

The thought of never walking again brought tears to her eyes. She had left the Tangletwigs for the last time, and it was as if she had left Lady Aspen without saying good-bye. The cairn in the woods would become a thing of memory. But she kept Lady Aspen's bracelet tucked under her blanket.

There was a sudden splutter of giggles from the mole maids outside. And what is so funny, thought Gleaner, about a poor injured squirrel lying here unable to walk? Then there was a loud knocking at the door, and, without waiting for an answer, Fingal burst into the room with his arms full of roses.

"Gleaner!" he cried. "Gleaner, wonderful, beautiful Gleaner, Gleaner of the Tangletwigs, the heroine of the island!" He saw the frown on her face, dropped the flowers into the water jug, and knelt to take her paws. "I'm not teasing you, Gleaner," he said. "You really are the island's deliverer. You're the one who killed the Silver Prince! Now, excuse me taking a liberty, but I promised this to whoever finished him off."

He wrapped her in his arms and planted a loud and enthusiastic kiss on each cheek.

"I salute you, Gleaner," he cried, springing to his paws. "Pardon me, but I have duties to attend to. But," he added, bending to whisper in her ear, "I think a picture in the Threadings is a pretty good chance."

The Threadings! Gleaner lay back, her face still tingling with whiskery kisses as he left the room. She turned her head so she could lie back and look at the water jug, and smiled, feeling happier than she could ever remember. Nobody had ever given her roses before.

Leaving the chamber, Fingal met Padra on his way down from the Throne Room. They were running down to the Spring Gate, when they heard shrieks and giggles of delight—very young shrieks and giggles—from a normally quiet corridor on the far side of the Gathering Chamber.

"Sounds good," said Fingal. "D'you think they'll let us join in, whatever it is?"

But by the time they reached the corridor, the giggles had stopped. Tay the otter stood there, drawn up to her full height, her arms folded. Looking up at her was Sepia, more cross than upset, with a huddle of bewildered little squirrels sheltering behind her. Some looked as if they had oil in their fur, some were soapy, and all were very wet.

"They have worked very hard!" Sepia was saying. "They needed time to play and have some fun, and I'm not supposed to watch them all the time. I had to go and see Urchin. Anyway, they haven't done any harm, and they're only little."

"What you think they need, Sepia," said Tay, "has nothing to do with the case. You are responsible for these animals, and I have never, never in my life witnessed such appalling behavior in Mistmantle Tower."

"Oh, I have," said Padra behind her.

Tay turned indignantly as if Padra had no right to be there. Fingal could tell from the tone of his voice that, for once, he would not try to be pleasant.

"I've seen far worse behavior than this in the tower," said Padra quietly. "I've seen battles and deceptions and an innocent captain convicted of murder and sent into exile, and so have you, Mistress Tay. So what's happening here? Hello, Sepia."

"I came down here," said Tay, "in order to ascertain the state of the building after the raven attack. Hearing much silly and inappropriate noise, I investigated and found these undisciplined little horrors— Sepia's choristers, all of them—sliding along the corridors. Really, Sepia, you ought to control them!"

Padra ignored her. He knelt down before two very small squirrels, one with an oily sheen to his fur and one crowned with such a froth of soap bubbles that her ear tufts were almost invisible.

"This looks very exciting," he said.

"Please, Captain Padra sir," said the boy. "Please, it wasn't Miss Sepia's fault, she wasn't here, and we'd heard all about, you know, about how the ravens got stuck in the Throne Room, and how, sir, Needle of the Cir.. Threa . . . Needle, sir, and Crackle the pastry cook put stuff on the floor and made it slippy and the ravens all went sliding about, and we thought—"

"You did not think!" pronounced Tay.

"Please don't interrupt, Tay," said Padra. "It sets the little ones a bad example. So, you two, don't be afraid. I'm not cross. You wanted to find out what it would be like to slide down the corridors, is that right? This one slopes downhill a little bit, doesn't it, and goes round the corner."

"Please, Captain Padra sir, yes, Captain Padra sir."

"They are running wild!" said Tay. "Sepia, you shouldn't have this choir if you can't manage them."

Padra turned to face her so suddenly that she flinched.

"Tay," he said, "nobody on this island speaks to Sepia like that. Leave her and the little ones alone." He turned to the animals again. "Tell me, what did you use to make your slides with?"

They exchanged glances. "We got a bit of oil that they use for lamps," said one. "But there wasn't much, and everyone got all stuck with it, so we tried some soapy stuff. It all got a bit mixed up."

"I see," said Padra. "Well, I'm afraid we have to get this corridor cleaned now; but let me tell you something: the best place for sliding is that long slope outside, beside the tower staircase. First, you need to ask Sepia if you may. Then you need tea trays. Go and ask very nicely at the kitchens, and take the tea trays back when you've finished with them. And be sure you all have a good wash. And thank you for singing so beautifully last night. Thank you, especially, Sepia." He waved a paw at a mole page hurrying from the Gathering Chamber. "Fetch Jig and Fig to keep an eye on this lot, will you? Sepia's been looking after Urchin and conducting the choir with the other paw. She must be exhausted."

The choir were soon on their way to the kitchens, the little animals looking up at Padra with squeaks of thanks and admiration. Tay marched away in disgust, and only Fingal, Sepia, and Padra were left. Fingal looked along the corridor. It shimmered wetly.

"My turn!" he said, and hurled himself along the corridor, gathering speed as he disappeared around a corner. There was a bump and a cry of "Oh, *yes!*"

"He's happy," said Padra. Now that Sepia wasn't standing up to Tay she looked droopy with weariness, and he noticed that her fur hadn't been brushed, but her tired eyes shone. "Sepia, you really are exhausted, aren't you? How's Urchin?"

"He's sitting up and talking," she said, almost too weary to smile. "He's tired of being in bed, and dying to walk. When I went down just now the king was with him, so I didn't stay—Oh, there's Juniper." Juniper and Whittle came into sight, earnestly discussing Brother Fir. "Juniper, don't go to Urchin; the king's with him."

Juniper, Hope, and Whittle arrived in time to see Fingal loping with difficulty up the corridor. The fact that he kept sliding back down didn't seem to bother him at all.

"You should have followed it around to the left," said Sepia. "You could have got out at the laundry room and come round the outside."

"Who cares!" called Fingal. "Anybody want a go?"

"No, thank you," said Sepia. "I'm scruffy enough already. I'm going for a wash and a little sleep."

"We all need a wash," said Padra. "The children smell of raven repellent, and the adults smell of ash. Hope, what are you . . ."

Hope launched himself down the corridor and vanished around the corner with a cry of "Ooooh!" then a squeak. Whittle hesitated, then joined in.

Juniper watched them, his healer's satchel over his shoulder. He was a priest. He still had wounded animals to care for, and Brother Fir, watched by the queen in the little turret room, was dying. But that meant that soon he would be the only priest on the island, and might never go on a slide again.

"I'll hold your satchel," said Padra.

The opportunity was too good to miss. Juniper gave Padra the satchel, pulled off his priest's tunic, and threw himself down the slide. Urchin was missing this. Pity. He'd have to take Urchin's turn for him.

Urchin was sitting up with a bowl of hazelnuts on the table at his elbow. Arran had made one last attempt to persuade him to eat fish, which she said would do him so much good; but Urchin couldn't stand it, and she had finally given up, afraid that he might be sick if she insisted. Then Apple and Filbert had come, bringing hazelnuts and dithering about whether to stay in the presence of King Crispin.

"Of course you should stay," said Crispin. "But he's only allowed visitors briefly, in case he gets too tired. We'll face the queen's wrath if we stay too long."

Apple and Filbert glanced at one another.

"Well, we did want to talk to our Urchin," said Apple. Crispin stood up.

"I'll leave you together," he said, and, from behind them, winked at Urchin. "I'll be back shortly to throw you both out, on the queen's orders."

"Oh, Your Majesty," said Apple, suddenly looking flustered,

271

"if you can spare a moment, me and Filbert would be most grateful if you'd stay, seeing as how you've always been so kind."

Crispin sat down again. Apple and Filbert glanced at each other, and it was Apple who spoke first.

"It's like this," she said. "I never thought a good squirrel would come along and find me, but he did."

"She's as good a squirrel as you'd meet in a lifetime in all the island, Your Majesty," said Filbert. "I'm a shy chap, never had the courage before to ask for a lady's paw. Besides, I never found one as nice as my old mum, and here she is; so Apple and me, we want to get wed. And it's not like we were important enough to need Your Majesty's permission, but we'd like your blessing all the same."

"And," said Apple, getting in quickly and folding her arms, "if my Urchin is happy with it, that's what we need to know, Urchin, because you're my little lad, and, come to think of, I'd probably marry Filbert even if you wasn't all right with it, but we'd like it a lot better if you was."

"Apple, Filbert," said Crispin. "Blessings on you both. I'm delighted."

"Yes!" said Urchin. "I mean . . . I'm astonished. But, yes."

Floundering for the right words to say, he imagined them under a tree root on a winter evening, sitting on either side of a crackling fire, roasting chestnuts, stretching out their hind paws to the blaze. Perhaps they would hold forepaws. "It's wonderful," he said.

"That's all right, then," said Apple. "Eat your hazelnuts and drink up your cordial."

In the evening, Crispin, Cedar, Catkin, Oakleaf, and Almondflower wandered along the beach. Oakleaf and Catkin skimmed stones across the water. Urchin and Juniper had taught them to do that. Almondflower toddled precariously along the beach, picking up pebbles to give to her mother. Then, when Cedar's paws were full, she put up her paws for Crispin to carry her. Tide and Swanfeather bobbed up to join them.

"All the island's been happy this afternoon," said Crispin. "Everyone's washing. Themselves, their children, their clothes. Washing the bitter taste out of their fur, washing away dust and the soot from the fires, washing the raven taint away. I've seen them all over the island, splashing each other in the sea and the waterfalls. It's wonderful what you can see when you're riding a swan."

"What will you do when Crown goes home?" wondered Cedar.

"Remember what my paws are for," he said. "But it's a good way of meeting a lot of animals in a short time. Corr's family is happy for him to stay here, if it's what he wants. They don't want to hold him back, and he'll still see them. His Great-aunt Kerrera is quite a character."

"I had a long talk with Pitter," said Cedar. "She desperately wants to stay, so I thought we could put her in charge of growing mendingmoss at strategic parts of the island. Crown says he'll speak to his father and the Swan Isle squirrels when he gets back, about letting her stay here.

But he doesn't want to go home yet either. He'll wait for Fir."

They walked on. In the evening sun, Thripple and Needle sat on the rocks, trimming hats. Myrtle sat drawing in the sand. When Crispin and his family came to them they stood up, and Needle popped a bonnet onto Almondflower's head.

"Thripple says we shouldn't even think about the new Threadings just yet," said Needle as the bonnet tipped over Almondflower's eyes.

"Quite right," said Crispin. "Give ourselves a breathing space." The bonnet tumbled off, and Crispin picked it up. "That's very pretty."

"It's a wedding bonnet for Apple," said Needle.

"You don't mean she's getting a new hat!" exclaimed Crispin.

"I offered to make her this one for a wedding present," she said. "But"—from the basket beside her she took a pale, dried rosebud—"she took these off her old one. She still has to have these wretched rosebuds."

They walked farther around the shore, stopping to take a deep breath when they came within sight of the mooring post where Catkin had been tied. The pain of that night stirred in them again, and when Catkin ran to Crispin's side, he hugged her tightly.

"Daddy," she said, "when I was tied up there" —she pressed against his fur as she said it—"I saw something in the mists, before the stars started. It might have just been the sunset in the mist, but it really, really looked like the Heartstone."

Crispin thought for a while. "It may be that you saw how the Heart is with you and cares for you, even when it doesn't seem much like it," he said. "Tell Juniper. Sweetheart, the choir is going to sing tonight, especially for Fir. Shall we go around to the battlements, where we can hear them? They should be just about ready by now."

The choir was not ready at all. Sepia had decided that they should wear their white robes tonight, and had assembled them in one of the maids' rooms. Moth the mole, whose two little daughters were in the choir, had come to help. Hope's sister Mopple and Needle's brother Scufflen led the choir into the maids' room, and Sepia stared in astonishment.

"Captain Padra said they should have a wash when they'd finished sliding," said Scufflen. "So they did."

The little choristers lined up to be given their robes. The hedgehogs simply looked a little soft about the spines, and the moles, freshly washed and dried in the breeze, were not quite as smooth as usual. The otters looked gently fluffy. But the young squirrels had frothed out until they looked like auburn thistledown. Their curved red tails were twice their normal size and three times as big as their bodies, and the smallest of them were almost spherical.

"Sweet!" said Moth. A small boy squirrel glared up at her. "Not you," she added quickly.

"Please, Sepia," said a little girl squirrel called Daisy, "we got very messy so we had a really good wash and we ran around in the sun to get dry and it was windy and we got all foofed."

"Foofed, Daisy?" repeated Sepia.

"Our tails went foofy," said the little squirrel. "And I can't get my robe on." Molted hairs lifted above her as Sepia wriggled the robe over her head and settled it on the soft fur. It seemed to float over her.

"It's like dressing a cloud," said Moth. "A little squirrel-red cloud." Daisy, her large eyes wide above the white robe, slipped a claw into her mouth and gazed up at Sepia.

"I want Brother Fir to have a present," said Sepia, and looked around quickly. "Excuse me." She ran down the wall, picked a few stems of pink sea thrift, ran back up again, and took Daisy by the paw.

"First," she said, "Daisy and I are going to take these flowers to Brother Fir, as a present from us all. Then we go to the battlements and sing."

Fir was, as Sepia had hoped, awake. Daisy pattered on clawtips to put the flowers into his paw, and curtsied. For a moment she stood, the candlelight shining softly on her fur, and her claw slipping into her mouth—then she turned and ran back to take Sepia's paw.

Brother Fir smiled. Sepia, seeing the wise love in those eyes, thought she had never in her life seen so beautiful a smile. The sight of that tiny squirrel, robed and fluffed with sea thrift in her paws, would be one of Fir's last sights on Mistmantle.

And this would be the last sound. She led the choir to the battlements, took a few deep breaths because she couldn't sing if she wanted to cry, raised her paw, and gave them their first note. As they sang, it seemed that the air shivered.

At sunrise, Brother Fir died quietly in his sleep. Crispin and Cedar went to kneel at the bedside where he lay. Animals went about their work quietly with thanksgiving and sorrow. Hope went to find Thripple, and they clung to each other, not needing to speak. Juniper put on his priest's tunic, went down to the Chamber of Candles, and prayed.

He had crossed the sea. He had made friends and faced the secrets of his past. He had even, in the last few days, seen one of Mistmantle's darkest times. Now it was time to be not just Fir's assistant priest, but *the* priest of Mistmantle. The thought of never looking into those deep, wise eyes again was heavy. He thanked the Heart for his friends, but knew that, in the future, he must face depths and darknesses that not even Urchin could understand.

He laid his heart before the Heart. What else could he do?

None of the choirs sang at Fir's funeral, but only Sepia, singing the lament for a priest. On the golden summer evening animals gathered on the shore, watching the procession leave the tower and cross the sand to where Juniper stood, the waves lapping at his hind paws as he stood by the long, sleek Parting Boat waiting empty, on the ebb tide, moored in place by four ropes held by otters. A fire had been kindled as near as could be to the water's edge.

Brother Fir's body lay dressed in the tunic Needle had made for him long ago, the pink sea thrift in his paws. He looked as if he slept as they carried him—the king and all three captains—across the sand to the boat, escorted by moles. The queen followed, and the Circle animals, Sepia and Hope, who had cared for him, and Corr the otter, because Fir had so enjoyed his company at the end.

Fingal slipped from the procession to the Spring Gate and appeared with Urchin close behind them. They had talked about this earlier that day.

"You don't have to go," Fingal had said. "Fir would understand."

"I do have to," Urchin had answered. "It's as much for Juniper as for Fir." And Fingal hadn't tried to talk him out of it, but only offered to prop him up, so Urchin had stood at a distance with Fingal, resenting his own weakness as he leaned on his sword and saw animals dab at their eyes. He was growing fitter and stronger every day, but he longed to be fully well again.

Sepia's song was carried away on the breeze. Gulls cried. The withered body was lowered lovingly into the small boat and covered with a white sheet, and Juniper raised his paw.

"Dear Brother Fir, servant of the Heart and of the island," he cried, "may your heart fly to the Heart that made you. We honor you with our fire, lament you with our songs, and lift you on our hearts. Be joy. Be peace. Be love. Be free!"

He took a brand from the fire and held it high, the flames leaping and trailing smoke. As he placed it on the boat, the otters released the ropes. In bright flames and lapping water, Brother Fir's body drifted away toward the mists. Urchin remembered the first evening he had spent in Fir's turret, and closed his eyes.

Cedar was the only one who noticed Crispin suddenly shudder. She glanced swiftly at him, wondering what was the matter—then she looked away, knowing that he would not want anyone else to notice.

Crispin closed his eyes and opened them again. For a moment it had seemed as if he had been following Brother Fir into the mists. It had lasted for only seconds, but it had been so real that he was surprised to find himself on the firm sand of the shore. It was as if he were being called away.

He understood, and wondered how long he had left.

CHAPTER TWENTY-FOUR

THE NEXT MORNING, ANIMALS gathered in the Throne Room. The king and queen were there, the three captains, and Needle, Juniper, Mother Huggen, and Urchin, who still needed help to get up the stairs. Urchin's left arm was still bandaged, but Cedar had carefully washed the blood from his fur and the bracelet. They talked briefly of crops, supplies, and repairs.

Finally Crispin said, "I think all of us in this room have worked it out now. Corr found the raven ship because he'd swum under the mists without realizing it. He may have been swimming under the mists and back all his life without knowing what he was doing. Fir's prophecies came true in him. For the first time in many, many generations—and I find it breathtaking that it's happened in our lifetime—the island has a Voyager, an animal who can come and go freely through the mists. The Heart alone knows where his adventures will take him."

"It's amazing!" said Juniper. "It's like the past coming alive."

"I assume that we don't want the whole island to know," said Padra. "Not while he's so young. Everyone would be goggle-eyed at him."

"We should definitely keep it quiet," said Crispin. "Catkin finds it hard enough to be singled out as a princess. Needle, if little Myrtle draws a circular boat in her Threadings, deal with it discreetly."

"Certainly, Your Majesty," said Needle.

"Oh, and if anyone can't call the Threadings Code to mind," said Crispin with a quick teasing smile, deliberately not looking at Urchin, "a circular boat is the sign of a Voyager. A circle comes back to its beginning, and a Voyager always comes back to Mistmantle. The other question is whether Corr himself should know who he is."

"There were prophecies about me," said Urchin, "but I didn't know about them until I was a bit older than Corr is now. I think it's probably better that way. If I'd known, I would have felt I had to live up to them."

"Or tried to fulfill them," said Juniper. "That could have been catastrophic."

"He's to stay here as a tower animal," said Crispin. "We can keep an eye on him and tell him his true nature as soon as he's ready. Urchin, train him as a page, will you?"

"Why me?" cried Urchin, and added, "Your Majesty."

"Because it's an order," said Crispin, and grinned. "I've told him to report to your chamber."

When the meeting was over, Crispin closed his eyes against the pain in his old wound and relived the morning long ago, the morning

281

after a night of riding stars, when he had stood in the waves at the water's edge with Fir behind him, scooping up something that looked like a starfish. In that moment, he had held the future of Mistmantle in his two paws.

In the chamber at the Spring Gate, Corr stood straight and tall before Urchin of the Riding Stars. He looked so freshly washed and dried, he reminded Urchin of Sepia's squirrels. But, more than that, Urchin was reminded of a young squirrel many years ago, knocking timidly on the door of Fir's turret, about to watch the riding stars with his hero, Captain Crispin.

Corr didn't know why he'd been summoned there. He only hoped he wasn't about to be sent home. Needle of the Circle sat at the hearth.

"So, Corr," said Urchin, "you're to be a tower squirrel. I don't suppose you'd consider being my page, would you?"

"Oh!" There was a moment of speechlessness that brought Urchin's past vividly back to him.

"I hope you'll say yes," he said.

"Yes, sir!" cried Corr. "Thank you—thank you, sir!"

"Fine," said Urchin. "We'll get a chamber sorted out for you and move you in. Run up to the storeroom by the laundry and ask for some bedding."

"Very impressive," said Needle, when Corr had gone. "And while you're giving orders, I've had one from the king. I have to teach you the Threadings Code."

"The Threadings Code!" cried Urchin. "All of it?"

"I had to learn it all," said Needle. "I don't see why you can't. I'll cram it into your skull somehow or other."

"Why?" asked Urchin. Then he thought of a reason why he might have to learn the Threadings Code—but surely it couldn't be that?

"Oh, come on," said Needle. "I know you've been ill, but make an effort. Who has to know the Threadings Code?"

"Oh!" said Urchin.

"Exactly," said Needle.

"But," he said, wondering if he'd really understood her, "I'm too young!"

"What, too young to be a captain?" she said. "You won't be by the time I've got the Threadings Code between your ears."

Corr flew down the stairs. If his paws hadn't been full of sheets and blankets, he would have turned somersaults. He had to tell Fingal—But no, I'm a page, I have to report to Urchin. He bowed to an imaginary animal on the stairs. *I'm Corr the . . .* No, start again, paw on an imaginary sword hilt—*I'm Corr the otter, page to Urchin of the Riding Stars.* He'd go back by way of the shore, just in case Fingal might be there.

On the beach, Myrtle left the picture she had been drawing. Her stomach told her it was lunchtime, so she wandered up the shore, dragging a stick of driftwood behind her to make patterns in the sand. The tide rose. A picture that looked like a boat, except that it was round, would be washed away before anyone could see it. A flower of pink sea thrift floating on the water washed up on the shore and lay there as if it shared a secret with the boat, and was smiling.